Praise for Elizabeth Eyre's
DEATH OF THE DUCHESS

"MOST ENTERTAINING . . . A RICHNESS OF HISTORICAL DETAIL . . . a plot that manages to combine aspects of *Romeo and Juliet* and *Othello* with more dwarves than ever lived in Oz." —*Chicago Tribune*

"A NICELY MACHIAVELLIAN LITTLE TALE . . . Readers will be cheered by it." —*Denver Post*

"THE PLOT COMPLICATIONS ARE DIVERTING . . . Interesting setting and customs, and plenty of murky secret passageways." —*Library Journal*

MORE MYSTERIES FROM THE
BERKLEY PUBLISHING GROUP . . .

THE INSPECTOR AND MRS. JEFFRIES: He's with Scotland Yard. She's his housekeeper. Sometimes, her job can be murder . . .

by Emily Brightwell

THE INSPECTOR AND MRS. JEFFRIES	THE GHOST AND MRS. JEFFRIES
MRS. JEFFRIES DUSTS FOR CLUES	MRS. JEFFRIES TAKES STOCK

JENNY McKAY MYSTERIES: This TV reporter finds out where, when, why . . . *and* whodunit. "A more streetwise version of television's 'Murphy Brown.' " —*Booklist*

by Dick Belsky

BROADCAST CLUES	THE MOURNING SHOW
LIVE FROM NEW YORK	

CAT CALIBAN MYSTERIES: She was married for thirty-eight years. Raised three kids. Compared to that, tracking down killers is easy . . .

by D. B. Borton

ONE FOR THE MONEY	THREE IS A CROWD
TWO POINTS FOR MURDER	

KATE JASPER MYSTERIES: Even in sunny California, there are cold-blooded killers . . . "This series is a treasure!" —Carolyn G. Hart

by Jaqueline Girdner

ADJUSTED TO DEATH	FAT-FREE AND FATAL
THE LAST RESORT	TEA-TOTALLY DEAD
MURDER MOST MELLOW	

RENAISSANCE MYSTERIES: Sigismondo the sleuth courts danger—and sheds light on the darkest of deeds . . . "Most entertaining!" —*Chicago Tribune*

by Elizabeth Eyre

DEATH OF THE DUCHESS	CURTAINS FOR THE CARDINAL

PENNYFOOT HOTEL MYSTERIES: In Edwardian England, death takes a seaside holiday . . .

by Kate Kingsbury

ROOM WITH A CLUE	SERVICE FOR TWO
DO NOT DISTURB	

CHARLOTTE GRAHAM MYSTERIES: She's an actress with a flair for dramatics—and an eye for detection. "You'll get hooked on Charlotte Graham!" —*Rave Reviews*

by Stefanie Matteson

MURDER AT THE SPA	MURDER ON THE SILK ROAD
MURDER AT TEATIME	MURDER AT THE FALLS
MURDER ON THE CLIFF	

CURTAINS FOR THE CARDINAL

ELIZABETH EYRE

BERKLEY PRIME CRIME, NEW YORK

This Berkley Prime Crime Book contains the complete text
of the original hardcover edition.
It has been completely reset in a typeface
designed for easy reading, and was printed from new film.

CURTAINS FOR THE CARDINAL

A Berkley Prime Crime Book / published by arrangement with
Harcourt Brace Jovanovich, Inc.

PRINTING HISTORY
Harcourt Brace Jovanovich edition published 1993
Berkley Prime Crime edition / October 1994

ISBN: 0-425-14126-8

Berkley Prime Crime Books are published
by The Berkley Publishing Group,
200 Madison Avenue, New York, NY 10016.
The name BERKLEY PRIME CRIME and the BERKLEY PRIME CRIME
design are trademarks belonging to Berkley Publishing Corporation.

PRINTED IN THE UNITED STATES OF AMERICA

10 9 8 7 6 5 4 3 2 1

CONTENTS

CURTAINS FOR THE CARDINAL

1

Where Was Her Husband?

"THE PRINCESS IS DYING. SHE CAN see no one."

She stood, the brocade curtain in the doorway leading to the bedchamber far less of an obstacle than her bulk in front of it. Her face was designed as a series of pouches—below the eyes, at the cheeks, and in layers under a vestigial chin. She now folded her hands on the ledge of her stomach and glared at this fresh nuisance in her life.

"I come from her brother, lady. From Duke Ludovico of Rocca." He held up the letter, its heavy seal dangling, that he had already shown to three people to get this far. He was a tall man, broad shouldered and quiet spoken. There was a quality about him that injected doubt into the dishevelled mind behind the pouches.

"Duke Ludovico." She put out a hand like a bunch of beringed carrots towards the letter, which in the same moment was withdrawn. The man gave a slight bow as if in excuse.

"His Grace insisted that I give this into Her Grace's hands myself. I carry private messages."

People who work in palaces know about privacy, a commodity so rare that it must, in general, be bought. The bunch of carrots closed over the gleaming little disc he proffered. She turned and lifted the curtain.

The room was as large as a princess's bedroom should be but given solemn darkness by the shutters at the windows. Only firelight and a vigil candle showed the expanse of marble floor and the coved ceiling. The bed on its low platform was also large but in this room looked to be of normal size. It was surmounted by a carved dome, poised on the heads of caryatids whose inlaid eyes glinted.

Two women, staring into the fire that burnt in the great

fireplace, whispered dully; one threw a handful of herbs into the flames, increasing the heaviness of the air. A priest, with a ragged frill of white hair round a bristling tonsure, knelt at the bedfoot, his prayers coming in mumbled bursts as if he were falling asleep. As the door curtain fell behind the Duke's envoy, the candle flame in the Virgin's shrine by the bed ducked, flickered, and sent a gust of smoke up to the Virgin's face, blackened and serene.

The tall man stepping quietly across to the bed was unexpected. The women turned their heads to stare, the priest woke up and was silent a moment before taking up a revitalised recitation; his eyes watched the envoy's approach, alert for an interesting distraction.

Over the pillows, the stout waiting-woman bent as she muttered to the woman who lay there. To the envoy's gaze, keen even in this dimness, the Princess had real need of the steady babble of prayers at the bedfoot—would shortly require those for the dead.

As the envoy came round the bed, a man stirred in a tall chair in the corner and rubbed his eyes. By his close cap and gown he was a doctor, and his standing up released a miasma of smells—herbal, spiritous, and fusty. He had a table there, with bowls, bottles, a flask of leeches, a bleeding-cup, and an astrological chart. He in his turn bent over the pillow. The Princess was, even in this state, beautiful. The envoy traced, in her fine haggard face, a resemblance to the brother he had recently served.

The eyes now opened and looked for him with an effort that spoke of the weight their frail eyelids had become. They were blue like the Duke Ludovico's—always a surprise among so many dark ones.

"Ludovico?"

The doctor drew back and plodded towards the fire. The envoy knelt on the dais beside the bedhead. A small greyhound on a cushion there looked up, blinked suspiciously but did not bark, as if considerate of etiquette in a sickroom.

The women had begun whispering again. The doctor rubbed his shins in the warmth. The flames' mutter, the priest's low chant, and the click of his beads made an undertone of soft sound.

"Highness. I bear a letter from the Duke, your brother."

The news raised a sudden energy in her as he had seen before in the dying. She half raised a thin hand and waved away the company.

"Go. Leave us. We would speak alone."

The nurse shooed the women towards the door. Neither the doctor nor the priest moved, taking it that their callings exempted them from the command. Her voice spoke again, with a peremptory power in its weakness.

"Go. All of you."

The priest stopped his prayers in midword, offended. He got up, catching his foot in his gown and stumbling against the bedfoot, which he took as a reminder that devils catch unfinished syllables. He crossed himself and finished the prayer as he went.

The envoy, watching them go, had two questions he did not ask: Why was a bishop not attending the Princess at this hour, and where was her husband, Prince Livio?

The curtain fell. The Princess and the envoy were alone with the shifting firelight, the sleeping dog.

"Is it Your Highness's wish that I read you His Grace's letter?" The smell of illness was strong, close to the bed, an acid smell stronger than the dried lavender strewn on the pillows and coverlet. A scent of valerian hung about. She would be drowsy.

He read her the letter in his deep voice; it might be wondered how much she was taking in. Her brother asked after her health, hoping that its sudden failing of late was a passing thing, hoping that she would be able to accompany her husband to her daughter Minerva's wedding.

Here the Princess moved her head, No. As the wedding of Minerva to Duke Grifone's son Astorre was to take place on the coming Sunday, at Colleverde in Grifone's duchy of Nemora, and as this was already Tuesday afternoon, it was wholly doubtful that the woman lying here would be present except in the spirit.

Duke Ludovico touched on the recent bereavement that prevented his own attendance there, and then recommended the letter's bearer to her, as one who had saved his life in the late conspiracy against him.

At the finish, the envoy paused, and the sunken eyelids lifted.

"You are that man my brother speaks of?"

A respectful bend of the head, a deep "Sigismondo, and your servant."

Her voice had hardly strength to reach even the oblivious greyhound. "He says he trusts you . . . you saved his life. . . . I have none left to trust you with but another's. Listen . . ." The voice failed. The eyes closed. After a little, she roused herself. "There is one at Fontecasta . . ." Again the voice dwindled. Another few heartbeats of silence, then another small surge of energy gave not strength but speed to her words, a confused and feverish stream. "What will become of my daughter? I wish I had never seen him, never. He betrays everyone, everyone, in the end. . . . *The Duke's eyes are shut.* We must pay for our sins, God protect the innocent! A fatal wedding, a fatal wedding—but what can I do now? The man is a monster . . . yet I did love him once . . . such jealousy! Poor Fabroni . . . such suffering . . ."

To hear her, he knelt with his head almost on the pillow and, outside the door curtain, the women and the doctor looked at each other in silent exasperation. She went on, her voice only a thread of sound. Her hand, shifting on the covers, found his arm and closed on it with startling fierceness.

"Fontecasta. Don't forget." Her hand let go. "Oh no time no time. He is in the dark . . . tell him . . . dark . . . take him to my brother . . . my daughter . . ."

"My daughter."

There was a Bishop after all; in fact, an Archbishop. The tapestry along the wall behind the bed billowed as the doors opened and the little procession entered.

This was no priest who could be dismissed. He came in robes that coruscated with jewels and gold thread, among candles borne by acolytes, under a canopy carried by priests, with the Host, with the ampulla, with a censer. Sigismondo rose, bowed profoundly, and backed away. He knelt again as the Host passed him and withdrew towards the doors by which the procession had entered.

The Archbishop, in a sonorous voice pitched to carry, proclaimed, "You must make your confession, my daughter.

Your time in this world draws to its close. Shed the concerns of this world and make ready your soul for the next."

He was now at her side. The procession remained at a distance to preserve the secrecy of the confessional. The white-haired priest, vested in full robes, had returned with them and reasserted his dignity by trying to arrange them in proper grouping. The other doorway had its curtain drawn aside and was crowded with kneeling women. Sigismondo was joined by the little greyhound, which had all the discretion of a natural courtier, but he noticed a stir of the arras behind the bed, suggesting the presence of other dogs less reverent.

The voice of the Princess had recovered a little of its fugitive strength so that it could just be heard that she was speaking, but the words could be audible only to someone close to her as she made confession.

Suddenly the arras behind the bedhead was dashed aside so violently that its hooks ripped from the wall. Its powdery dust made an aura round the man who emerged into candlelight. He stood for a long moment, in black and cloth of gold, his pallor emphasised by the black hair and beard, the wide dark eyes. He moved, trying to speak. The Archbishop had recoiled but, as the Princess's voice did not falter, he leant forward once more, though staring still at the apparition.

At last the Prince had made his entrance.

His sword was clogged in its scabbard like the words in his mouth. He dragged at it, as the Archbishop rose, arms spread to protect the dying woman; but Prince Livio's intent was elsewhere.

His sword was out. He followed it at a rush to the doors where Sigismondo stood. Boys in cottas and cassocks hurled themselves from his path, to be thrust away in turn by Sigismondo who, at the Prince's heels, heard his hypnotized whisper: "*Betrayed me! Betrayed me! Bastards! Bastards!*"

Along the dim, vaulted corridor he went. From a doorway that he passed, a girl emerged and breathed "Father?" towards his back. In a cloud of fair hair and crumpled gold dress, she clung to the doorjamb, and as Sigismondo passed she followed.

There was a brightly lit anteroom at the end, opening onto a chapel from which a number of courtiers came. The Prince hurtled towards them. Faces of men and women, courtiers who had been praying for their Princess, became masks of shock or fear as they saw his face, his sword. One came forward alone. The face, so like the girl in the doorway, so like the Princess, marked him as her son. His rank showed in the velvet tunic scrolled with golden arabesques and the collar of smouldering rubies round his neck.

"Father! Is she—"

The Prince's sword violently swept, dividing the chain of rubies from the cloud of gold hair. A lady who had sunk to the ground in a terrified curtsey at sight of the Prince received the boy's head in her lap and, screaming, jerked it to the floor; it rolled until it lay staring as if in surprise at the man it had called father.

The body dropped. Blood had rained everywhere, its smell mingling with the incense and the candlewax.

"Eugenio! You devil! I know the truth!"

The Prince's sword, pointing at the head, dripped into the fair hair. Courtiers crowded back, leaving a tall handsome man, pale as his shirt, isolated, gazing in fearful astonishment from the Prince's distorted face to the head, as though Hell gaped before him.

"Highness!—"

The Duke's envoy did not wait. He had heard a movement behind him. The girl had come to the anteroom entrance. She had seen, and lay crumpled at the foot of the archway.

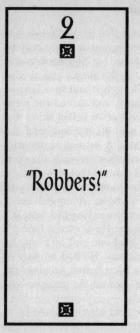

2

"Robbers?"

UNNOTICED AMID THE SCREAMING, the scattering of courtiers, everyone rushing, some falling, he picked her up and carried her into the room from which she had come.

He shot the small brass bolt on her door, although it would be ineffective against any serious assault. Laying the unconscious girl on her bed, he looked around and picked up a dark cloak that lay on a painted coffer nearby. He opened the shutters on the evening light and, after a moment's reconnoitre, turned back. Swathing the girl in the cloak, he picked her up and went out onto the loggia. The shuttered windows of the Princess Oralia's room offered no danger, but a gardener with a can was below, scooping water from a fountain basin and trudging to the parterres. Beyond him was a gate in a high wall.

Sigismondo hoisted the girl over his shoulder and strode to the loggia's end, where a vine had established its branches for years up the wall from below. He constantly turned his head, watchful for eyes. The climb down would be a vulnerable time, but he could afford no pause.

From the anteroom, the uproar burst into the Princess's chamber. The gardener, and another man from under the loggia, stared up at the shuttered windows. Sigismondo drew into the shadows, and there hidden looked at them through the balustrading until both of them, in loud argument, ran into the Palace. Sigismondo's passage to the ground was in the nature of a controlled fall—his burden forcing him out from the wall, his feet making footholds in the vine's branches and the trellis where they might. His face showed nothing but vigilance as he strode through the garden, unbarred the gate, and went through.

He shifted the girl's weight and set off along a pleached

alley. Uproar in the Palace might mean that the girl's loss had been discovered and a search had been begun; it might only be the reaction to what the Prince had done, but Sigismondo was now moving fast. Another solid gate at the alley's end needed unbarring and unlatching; he was through it and in a narrow dusty lane. He took the girl in his arms and tucked the wrap more securely round the betraying gold-sewn velvet skirts and over her face. As he walked on, he bent his hooded head and went swiftly through the narrow streets. A woman seeing him crossed herself. She saw a stricken mourner carrying a corpse.

He turned a corner and descended a street that was shallow long steps. A bird sang in a cage; Sigismondo walked through shadows of washing from the lines above. A ragged child, seeing someone well dressed, ran after him crying in a beggar's voice until he strode out of her territory. He skirted a tanner's vat that reeked on a corner, and crossed one end of a square. People glanced; some crossed themselves. He had no way of knowing, in a town where he had not been before, whether the carrying of a corpse by daylight was against the statutes—he had met such a law elsewhere.

He reached a maze of small alleys, but after a minute or so he came to a slight widening in the street and turned to the right and whistled as he passed the trees and fountain.

It was towards evening. The town clock had already struck six. It had doggedly insisted on its own time for some years now, and the townspeople of Montenero cherished it for warning them in advance of what time it was going to be, thus providing an illusion of being prepared. The small grubby man sitting on the steps of the fountain had been lulled by the afternoon sun's warmth and the splash of water into dozing. The bell of the clock roused him. His business was to be prepared, and as working for his master had so far taught him that he could seldom, if ever, tell for what he was to be prepared, he sat up, splashed his face from the fountain, and looked about him.

The horses at least were still there, reins looped round his wrist, but although he looked half-witted, he well knew that a sharp knife could have taken care of that; had he really fallen asleep there might have been no horses at the reins' end. There was a boy patting the nose of the big dun as it was. Benno twitched the reins, the horse jerked its head, and the boy stepped back.

A weary-looking party of pilgrims straggled up to the fountain and started to drink, fill their water bottles, wash the dust from their faces, and argue about which hospice to try for their lodging. Their arrival raised the hopes of a woman sitting nearby on a doorstep with baskets of dried plums and olives, and she raised her voice and her prices accordingly. One of the pilgrims, a stout woman sweating under her long-flapped linen cap, let herself down on the steps beside Benno and nursed a foot, groaning.

"What roads! It'll be remembered to me in Purgatory, these roads." She turned a red moonface towards him and talked on as she took off her shoe. "I'm doing this for my daughter, you know. I've left her at home with my mother, too ill to move." She stopped as she took in Benno's vacant gaze and hanging jaw, decided that more gossip was wasted on a mind that might not have room for it, and went back to massaging her foot.

Benno, his own hunger stimulated by the sight and smell of the pilgrims noisily eating their olives and dried plums, delved into the recesses of his tunic and produced a heel of a loaf and some cheese that had both contributed to the smell of his clothes and gained something from them. He ate with relish and listened to the pilgrims squabbling.

He was beginning to wonder about his own journey when he heard the whistle.

It brought him to his feet. A little dog that had been foraging from group to group, eating anything that was offered and anything that was not but was in reach, pricked up its one ear and rushed to follow him.

Benno saw, amazed, that his master was carrying what, from the swathing that could only be skirts, must be a girl. His master had never had to steal a girl so far. He found, too, when he had to support her weight as Sigismondo hoisted her up before him on the big dun, that she was no mere slip of a thing. Benno clamped his mouth shut, picked up the dog Biondello, and mounted. They rode at a brisk unhurried pace out of the city by the nearest gate.

Sigismondo turned off the road as soon as they came to

woods. The girl was stirring. Benno dismounted, and she was
lowered into his arms. He put her down on a mossy bank under
a beech, and the cloak slid away showing a gold dress richly
embroidered. Benno stared as Sigismondo dismounted.

"Hmm-mm! Well done, Benno—not one question!" As he
bent to look at the girl, he said: "You'll get some answers in a
while, but be warned, ask nothing. I have as many questions as
you."

The girl opened her eyes. Her last glimpse of the world had
been her brother's head staring up from the marble floor; this,
now, was two dark figures looking down at her, silhouetted
against a pale violet sky seen through branches. Her mind
refused to provide any solution and, shying like a frightened
horse from that last image of horror, told her that she was
dreaming.

"My lady . . ."

Her body, unfortunately, began to contradict her mind,
informing her that the bank under her was cold, perhaps damp,
and full of roots or stones; that the evening breeze chilled her;
that the man now bending over her, whose face she could not
see, had definitely spoken to her. He took her hand in a warm
one that could not belong to a dream.

"My lady, we are your friends. You must trust us."

She sat up, so swiftly that it made her dizzy, and snatched
her hand from his. Robbers! Thieves! Somehow they had got
her from the Palace to this wood. They would ask her father for
ransom.

Again she heard the noise of the sword, heard the screaming,
and saw her brother's eyes staring from the scarlet floor. She
took hold of her own head and would have let herself slip into
the safe world of darkness, only the big robber was holding her
up, kneeling at her side, and pressing the rim of a flask to her
lips. She tried to avert her head, but he tipped the flask so
quickly that liquid ran into her mouth and automatically down
her throat. She had never drunk anything so fiery. She coughed
and held her mouth as he lifted her to her feet.

"We mustn't stay here. Your father will have men out
searching for us."

There! Robbers . . . ? Again she saw the flash of the sword
and that half-view of her father's face, distorted as he swung it.

She stared up at the tall robber and shrieked: "He killed him! I saw! He *killed* him!"

"Come, my lady. Come now, or he may kill you too."

She stood, in the near dark, staring at the men she could not see. "Why did he? Why? Is he mad?"

"Perhaps. I think he believes your mother betrayed him and that you are not his own children. That's why he's likely to seek you out—to kill you as he killed your brother. As for me, I was sent to your mother by your uncle, Ludovico of Rocca, and I'll take you back to him. Come."

She did not resist as he led her towards the horses cropping at the edge of the wood. He supported her again when she tripped on the uneven ground; but when he had mounted and reached for her, she baulked and cried: "My mother? It's not true! She is a saint, and he loves her."

She was pulled effortlessly up, the strong arms closed round her, and the horse began to move under them. She said again, "*He loves her!*"

The man's chest seemed to vibrate in agreement, but he also shook his head. "M'mhm-m. He loved her, my lady; but he was jealous. Nothing so bitter as jealousy. If he believes you and your brother are not his children, that may be what has sent him beyond all reason."

She drew breath sharply, remembering that half-seen face, distorted, not like father's at all. He must have looked like that when he killed the musician Fabroni, her mother's lutanist. Suddenly she started, so instinctively his arm tightened.

"My mother. I must go back. I must!" she said imperiously. "I must see her—she's dying. . . ." She looked up into the dark, strong face, seeing for the first time the hook of the nose, the curve of the mouth, but taking in only his expression. She looked away, over the shadowy countryside to the rim of orange and green on the horizon. It all blurred.

"She's dead. She died, and I wasn't there." She stared out at the countryside, silent, and wiped her tears away with her fingers again and again, while he rode on in the dusk.

Benno came alongside as the path allowed it. He rode with his face turned towards his companions, his mouth open as though all he had heard stretched his jaw as much as his wits. He ventured a hoarse whisper.

"She the Princess's daughter?" He knew his master disliked questions, but at this moment he needed to know. Sigismondo's confirming nod gave him ground for piecing the rest of all he had heard together, and the result did nothing to close his mouth. Another piece of information became vital.

"Where we going then?"

"To see a man whose name I don't know."

"Does he live far?"

"We'll find out. A place called Fontecasta."

"In this direction?"

"We're trying this one to start with." And Sigismondo, holding the weeping girl more firmly, spurred his horse.

3

"Who Is My Father?"

BENNO HAD HEARD ENOUGH TO make him frankly sorry not to have witnessed the dramas—provided he'd been in no danger of getting involved. He was also sorry for the girl with a dead mother, a slaughtered brother, and the mad father who wasn't a father perhaps. It relieved his mind to realise that, exhausted by what she had been through and lulled by the steady rhythm of the horse, she had fallen asleep.

He glanced at the risen quarter moon, pale in the almost dark sky.

"So they'll be after us? Looking for *her?*"

"Mm-mm . . . perhaps. The Princess Oralia was much loved."

Benno scratched his beard. "You mean they won't *want* to find us? Have to try all the same, won't they, right? Not going to tell the Prince they don't feel like it, when he's got his sword out. You reckon he's killed anyone else?"

"Who could stop him? A prince is his own justice." Sigismondo glanced down at the sleeping girl. "I heard in Rocca that Prince Livio is given to sudden seizures of violence—that he killed his wife's lutanist a year or so ago only for being in love with her. He believes he knows his wife's lover, and I hardly think that man still lives."

"He believes?"

"It may be that he listened to the Princess Oralia's confession, behind the arras."

"Listened to her confession?" Benno was horrified.

"Mm-hm-hm-hm."

"But he only believes?" Part of Benno's cloak moved abruptly, and the small dog poked its head out to look round and sniff the night air. As if in sympathy, a dog barked miles away. "You think it's not right, then? Bit late for whoever-it-was, sorry, my mistake, here's your head back."

Sigismondo, in the midst of an appreciative hum, checked his horse and, putting back his hood with one hand, turned his head to listen.

"If we want to keep ours, we'll move into that wood."

Benno had been about to put the little dog down for a run. He caught him back in midspring and stuffed him under the cloak again. They moved off the track and under trees, down into a convenient dip in the ground. A small stream, silver in the early moonlight, ran through at their feet. After some minutes, the birds they had disturbed stopped scolding them, and they could hear horses in the distance and see, through the trees, a confused glow of torches approaching.

The girl had half-roused once the horses stopped moving. Sigismondo breathed a word or two in her ear, which kept her silent as they watched the party of horsemen ride by. The little dog extruded a nose that twitched vivaciously, but he had long known the wisdom of silence when danger was near. In any case, the horsemen were making such a noise, calling out to each other over the clatter of hooves on the stony path, that a little barking might have gone unheard. Certainly no one paid heed when Benno's horse stamped. Benno imagined the horsemen had plenty to discuss, events such as had occurred, even under their Prince, not happening with much frequency. Also they would be aware, like all travelers by night, that other creatures that might not be human, or even animal, were abroad in the moonlight, and noise had a sustaining power on the spirits. No doubt, even if not anxious to find the Princess's daughter, they were very anxious not to return and confront their Prince before his temper had time to cool.

The noise died to almost nothing. Sigismondo said, "Stay, Benno," and rode his horse up to the bank. He could be made out, in the dapple of light, standing on his saddle beneath an oak. The girl, with the reins in her hand, lifted a pale face in a cloud of silvery hair to watch him hoist himself into the branches and climb.

Suddenly he was lowering himself to the saddle again. "We'll follow them as far as a branching track. They've just passed it—too steep for them, and I dare say they're on the direct route to Rocca. But for us—hey, we'll not waste the moonlight."

Benno's horse caught up with Sigismondo's on the path. The dog, settled under his cloak, put out its head and barked, once. The girl gave it a dazed glance—it was another odd thing among so many—but she was beginning to rouse to curiosity.

"I'm not sure I know why I should believe that you saved me, that you mean me well, that my uncle sent you. Who are you?"

"Sigismondo is my name, Lady. And I promise I will take you to your uncle, Duke Ludovico of Rocca, whom I have served."

Benno recalled perfectly well that his master had spoken of going to see a man whose name he didn't know, in a direction he didn't seem to be sure of. Like the dog, however, he knew when to stay quiet. The girl was thoughtful.

"Why should my uncle send you? I've never seen you before." She turned to look up at him.

"I came with a message from His Grace of Rocca to your mother. He was anxious, having heard that all was not well with her, and because of his mourning he would not be meeting her at Colleverde."

This oblique reference to what was to happen at Colleverde plunged her into more uncertainty: her marriage . . . if she were not her father's daughter . . . all her world had been turned upside down.

Her tears were once again silent, and she wiped them off with the back of her hand. Her rings of pearl and diamond gleamed as the moon caught them in a kindred light, and Benno thought comfortably: We shan't go short of food.

Less than half an hour later, Benno was feeling nearly sated as he sat toasting his shins at a small fire and combing his beard with his fingers. Biondello sat at his feet, lopsided head between Benno's knees in case bits of food dropped to him. Sigismondo, who had led them into this rocky hollow, off that side track the search party had not taken, was drinking wine. His saddlebags had yielded a number of things: a thicker dark cloak for the girl that completely covered the crumpled gold velvet, a flat round loaf, cheese, hard-boiled eggs, and half a cold chicken, as well as the piece of smoked sausage Benno had eaten and the wine that at first was all the girl would take.

The firelight showed her younger than Benno had thought. The smooth curve of cheek, chin, and neck, the rounded forehead under the crimped hair, held promise rather than fulfilment of beauty. Suddenly she sat up.

"Who *is* my father?"

4

To Call on a Dead Man

THE QUESTION WAS ABRUPT AND delivered with energy. She turned imperiously on Sigismondo, who wiped his mouth with the heel of his hand and capped the flask, while she moved impatiently.

"Possibly it was the Lord Eugenio, Highness."

She looked startled but, as she considered it, not displeased. The Lord Eugenio's rank and person evidently weren't despicable; that he was not a prince might be a detraction, but still she was the daughter of a princess. Perhaps she was glad not to be the daughter of Prince Livio after what she'd seen.

Her face contracted suddenly as if she'd seen it again. Almost hastily she said, "Does my— the Prince know?"

Sigismondo's voice was matter-of-fact. "The Prince believed that Lord Eugenio was your father, so I don't think he would have let him live."

She shut her mouth hard. She had seen the sword used and did not doubt it would be used again.

"You said, 'Possibly.' You meant it may not be the Lord Eugenio?"

"Even princes can be wrong."

"Did my mother *tell* him? Surely she'd never have told him. She'd know it would put him in a fury, and we'd not be safe—" Sigismondo's hood fell back as he turned to put the flask away, and she gave a soft cry of astonishment. "You're a priest! Did my mother confess to you? Do you *know* who my father is?"

Sigismondo passed his hand over his shaven scalp and smiled. "No, Highness. I am not a priest, and your mother did not tell me who your father is. She may have wanted me to find him."

"Then he's not dead?" She was leaning forward. "Take me to him! He will protect me from—" She stopped, as if she flinched.

"I do not know that the man your mother spoke of to me is your father. Her Highness gave me to understand that he is in danger and that she wished me to take him to Rocca. I don't know for certain where he lives, but Heaven send we can find him before the Prince does."

He offered her a piece of bread folded round a wedge of chicken, and she took it, almost absentmindedly. Terrible images in the brain do not always prevent the body from asserting its right to be fed, particularly not at fourteen.

She accepted the flask, after Sigismondo had courteously wiped the rim with the cloth that had wrapped the bread, and she even giggled at the inexpert swig that sent some wine trickling down her chin to drop on the gold velvet. She held out her hand for the cloth to wipe her face but did not bother with the dress. She had always been served on bended knee from a goblet and had certainly never had to remove a stain from a dress. There were maids to clean such, with feathers soaked in hot water; she had watched them do it. Now she took more chicken and spoke resolutely.

"I thought I would have seen my uncle Ludovico this Sunday in any case, at my wedding. You will have heard he was going to be a guest of Duke Grifone when I marry his son in Colleverde."

"When you marry the Lord Astorre." Sigismondo did not suggest that the marriage might not now take place.

"I was betrothed to his older brother Ercole, who died. I was eight then. Ercole was fourteen and very ugly. I wished even then that it was Astorre instead. He was eleven and very handsome. . . ."

Her voice faltered on this childish confidence, born of wine and shock. The marriage had joined all the uncertainties of her life. It was true that the bastards of great lords were almost as much valued for marriage as were their legitimate children; the bastards of their wives were a different matter, although a Duke's niece . . . she felt adrift, her status in question and, deeper than this, the foundation of her very self. She went on more resolutely still: "My mother"—she stopped and gave

Biondello the last piece of chicken, which she had been going to eat— "my mother took me there." She looked round. "It was at just this time of year, only there was a full moon; we stopped on the way home because my mother saw that man stumbling among rocks in the distance."

"A man, alone? Why did your mother stop?"

"She thought he was ill and needed help, that perhaps he'd been robbed and left to die. My mother was a *saint*," she added defiantly, as if to remind them that Christian charity must outweigh adultery.

Sigismondo bent to put more twigs on the fire.

"And had he been robbed?"

She shuddered. Here was another image she would never forget.

"They brought him up to our litter. I remember how slow they were, and I was so anxious about the escort going ahead if there were robbers, and she wouldn't let me call out to them, and I wondered why. And the baggage mules were far back, they'd stopped, and I could hear the men quarrelling. We were nearly alone . . . they brought this man right up to our litter and showed him to my mother. There was blood all down his face. It looked black by the moon, but the flambeau made it red . . . Mother had him tended, of course."

"What happened to him after that?"

"I don't know." She shrugged. "Mother thought I shouldn't know. She was very distressed, but she didn't want me to fret over strangers even with blood all over them. She told me he would be taken care of. I didn't see him again. I had bad dreams about his face, but I'd nearly—in a way—forgotten him until tonight, because it's like then. It was cold then too."

She spread out her hands to warm them and drew back with an "Oh!" as Sigismondo, with a branch she had thought he was adding as fuel, raked the fire away from her and broke it up, spreading the embers, that at once dimmed. He bowed with a courtier's grace.

"Highness, we must move on. It was necessary to rest and to eat, but we must wait until we are on safer ground before we sleep. The party searching for you will return, and though our fire was hidden, the smell of smoke drifts a long way down the wind."

She made no objection. Benno, passing Sigismondo on the way to replace the saddlebags, asked in a low mutter, "We off to Rocca then?"

"I think," said Sigismondo, faceless in the shadow of his hood, "I think we are going to call on a dead man."

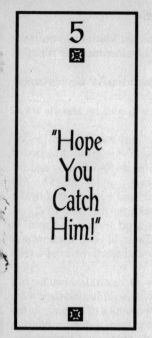

5

"Hope You Catch Him!"

AN ADVANTAGE OF NOT SLEEPING, Benno reflected as his horse picked its way up the stony track they were following, is that you can't have nightmares. If the young lady has seen her brother killed, it's odds on she won't dream of nightingales and roses.

He was still trying to work out how urgent the danger was. What about this calling on a dead man? Benno put nothing beyond his master, even witchcraft, but the idea of conjuring people from the graves where they belonged failed to appeal. In the kitchens and stables where he had listened to stories, Benno had formed an opinion that Tuscan ghosts were the superiors of their kind. He had much rather not disturb them.

"We must have you out of those clothes, my lady, as soon as we can."

Dazed as she was from the extraordinary experience of riding through the night in the arms of a man she had never seen before—even to touch a man other than her father had been unthinkable for the virgin daughter of a prince—this roused her. She sat up straight, her eyes fierce in the early dawn light.

"What do you mean? How dare you!"

"Forgive me, Highness." The deep voice was amused. "My meaning is that you must not be recognized. By now the Prince will guess that you've had help to escape him. By now he may have heard that the Princess, your mother, received a messenger from Rocca. Nothing more likely than that such a messenger, who was gone so swiftly, will be taking you to Duke Ludovico. We shall be looked for on all the possible ways to Rocca."

"I think," said the young lady, and her voice had unexpectedly a trace of a giggle, "that I might be as noticeable riding in my shift."

"A young lady such as yourself would be noticeable anywhere."

This was gallantry of the sort she was used to, and she asked no further explanation.

Perhaps an hour later, when the sun was up and the air beginning to be warm, they came upon the pilgrims. Voices and a sound of splashing had been audible as Sigismondo and his party came through the trees cresting a small hill. The girl instinctively made sure her dress and head were covered by the cloak. The last journey she had taken on the open road had been at the age of eight, and, quite apart from any danger of being recognized, she felt that almost anyone encountered outside the Palace might display some characteristics of a wild beast.

A number of the pilgrims they saw as they rode down the hill had, indeed, one thing in common with wild beasts: they wore no clothes. They had seized the opportunity of bathing in the waters of the holy spring that bubbled from a stone conduit to make a pool overhung by bushes of juniper and bordered by reeds. It was the holy spring that had made them choose an awkward and stony track they would normally have avoided, and total immersion not only ensured that they would reap the maximum spiritual benefit from the water, but, such was the grace of God, they could also wash away the dust of the journey and even ease the inflammation of the fleabites acquired on their travels. Rosemary bushes on the slope of the hillside sported drying shifts and shirts. One of the pilgrims had just struck up a rather dreary chant, to which a couple more responded, but most were simply enjoying the water. A boy who began larking about and splashing others was suppressed by a tonsured bather.

Seeing strangers ride up, one or two of the women crossed hands over their breasts or gave at the knees so that the water covered them further, but most gazed, without concealing their curiosity or themselves. A burly fellow, most likely their hired guide, who had not stripped like the rest, rose from near the bushes, holding a pilgrim's staff that looked like a possible weapon, and hailed them.

"On your way to Colleverde too? For the relics and the wedding?"

Sigismondo reined up, dismounted, and took the bundled girl in his arms, the cloak wrapped firmly round her. "My daughter's health and strength are what I seek. Anything that can restore that, I'll visit."

The pilgrims responded heartily. "Carry her into this water— it's under the protection of Saint Luke and Saint Christopher!"

"Bring her into the water."

"The saints will help the poor child."

Sigismondo strode forward, and Benno detected an effort at kicking in the swathed feet; he had been servant to a young unmarried lady in the past and had an inkling of what a Princess's daughter might be feeling as she was borne towards a bunch of naked peasants anxious for her to join them. His master, however, arranged all with great decorum, holding up the cloak, his head averted while his supposed daughter shed her incriminating dress. She had at first, when Sigismondo put her feet to the ground, stood rigid. She might have been invoking the saints of the spring to provide a very sudden landslide, not sparing her rescuer. She would not move to undo her dress until he spoke a few words in a low voice that set her fingers working under the cloak. Benno hoped she could undress without maids and had proof of her competence when she kicked a crumpled bundle of gold velvet out behind her from under the hem of the cloak. Benno crouched to retrieve it and had clasped it to his bosom, partly stifling Biondello, when he was poked sharply in the rump by a staff.

"Respect the lady's modesty, rascal! No peeking!"

Sigismondo gravely thanked the pilgrims' guide. "The fellow has but few wits, and he is a born lecher."

Benno, who had matched his expression to the first part of the statement, had no difficulty in letting his jaw sag still further at the injustice of the second part. Sigismondo continued, "I am taking him to Colleverde in the hope that the relics may have some power over his nature." He tossed his cloak at Benno and picked up the girl, shrinking in her shift. The guide escorted them down to the poolside, where the pilgrims had

crowded forward with kindly enthusiasm. A woman with her
head tied up in a cloth like a pudding was especially solicitous.
All attention was on the girl, hiding her face in her hair, and
after her father had explained that to carry her into the water
might bring on one of her seizures, the pilgrims were quick to
offer her the water to drink and, cupping their hands, scooped
the water over her with energy. The little ceremony incited the
chanter to start up again, and soon nearly everyone, Sigismondo's voice deeper than all the rest, was singing. The girl sat on
the bank where Sigismondo had put her, shivering, possibly
with rage. Sigismondo helped her to her feet.

Suddenly, the sound of their singing was broken into by the
thudding of hoofbeats, and all turned to see if another traveller
had come to seek the holy spring. What they saw was Benno,
flat to the neck of his small grey, galloping furiously into the
distance along a track among the trees.

Sigismondo was the first to shout out. He had run to beat
among the bushes. "Villain! He's stolen my child's dress as
well as the horse!" He strode back, picked up the girl and
carried her to where the great dun waited patiently by the track,
unlooped the reins from the tree branch, put the girl up, and
mounted, while the pilgrim guide shook his staff and shouted,
"You're lucky he hadn't the wit to steal both horses!"

Sigismondo, wrapping his own cloak round the soaking girl,
scowled at the joke as he shortened the reins and dug in his
heels. The pilgrims, like so many wet piglets, clambered from
the water to search among their own clothes.

"Hope you catch him!" was shouted into the dust kicked up
by the big dun as it set off furiously after the grey.

The pilgrims, collecting and sorting their clothes, drying
themselves and dressing, rehearsed the event over and over.
They reckoned themselves lucky the half-wit hadn't stolen
even more. The boy seemed to be the only one to have lost his
clothes, and one of the pilgrims, a stout man prudent and rich
enough to be carrying a spare tunic in his pack (for he felt the
cold), had his Christian charity stretched to the uttermost when
public opinion decided he should offer it to the boy, with no
more recompense than a future blessing from the saints.

6

"There's the Witch"

THE DAUGHTER OF THE PRINCESS Oralia was so angry she could have spat in her rescuer's face—if indeed he were a rescuer and not a common robber as she had first thought; his half-wit servant had after all just proved to be a thief. She had suffered the humiliation of being soaked to the skin by a crowd of officious peasants while he stood by *and encouraged* them—and to be jolted, helpless in his grip as they thundered along the track! Difficult to stamp the foot and let fly one's feelings when one was seated painfully on the saddlebow of a speeding horse with one's face in a leather jerkin; but as soon as the pace slowed, and he wheeled off the track among trees, and she opened her mouth to begin, there of all things was the half-wit waiting for them and grinning. Was he so much of an idiot he expected praise for stealing?

"Well done, Benno."

"Well done? *Well done?*" She heard her voice run up into a squawk.

"Give me the dress."

Sigismondo lowered her to the ground, where to her fury she stumbled. He dismounted, took the dress, and looked about. The dress was a crumpled ruin and moreover stinking wet, a circumstance explained by the eruption of the woolly grey dog from Benno's bosom, leaping to the ground. Sigismondo went off a few paces among the trees and thrust the embroidered velvet at arm's length under a tree root between rocks and began to fill the hollow with stones.

"What are you doing? That's my *dress!* Am I to die of cold? Is that what you've planned? Have you forgotten who I am? I'm not to be treated like this!—" She was about to remind him who she was, and of her title, when it came to her that her father, the source of her standing, had disowned her.

"I am not to be treated like this!" she said bravely, after her hesitation.

"Hadn't she better be quiet?" the half-wit asked anxiously. Sigismondo shrugged.

"If they could hear her, they'd think she was having a seizure." He turned to the girl with a tinge of severity in his voice. "My Lady, our actions have reason. I said you must change your clothes."

Benno was pulling a crumpled mess from a saddlebag. She saw with disgust it was peasant clothes: grey linen, drab cloth, thick woollens, with rustic embroidery in coarse wool.

"We'll have to find or make you new shoes as soon as may be, but your own slippers will have to do until then."

"I won't wear that. I'd rather die of cold than let those awful things touch me. How dare you think of it? How dare—"

"Highness." The deep voice cut in harshly. "Your life is in danger. The choice of dying of cold or at the hands of Prince Livio is no longer yours—"

Her mind echoed the sound of a sword blow; her brother's face stared from the ground.

"—it is mine. Put the clothes on."

She looked at him, at the steady dark gaze, the firm mouth, the whole uncompromising strength of will. After a moment she held out her hand, and Benno brought her the loathsome bundle.

She shook the things out, as the horses stamped and one tried to browse the early buds of a bush. She could not make sense of what she held; then she exclaimed, "These are boys' clothes!"

She looked at Sigismondo and saw that he was smiling. "A disguise," he said, his voice suggesting intrigue, adventure. "They will be looking for a girl." She still hesitated between the repellent clothes and his conviction that she would wear them.

"I don't know how they go on."

Sigismondo proved to be a competent, impersonal lady's maid. After she had put on the shirt behind a tree, drying herself on her damp shift, he directed her tying of hose to shirt and the lacing of the tunic. Her skin crawled at the contact of coarse, unclean woollen, but she thought, when it was finished, that she might at least get his *Well done* or some acknowledgement of her compliance. The dark eyes looked her over. "Can you walk like a boy?"

She envisaged strutting like a young man at court. She would look a fool. "No," she said flatly.

He put her up on his horse, shortening the stirrups, and took the bridle. She expected him to turn back to the track, but he looked about and turned the horse's head uphill and led the way across the hillside. At first he picked a way among rocks, then they came out of scrub and saplings to a hanging wood of beeches, where the horses' feet thudded on a century of mast. A bird chirruped, but the woods were curiously quiet, and when a pigeon took flight, Benno's horse pranced and the girl was startled.

"Where are we going?" she asked. Nobody answered. She kicked the horse to urge him forward and force Sigismondo to react, but the horse knew well enough that, whoever was on his back, the master was at his head, and it did not respond. Still they climbed and by the sun were heading back the way they had come but higher up across the hill.

Now they were among juniper and cypresses. A path, or a dry watercourse, or both, seemed to lead in their direction and he took it. She had to lie along the horse's neck as the path climbed beneath strange-shaped rocks.

Sigismondo stopped without warning and, putting a hand down, drew a knife from his boot. They were silent, waiting. Then she heard pebbles rattling and little pattering footsteps. Into view down the track came a black-and-brown goat that stopped abruptly when it saw them. A boy came alongside the goat—to her aristocratic eyes an extravagantly filthy, ragged boy, who eyed them with a distrust identical to that of the goat. Clad in a goatskin and rags, he carried a staff.

"Where does this lead?" Sigismondo sheathed the knife and nodded at the pathway.

"Nowhere you'd want to go."

"I'll choose that for myself. Where does it lead?"

"There's the village. Lot of strong men and dogs there, I can tell you. And it's a good long way." Clearly strangers had a hard time around here.

"What else?"

The boy made a quick gesture and fingered his breast as if he had a talisman.

"Fontecasta. You keep off the villa, that's all." The goat bleated in baleful confirmation.

"What's at the villa then?"

The boy looked over his shoulder, fearfully, as if someone might be listening. "There's the witch."

"The witch. Yes?"

"And dogs that aren't dogs. And devils."

"Mmm-hm," said Sigismondo with faint derision.

"It's *not* nothing," said the boy. "*He* lives there."

"He?"

"The dead man."

7

"I Must See Her"

THEY FOLLOWED THE HIGH WALL round. It was tiled along the top, but tiles had slid off and lay in the rough brown grass. Benno's horse trod on one, with a crack that made the girl jump. Rosy brick showed through where patches of plaster had crumbled away. They came to the gate. Stone pineapples that topped the pillars were chipped as if some great bird had fancied a titbit.

Sigismondo helped the girl to dismount and handed her the reins to hold. She took them with a sense of shock—her first menial task—and watched him knock three times on the sun-bleached wood. Distant dogs barked within. A bird called as if in warning. Benno crossed himself.

Sigismondo knocked again, thrice, and then stepped back to scan the top of the gate and the wall, as though considering a way over, when the girl drew a sharp breath.

The wood panel behind the rusted grille of the wicket had slid back, without sound, and an eye was peering at them. It was black, hooded with wrinkles, and malignant.

They could hear muttered words, only a few of which made sense. "Be off. I'll set the dogs on you."

So far the threat was human, although the eye looked well able to conjure more mischief than this.

"I have business with your master. From the Lady of Montenero."

The panel, checked halfway in sliding home, was slowly put back again. The head moved to let the eye see all three of them.

"Montenero?" The voice, rusty as the grille, might have been unused to framing intelligible words. Sigismondo stepped nearer, his own voice softened and persuasive.

"We come from the lady, the friend to your master. She has

sent me with messages, and they are urgent. He is in danger."

For a moment the girl thought he had failed; the panel slammed closed; but the noise of that was followed by the creak of a bar, and the gates shifted a little. Then came the squeal and thud of bolts drawn back. The wicket door opened.

The woman holding it was not as old as her eye had suggested. The white hair under the cap was abundant, and her movements showed vigour. If Benno had not known she was a witch, he might have thought the rosy brown face behind the scowl not unattractive. She was holding a hoe like a weapon.

The hoe indicated Sigismondo, and she grumbled under her breath as she jerked her head towards the house behind. Bending his head, Sigismondo stepped through the wicket without a backward glance. The hoe was shaken, with menace, at the others as the gate shut. Benno and the girl were left staring, listening to the thud of bolts. At once the girl handed the dun's reins to Benno. She was not going to play page in front of nobody. Benno freed a hand to fish in the bosom of his shirt, where he found a holy medal and pressed it to his lips. The dog's face showed, but it did not emerge. Benno pressed the medal to its brow and to its muzzle, and it sneezed devoutly.

The girl was cold. Her legs were not used to the air, and in the shade of the wall and the encroaching trees she longed for her skirts, for warmth and comfort. That man had simply deserted them here! Besides, her incredulity of peasant superstition about witches had been uncomfortably shaken by the old woman. It brought images from childhood too deep to remember clearly.

My master all over! Benno thought. He rejoiced in Sigismondo's cleverness in leading them here, uphill from the pilgrims' "holy waters" to find the stream's source, the pure spring, *fonte casta*.

The girl began to pace up and down, practising a boyish stride, and rubbed her arms. She did not want to shiver, but she was chilled and hungry. She had been, two days ago, sure of her world. Now not only her past but her future seemed to have vanished. She was orphaned, lost, disguised, bewildered, and determined not to cry.

†   †   †

As Sigismondo crossed the mossy cobbles of the courtyard after the old woman, a pair of doves rose from the roof tiles with a clap of wings and beat over their heads. The barking of dogs was louder now, and he could hear the snatching rattle of chains as they leaped to free themselves and rush to sample the stranger. Nothing else stirred. Nobody looked from a window or came to see what the barking was about.

The old woman pushed open half a tall pair of doors under the pediment of the shuttered housefront, beneath a coat of arms Sigismondo did not recognise. No one was in the dim stretch of hall. Busts of Roman emperors stood in niches along the walls, stony eyes wide as if in surprise at one who had dared to enter this place of ghosts. Empty rooms, almost unfurnished, with straw and leaves on the floors, opened off the hall, dimly lit by shuttered windows. A dank chill pervaded the place.

The old woman had leant her hoe outside the doors, and she walked with her arms clasped one over the other at her waist, trotting forward, grumbling all the time, a throaty noise like an animal chewing at food and warning off others.

This end of the hall was painted with peeling frescoes of hunting scenes: pearl-pale Artemis bathing, Actaeon pulled down by his hounds against a terra-cotta sky. Sigismondo followed the old woman up a sweep of stairs round the apse of the hall, an adequate but not grand flight. From an archway at the top, a man appeared.

"Who's this?" He was small but stockily built, balding, with intense brown eyes. He gave the impression that some inner violence had knotted his forehead, thrust forward his jaw, and worn away his fuzzy hair.

The burst of gibberish from the old woman had one intelligible word, *Montenero*, in it, which made the man's eyes burn even more suspiciously at Sigismondo. One hand already rested on the knife at his belt; the other came forward, palm up.

"The token?"

The old woman shrugged, holding her arms by the elbows and releasing a stream of angry nonsense that made him frown and step forward. He had not taken his eyes from Sigismondo, who now spoke.

"The Lady of Montenero has sent no token this time. She is dead."

The man's head came up as though he had been struck. "Dead!" He crossed himself, while the old woman rocked and bobbed, muttering words that might as easily have been curses as prayers.

"How did she die? Why are you here? Who are you?" His voice grated; and his hand did not leave his knife. It looked at home there.

"My messages are to your master alone."

A voice beyond the half-open door spoke, a harsh voice, unhurried, full of authority. "Let him in, Massimo. I will see him."

"Yes sir. Of course. In a moment, sir."

This might have been addressed to the man within or to Sigismondo, for Massimo slipped into the room, closing the door in Sigismondo's face. He was out again in a moment, bowing, holding the door wide into darkness beyond.

"My master's eyes are poor, sir. The physician is firm that he must avoid the daylight. Will you please go in?"

Sigismondo did not comment that Massimo's master had to avoid daylight only when visitors came. He had heard the curtains being drawn. He went in, taking the door from Massimo's hand and shutting it against resistance.

He stood there, his back to the door, accustoming his eyes to the near-dark. A narrow line at the edge of the curtain allowed greyness to filter past, letting him make out someone sitting in a tall-backed chair, someone who carried his head slightly to one side, as if listening. The harsh voice spoke.

"I heard you say the Princess is dead."

Sigismondo crossed the floor and bowed. "I saw her dying, sir. Her last thoughts were for her children and for you. She feared for you both."

"Does her husband know you have come here?"

"I believe that the Prince knows nothing." But that depended on how long he had been behind the Princess's bed, and whether her confession had been the only thing he had been able to hear. "He will certainly put the people of the Princess's household to the question. I would advise you to leave this place. Princess Oralia wished me to escort you to Rocca, to Duke Ludovico."

Now that his eyes had adapted, he could see a strongly marked profile against the deeper shadows beyond, the face slightly averted now that Sigismondo had come to stand by the window. There was silence while his offer was considered.

"What is this danger?" There was a wry amusement in the tone, as though the man knew the answer but was curious to know what this visitor thought.

"Prince Livio has killed both the Princess's son and the Lord Eugenio."

The man swung his head round, startled.

"Has her death crazed him? Jealousy's made him kill before now; I have always known I am a danger to her." The strange voice cracked as though he acknowledged for the first time the effect of her death on him. Sigismondo hummed and wagged his head.

"It may be. He believed the Princess betrayed him and that her children are the Lord Eugenio's."

"By the Nails and Blood! Is the girl dead too?" He had started to his feet, turned towards Sigismondo.

"I brought her away, sir, for safety's sake disguised as a boy. I am taking her, as the Princess wished, to her uncle at Rocca."

"She is with you? I must see her."

There was longing and restless energy in the voice. Sigismondo had already grasped the velvet curtain in one hand. Now, he lifted a swath of it silently, admitting light full on the face. It was a noble face, handsome, deeply lined, framed in dark hair streaked with grey, but the eye sockets had shadows for eyes. This man would never see anyone again.

8

The Coming of the Cardinal

THE DUST FROM THE PROCESSION could be seen for miles. However, they were lucky at this season not to be walking in rain and mud, though "luck" was not the word to be using. They travelled, as they could not forget, under heavenly protection. They bore sacred relics.

Dust advertised their progress, but it was supererogatory. Word had spread long before that, and people responded in more ways than by leaving their work in the fields to come and kneel by the wayside as the relics passed. Groups were leaving their homes in village and town to follow the procession, so it moved with a glittering head and swollen dun-coloured tail. Pilgrims on the way to Colleverde had joined on early, avid to miss not a moment of the saints' blessings.

At Colleverde, the relics were to be lodged in the Cathedral to await the arrival of Duke Grifone, their purchaser. He intended their final resting place to be in the altar of his still half-finished cathedral at the capital city, Nemora, but until its consecration, they were to remain at Colleverde. There they would bestow a blessing on the marriage of his son Astorre to the daughter of Prince Livio of Montenero. The pilgrims who were streaming towards Colleverde had a lively anticipation, therefore, of wedding junkets as well as spiritual benefits.

Duke Grifone already had a respectable number of relics. His life was such, however, that the intercession of a really powerful saint had become a matter of urgency, and Saint Bernardina, by popular agreement as well as by consensus in the Church, stood high in the ranks of Heaven. A word from her might make the difference to Duke Grifone between a rather tediously long time in Purgatory and certain damnation. He had burnt enough people alive to appreciate the difference.

Duke Grifone's subjects saw the chance to expiate their own sins and thought him a sensible man to take out such death insurance now that he had against all odds arrived at his forties. At his present rate it was even odds whether disease or revenge from his victims' relations would bring about his end first. On the recent death of his confessor there had been some laudably modest back-stepping among those suitable for the post.

Nevertheless, most of his subjects were philosophical. They reckoned that, since they were not lucky enough to be ruled by Duke Ludovico of neighbouring Rocca, there was little to choose between their own Duke and Prince Livio of Montenero. Those who remembered the old Duke, Grifone's father, mourned his loss—he and his counsellors had kept on happy terms with Duke Ludovico and other neighbours, and there had been no uprisings in his reign as in this one; though Duke Grifone and his formidable Cardinal Petrucci had, by a programme of burning and hanging, imposed a peace on Nemora not relished by all. There may have been some prayers by the wayside for a quick death for the tyrant, in the hopes that his son would prove a kindlier ruler. The more cynical majority believed ruthless tyrants were good for business; they kept the peace, and peace was what you made money in.

The parts of Saint Bernardina that had been acquired were travelling in a little gold house with latticed windows of rubies and emeralds and a spire of diamonds, carried on a bier spread with scarlet velvet and veiled for the journey in an embroidered and braided scarlet velvet mitre. The bier, heavy enough to combine mortification with privilege, was carried by relays of four priests in blue robes bordered with gold. Minor parts of minor saints on lesser biers followed, and ahead went acolytes swinging censers, the smoke from which was almost invisible in the dust. Banners with the saints' pictures were borne ahead of each bier, and in the forefront of all rode Cardinal Petrucci and his train.

After the relics came more priests and an escort of the Cardinal's men, hired in Rome and wearing his grey and scarlet livery; his own personal guard had been sent to his palace in Nemora to spare his sister, Princess Corio, the inconvenience of putting up so many in Colleverde. After them trudged the baggage mules and servants needed to maintain all this pomp,

and at the rear the pilgrims and worshippers. A constant chant
rose up with the dust, though many by the wayside, the men
with hoods pulled back or caps clasped to their chests, were
silent, eyes wide to take in the glory; a child here and there,
among those lifted up by the women, bawled and kicked in
terror at the strangeness of it all.

Much of the dust and noise was avoided by the Cardinal
riding in front. What was novelty to the peasants had become
wearisome to the man responsible for fetching the relics from
Rome. The journey towards Rome had been accomplished in
reasonable time, but the journey back was a different matter.
The Cardinal was a man of active temperament. Both his mind
and his body abhorred a slow pace—even now, as they began
the climb up from the river that was border between Nemora
and Montenero and could see in the distance the valley that hid
Colleverde, he was looking for a way to leave the road and the
procession for a half hour's swift trot with only a few of his
followers. He pointed with his whip towards a likely track
leading off among scattered trees into dense woods and bent to
ask a question of the page at his stirrup. The boy, as he knew,
came from Colleverde and could assure him that the path—
though a poor one and taking a sweep round the hill for some
distance—joined the road from Nemora quite close to Colleverde itself. The Cardinal's mule, a beautiful beast, silvery
grey under its scarlet trappings, was quite capable of taking the
Cardinal there in time to head the slow procession into town.

He sent the page back to prevent the long train from blindly
following him and, with no more than a flourish of his red
glove to his immediate followers, put his gold spurs to the mule
and wheeled into the side track at a fast clip, his scarlet cloak
taking the wind and, lifting from the mule's rump, billowing
like a sail behind him.

His nephew Torquato followed him with relief. He had his
uncle's dislike of crowds, except on the briefer ceremonial
occasions, and he shared his uncle's enjoyment of the more
private arts of intrigue, which were better practised on a few,
no matter what the later results on the many. Torquato had
never ceased, all this long and monotonous journey, to regret
their leaving Rome and the absorbing negotiations with the

Pope over a fair price for such pieces of Saint Bernardina's bones as were on offer.

Various sessions of discreet haggling had been necessary; the money confided by Duke Grifone, although considerable, was not enough to buy as much in the way of relics as the Duke would have liked to possess, so that at times he was reduced to bargaining for bits of garments rather than bits of limbs. Torquato had been employed by his uncle as a go-between in securing such portions of saints, or their clothing, as he could without committing all the gold they had brought. He had done very well over a splinter of Saint Ursula's wheel, but on other occasions had been beaten down from a finger to a fragment.

In these activities he had met various princes of the Church, and, without flattering himself, he was sure he had made a good impression. Rome was an exciting place; he had looked round during Mass at Saint Peter's on the hundreds of bowed heads before the Holy Father and had experienced an almost physical surge of ambition. Priests more obscure than himself had become pope . . . it was true some of them had had to wait till they were so old that the Curia considered them a safe bet for a stopgap, but Torquato had no intention of waiting that long to exercise his own powers.

It was dreary to be on his way back to Nemora, where the Cathedral was half-finished and the Duke, it must be admitted, half-mad. Grifone had swept away opposition both real and putative—one of his counsellors, Torquato had heard, had been hung up in a cage on the castle wall; another torn apart by two teams of labouring horses in the city square; another, blinded and with hands chopped off, had been thrown to the wolves. Dismemberment of others made Grifone quite at home with the thought of relics.

His uncle's voice recalled him from these absorbing thoughts.

"Have you ever seen the villa at Fontecasta?" Petrucci had slackened his pace at last and waved him alongside. The afternoon sun was hot. He had thrown back his cloak and was looking about him with interest, his lean face dappled in the light shade of the trees overhead.

"Fontecasta? We passed the village a little way back, Eminence, and the holy pool. Is there a villa?"

"There was one, certainly. Belonged to a man called Giraldi, of ancient family with connections in Rocca." The Cardinal pulled off his scarlet gauntlets and handed them to his nephew to carry. "It's only a hunting lodge but a fine one. I remember the late Duke Ercole being entertained there once by this Giraldi. He must be very old by now—I believe, in fact, your aunt told me he was dead."

Torquato's aunt, the Princess Corio, was the Cardinal's sister. If she had made a statement of any kind, it was either likely to be true or politic to pretend it was.

"Indeed. Had the old man any heirs?" Torquato looked at his uncle sidelong, not out of slyness but because it was habitual with him. He did not need it to be spelled out that his uncle, more fond of hunting than might be thought apposite for a churchman, was attracted by the idea of a hunting lodge on the outskirts of Colleverde. There were wild boar in the surrounding hills.

"We must find out." The Cardinal spurred the mule again, pointing with his whip to a wall now visible beyond the wood, a wall with patches of plaster peeling from the brick and tiles missing along the top.

9

In the Dark

PAST EXPERIENCE HAD DEVELOPED in Benno a profound faith in his master's ability to come safe, and even victorious, out of impossible situations. But for this faith, the time he and the girl spent outside the villa's gates would have been more anxious still.

He walked the horses, let Biondello out for a run, and wondered if, now that they had seen the witch and presumably at this moment Sigismondo was viewing the dead man, there would be a sight of the devils the goatherd had talked of too. He had tried to say a few words to the young lady— he could not think of her as Sigismondo had instructed, as a boy—but she ignored him. True enough, it wasn't for him to address the daughter of a Princess until she spoke to him; he understood her not replying, but all the same she was looking miserable, sitting under a sapling in front of the gate, hugging her knees, and he'd thought they could be more cheerful being miserable together.

The squeaking of the gate bolts made them both jump. Benno stopped breathing until he saw it was the witch again, grumbling furiously. She beckoned to Benno, making an explosive little sound under her breath, "Po-po-po," and then to his horror pulled his sleeve. Following her gestures, and catching the word "gate" among the gibberish, he understood that she meant him to open the gate proper so that the horses could be led in. He would have been happier to see Sigismondo to be sure these were his orders, but you don't contradict witches. He hitched the horses to the ring outside and did as she told him.

He helped her to shut the gates again after the horses went

through and the young lady had been peremptorily pushed in by the witch, not, he could see, a thing she at all cared for.

Whatever might be happening inside, and whatever might be there, they were now drawn into it. If the dead man was having his master for dinner, they were dessert.

The witch drove them before her across the courtyard's cobbled expanse. She pointed out a ring where Benno must tie the horses, next to the water trough, then she chivvied the two into the villa, along a hall and up a flight of stairs. Benno had scarcely time for a fearful glance at open doorways when he was relieved to hear the deep, calm tones of his master talking to someone. As they arrived at the stairhead a small stocky man straightened from the keyhole of a big door on the landing and turned an angry face on them. Sight of them did not soften his expression but, grudgingly, he opened the door and ushered in the young lady. The half-wit he stopped with a hand to the chest.

"Stop where you are, knave. You're not wanted in there."

"M'mhm. Benno."

Sigismondo was there in the doorway—tall, broad, the amused face infinitely comforting. He closed the door at his back, and Benno felt sorry for the young lady, abandoned in the darkness to whatever else was there. Sigismondo turned to the small, angry man.

"Massimo. Your master wishes that food and wine be provided for his guests."

Massimo stood for a moment, as if unwilling to accept an order he had not heard directly, but he eyed Sigismondo, and it decided him. He turned and ran briskly down the stairs. The witch had already disappeared, perhaps to the lower regions of the villa. Benno speculated on what sort of objects would hang from those beams. What concoctions on the shelves? Would they have to eat what she prepared?

"Hey, stop *sweating*, Benno." His master's hand gripped his shoulder. "The bat's not been born whose blood you can't drink. Give it a whiff of the piece of cheese you keep under your arm and it might even come to life again." He led Benno by the shoulder along the upper corridor and out onto a loggia overlooking the courtyard and the gates. The horses below, recognising his voice, stamped and whinnied.

Sigismondo leant his arms along the balustrade and looked down. "You've got questions. Ask them. I don't want you to explode out here and frighten the horses."

Benno came close to Sigismondo and looked back along the corridor, jerking his head at the door from which Sigismondo had come.

"Him." Automatically he spoke in a lower tone. "Is there a dead man? In the dark? I suppose if he's dead he won't need to see."

"He doesn't."

"Is it safe for *her* to be in there with him?"

Sigismondo bent to pick up something his foot had encountered between pillars of the balustrade. He turned it in his hands and showed it to Benno. It was a large gourd, about the size of a human head, with inverted triangular holes for eyes and a gash for a mouth carved into the dried flesh. He upturned it, to show the smudge of candle smoke inside. It reeked of tallow.

"You come up to the villa at night, Benno, the villa where the dead man lives, and what do you see?"

"Devils," said Benno promptly.

"Mm-hm-hm." Sigismondo put the gourd on the balustrade. "And who peers through the wicket?"

"The witch."

"They protect him very well. Tricks for children, but they work."

A door opened in an archway to one side of the courtyard, and another small, stocky man, but this one with white hair, came out. He unhitched the horses and led them in. The door shut. Sigismondo leant his arms on the balustrade once more.

"They protect him well, Massimo and the old woman; but we must do more. The Princess Oralia told me to take him to her brother and spoke of her husband's jealousy. There are good reasons why this man should be thought dead."

Benno unloaded Biondello and stood, digesting ideas and scratching his chest.

"Was this man the Princess's lover, then? Prince Livio would whop off *his* head double-quick if he finds him, right?"

"Mm-mm. There may be others who would kill him but that they think him dead. He is a friend to Rocca—and Duke

Ludovico knows nothing of a conspiracy that seems to be forming. The Princess told me '*the Duke's eyes are shut*' — but which duke did she mean?"

He bent to pat the small rump of Biondello, who had come to stick his head between the pillars of the balustrade and sniff the air enthusiastically.

"Who is he?" Benno nodded again along the corridor.

"Mm-mm . . . The Princess Minerva was eight when she was betrothed, which must be six years or so ago. Six years or so ago, Duke Ercole died in Nemora, and his son Grifone succeeded him. A conspiracy against the new Duke was discovered by the Bishop of Nemora, now Cardinal Petrucci. The old Duke Ercole's most trusted counsellor, and also a friend to Rocca, was Lord Mirandola. Petrucci named him among others as a conspirator. Grifone had him blinded and turned out of the city for wolves to devour."

"I've heard of that," said Benno. "Had his hands cut off too."

"If our dead man is who I think he is, that detail is inexact. Perhaps Duke Grifone thought our friend shouldn't die before the wolves turned up for dinner. You'll remember what the Princess's daughter told us about the man found wandering with blood on his face."

"She saved him? The Princess Oralia saved him? Why didn't she send him straight to her brother at Rocca?"

"It may be that he was too ill to travel or in too much pain. It may be for reasons we'll discover. It's not easy travelling with a man with no eyes, particularly when he's just lost them."

"We have to get him out of Nemora on the sly, then, don't we? You reckon anyone would know him again still?"

"We must avoid going by way of Colleverde, because Cardinal Petrucci certainly would."

Benno dived to pick up Biondello, who was about to explore the corridor. "And I wanted to see the relics. The wedding would've been good fun too." He was plaintive but resigned.

"Mm. I've heard Petrucci is a great huntsman, and no hunter likes to find his quarry has escaped him." Sigismondo pinched a sprig of thyme that grew in a pot on the balustrade and sniffed his fingers. Then, sharply, he raised his head. Both men listened.

The drum of hoofbeats and the clink of harness came faintly on the wind.

Sigismondo strode down the corridor. As they came near to the room where the Lord Mirandola sat talking to the Princess's daughter, the door opened and the harsh, distinctive voice was heard, raised in urgent summons.

"The Princess is ill. Help me here; she has fainted."

Outside the walls along the track came the sound of riders.

10

"We'll Kill Your Master"

CARDINAL PETRUCCI WAS AMUSED. His little digression from the route was proving worthwhile. His nephew had dealt with the old crone at the wicket by threatening to light a pile of faggots under her to brisk up her wits. She had taken one look at his own scarlet robes and scuttled for her life, squawking. There was an annoying delay. Then a couple of surly rascals opened the gates and let them in.

As they rode in, clattering over the cobbles, the Cardinal cast an appraising eye round. A few workmen from Colleverde could restore and paint the whole place in time for him to entertain the Duke before the summer. Whoever might be living here, now that the old man—Giraldi?—was dead, obviously had not the money to keep it up and would therefore be glad to part with it. The Cardinal had spent his Duke's money on sacred relics, but he himself was far from penniless.

"Who's your master, fellow?" How extraordinarily uncouth these peasants could look. This one resembled some ferocious animal at bay.

"The Lord Giraldi—Eminence." The title was given him with a choked splutter, as if it came with difficulty to his tongue.

"I had heard that he was dead."

Another voice spoke from the doorway, and Petrucci wheeled his mount.

"Not dead, Your Eminence, although nearly so." This, though foreign, was no rustic accent, and the man who had appeared in the doorway, lit now by the westering sun, was an entirely different proposition from the squat peasants. He had the build of a fighter, the height, the shoulders to carry armour, but the shaven head of a man who had perhaps taken a vow. The Cardinal was used to the company of priests, and, the clothes apart, he did not think this man was one. The face was hard to read: the strong nose spoke of will, the dark eyes held intelligence, even calculation; the curved mouth was sensual, suggesting a weakness but that the underlip had less fullness and closed with restraint. This was a man for secrets, after his own heart. What could he be doing here, in this decayed villa? He had seen faces less remarkable in Rome, in the Curia itself.

"Not dead, but nearly so?" Petrucci dismounted and flung the reins to one of the oafs. "Then has he a priest for the last rites?"

"The priest came and has gone, Eminence; but my Lord yet lingers." The man came forward with a bow that would have done credit to any accomplished courtier. "He can scarcely speak and must lie in the dark as any light gives him pain. His soul struggles to escape."

The Cardinal stood on the cobbles, not as tall as the man before him, and pointed to the doorway with his whip.

"I will see him." It should be possible to drive a good bargain with a dying man, to persuade him to give to the Church—or to its representative at least—what would otherwise go to his heirs, in return for such remittance of Purgatory as the Cardinal could obtain for him. It was a very good bargain for both, and Torquato could be witness to what the man might be induced to say.

"I regret, Your Eminence, that it cannot be done."

Petrucci stared. Torquato exclaimed. The escort looked at one another uneasily. No one told a cardinal that something could not be done; yet this assured stranger merely bowed again, frowning.

"We do not know—the Lord Giraldi refuses to consult a physician—but we fear now that there is contagion; that his illness can be dangerous to others. A servant collapsed today and is now abed with fever."

Petrucci stood still. Then he felt for the gold pomander at his sash and held it to his nose. If the old man were dying not of natural causes—if he had a malignant fever—the word *Plague* whispered in his mind. . . .

He said to Torquato, "My gloves, if you please," and put

them on. Only then did he take the reins and mount. He said to
the man: "What are you here? The major-domo, I suppose."

The man bowed. Petrucci liked a supple back. He said,
"Bring word yourself of his health, tomorrow to the Palazzo
Corio. Perhaps I can send a physician"—who might shorten
the poor man's sufferings; not his own physician, of course. It
would be sensible, if there were contagion, to send another.

He wheeled his mule and led the little party out of the
courtyard at a lively pace. The second servant hobbled to shut
the gates.

Massimo came abruptly to Sigismondo, took his hand, and
bent to kiss it. He looked up at him with that fierce gaze and
said, "*I would have killed him.*" Sigismondo, turning with him
towards the house, gave a deprecatory hum.

"I would have done so!" He made his hands into fists. "He
might have burnt us all alive! Do you know what he did
eighteen months ago at San Sevino? They didn't like Duke
Grifone's taxes, and they held out against him, and when the
town fell, the people took refuge in the tower—men, women
and children, and the old and ill." Massimo paused, as though
choked, then burst out, "He burnt it down! He burnt it down!
Those who jumped from the windows his men hacked to
pieces. It all burnt." He thrust his face close to Sigismondo's
and spoke hoarsely. "There wasn't a soul left alive in the whole
town when that man of God rode away."

"Mm-mm-m," said Sigismondo. "If you had killed him, the
others would certainly have burnt this place down—and your
master in it. What concerns me is another matter. What did he
want here?" Sigismondo stood for a moment, brooding, forefinger to lip, while Massimo and Benno gazed at him with
something of the same air of trust. The dark eyes lifted to
survey them, and he smiled.

"I have it. He has no reason to suspect who's here. He wants
this villa. Did you see him looking round?"

"What do we do?" Massimo, urgent and hopeful, was ready.

"Hey, we *give* him the place, of course."

"Give . . . ? But my master? What's to become of him?"

"We'll kill your master, Massimo. Today, perhaps."

Massimo stood back, his face clamped into its anger and
suspicion, his hand on his knife. Sigismondo held up his own

hands soothingly. "Your master has been dead before, which worked very well. Cardinal Petrucci may be sending a physician or one of his men to spy the ground. He must see a grave. Go and dig one."

11

⊠

The Relics Come to Town

⊠

THE DAY ON WHICH THE RELICS came to Colleverde had been declared a public holiday by the town council. All citizens put on their best and prepared to enjoy it. Some took their prudent packages of food and wine to the North Gate, by which the Cardinal would enter, to welcome and join the procession, but most collected in the great square outside the Cathedral, where the relics would be lodged until the Duke could take them to his capital of Nemora.

There were already rumours that the Duke would be delayed. Some gave as a reason that he had missed a prisoner whom he was lashing with a spiked whip and caught himself across the back of the legs instead; others declared that those legs had, not unnaturally, refused to carry a body so stained by sin towards anything so holy as the relics. The opinions of the Colleverdese on the subject of their Duke were divided, most being grateful that he chose to live in Nemora and rarely visited his other towns. Quite a few were proud of the reputation that made other princes reluctant to tamper with Grifone's territories. You had to admire, they said, a prince who had managed to do so many appalling things in the relatively short time since his accession.

There was a dearth of well-born unmarried girls in the city; judicious parents had thought this an excellent time of year for a spring visit to country estates or to their relations in distant convents.

Everyone agreed, almost complacently, that no one needed the intervention of Saint Bernardina more than did their Duke. Her blessing would also come in handy for his son's wedding on Sunday and would be vital if the Lord Astorre took after his father.

There were also those in the crowd who had serious need of intercession themselves and were determined to secure a place on the route of the procession. A couple of bravos—who had lately murdered several travellers on the road to Montenero and who were in town for very dubious reasons, which they were keeping to themselves—employed their elbows much as they were used to employing their daggers and were soon near enough to preempt the first benefits of a blessing before its dispersal over the crowd. One, who had shoved a large woman back into the throng, picked up her child and set it, alarmed but pleased, on his shoulders, to attract the attention of the Saint. His partner, from a similar motive, dragged a cripple painfully forward and linked arms with him.

Another party, stonemasons on their way from work at Berano Cathedral to their homes in San Sevino, were also in town for reasons they hoped would not become known. When such an obvious draw as the coming wedding of the Duke's son existed, they believed themselves safe.

It was saints' weather too. The spring rains had held off, and it was sunny enough for standing out for hours without need of shelter; yet the breeze was cool, fluttering the women's coifs over the square like the foamcrest of a wave, with a veil or two getting half-free like a sudden banner—cool enough for best clothes. It was also cool enough to provoke the need for mulled wine, hot sausages, chestnuts, pigs' trotters, and anything that could be cheaply got and quickly sold.

The beggars were out in force. The Duke had not attended to the merchants' protests about their poor effect on trade. His officers were content to lay a tax on them all, on those who were disabled and those who pretended to be, those who had disabled themselves or had others do them that service while they were still children. On such a day they rejoiced. The Saint might cure them, which would win benefits from affected witnesses; and if she didn't, they would be sure to profit from the ostentatious charity of bystanders trying to impress her. Bandages were unwound from stumps for maximum effect, sores were smartened up with blood from the shambles where the butchers ran it from their shops into the gutter; some, insufficiently mutilated, invented wounds with a little stolen wax.

Along with the pilgrims, beggars, bravos, traders, and townsfolk, there were entertainers, in Colleverde because of their nose for a crowd and their knowledge that an appetite for spectacle, even when provided by relics, celebrations, or weddings, can never be entirely satisfied by processions, however glorious, or in this case by the presence of bones, however holy, encased from sight in encrusted silk, bullion, enamel, and general orfevrerie.

Spectacle must be immediate and on tap.

A dancing bear had proved very popular up to the point when the crowd began to thicken and the city guard decided to make the processional way clear. This involved marching in double file through the crowd along the processional route, executing a half-turn outward, laying their pikes across the first ranks, and leaning forward as they took six paces. This compressed the crowd, and people objected to the propinquity of the bear. Its owner was forced to lead it away and miss the procession.

The stilt walkers were going to get the best view of all, except one who had accidentally upset the brazier and therefore the temper of a hot-chestnut vendor and who was, in fast order, pulled down to sit on the embers. He was then crudely invited to display his backside for the Saint to heal.

A team of dwarfs had found that a house facing the Cathedral was being repaired and were using the scaffolding as platforms for a series of tableaux featuring incidents in the life of Saint Bernardina. Her part was naturally played by a male dwarf, veiled modestly and dressed in white pillowcases, and the scenes in which the Saint was saved by angels from violation by the husband who refused to respect her virginity, and in which she offered herself to be tormented by devils with pitchforks and grotesque masks in order to save her cruel father from longer years in Purgatory, drew the most applause, and coins, from the audience.

Before the crowd made such displays impossible, jugglers had juggled and dancers danced. A dog, as small and dirty as Biondello but boasting two ears, had danced, wearing a painted ruff. One fortune-teller attracted more custom than the others together because he danced, expertly, to a tambourine as advertisement before he offered his tarot cards, and because he had the features and golden hair of an angel. He had also the wit to see, in the cards, those past misfortunes that everyone believes they have suffered and dramatic changes for the better shortly to arrive, which was nicely coincident with what everyone hoped from the relics.

Balconies and windows round the square were filled with the owners of the houses, their families, and friends. Carpets had been laid over the balustrades and windowsills and refreshments prepared. Caged birds had been brought out to share the blessing, children ran round the feet of the grown-ups and spat sweetmeats they did not fancy onto the crowd beneath. One merchant, who had pulled off his velvet hat to scratch his head with greater vigour, thought for a moment that the saints' weather had broken, until he found that what he took for rain was a small boy relieving himself through the balustrading above.

The really important people—except for the Bishop—were already inside the Cathedral. The Princess Corio (sister to Cardinal Petrucci and widow for many years of Prince Corio, a rich nonentity) enjoyed the best position available to the laity, not only by right but because nobody would have been willing to dispute it with her. She waited in conscious dignity, aware that until the relics arrived she was going to attract most of the attention, dressed as she was in burgundy velvet quilted in gold arabesques, her head swathed in a large turban of cloth-of-gold wound with strings of pearls and with a huge gold cross pitted with rubies pendent on her breast.

Part of her mind, as she sat glittering in the candlelit gloom of the Cathedral, was occupied with anticipation of her brother's arrival, but part, it must be admitted, was wondering whether her steward had managed to obtain enough gold leaf to cover the main courses for both the splendid dinner she was giving tonight and for the fine dinner tomorrow that must strike the right compromise between splendour and Friday. A great deal must be saved for the feast she intended to give to the Duke and the wedding party after the ceremony on Sunday, but she was determined to do her brother honour. At least she had provided for tomorrow a huge dish of his favourite larks wrapped in forcemeat on which goldfish scales had been carefully stuck.

Cardinal Petrucci was also in the mind of Bishop Taddeo, riding out of the West Gate to meet the relics and bring them, together with the Cardinal, to their lodgement in the Cathedral. The Bishop was a man of the mildest temper, who asked little more of life than to be permitted to carry out his duties without overmuch interference. It was his fate that, as Bishop of Colleverde, he was forced to live in the same city as the Princess Corio. Her nature was far from mild, and she seemed to conceive it as her especial duty to keep surveillance on all the Bishop did in order to report anything she considered lax or unorthodox to her brother in Nemora. The Cardinal was, in consequence, a bugbear to the Bishop. He had, on occasion, nightmares of him in the full flood of sacerdotal reprimand and wearing his scarlet hat. Bishop Taddeo was not looking forward to seeing the Cardinal again in the flesh, and he was grateful that at least he was not responsible for the feast tonight. Had the Princess Corio been guest, not hostess, nothing would have gone right.

In the town, people waited for the relics. Outside, the relics advanced at a solemn pace to the West Gate, where the Bishop, fussing with his vestments, also waited. The Cathedral had been prepared, as far as it could be prepared in advance of the relics' arrival, and in Colleverde itself there were other, and more sinister, preparations taking place for events of which the crowd was ignorant.

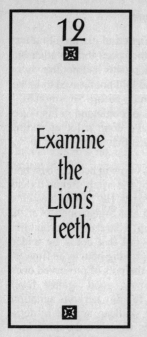

12

Examine the Lion's Teeth

BENNO'S EXPERIENCE OF GRAVE digging had been, so far, confined to providing a small pit under a rose tree for Biondello's predecessor, but one look at Massimo and his father, Gruchio, removed any objections he might have made to helping them with their master's grave.

Gruchio had an unmistakable resemblance to his son, although in his wrinkled face the eyes were even smaller and closer together. They all dug the grave in silence, and Benno was glad that Biondello kept at a cautious distance. It might be Gruchio's idea of a joke to pick the dog up by the leg and toss him in before they shovelled the earth back. As they grunted and dug, he had, in fact, suggested they should leave the pit open until the Cardinal's physician arrived, then tip him in sooner than waste it. He and Massimo would, they made clear, eagerly get rid of anyone connected with the Cardinal; and if Petrucci had, in fact, engineered their master's downfall and blinding, Benno was with them all the way. However, since the point of the exercise was to convince the Cardinal that "Giraldi" no longer existed, the idea had to be abandoned so that the physician, if one did arrive, could go back with the news.

What would happen to the Lord Mirandola if the Cardinal should decide to take over the villa? Unless Sigismondo could escort him to Rocca, the blind lord had little hope of escape.

Benno pondered on the devotion father and son showed to their master, since he was not the Giraldi whom they had served but a comparative stranger who had come first as Giraldi's guest, sent by the Princess Oralia. This devotion said something about the ex-counsellor to the Duke of Nemora.

So did another thing. The best plan for Sigismondo would

have been to take to the road that night and get the blind lord and the Princess to Rocca with all the speed that weather and secrecy permitted. He would have done this had not the young lady fallen ill of a fever, and the blind lord not refused to let her be made into a sick parcel and taken up before Sigismondo. It had been interesting to hear the note of command in his voice; you had to be born a lord and have done a lot of serious ordering of people about to acquire that note—and to see Sigismondo bow in silence.

This meant that the young lady was now in bed, the best bed, the blind Lord had insisted, tended by the witch. Benno did not envy the young lady this in the least. He had witnessed a curious colloquy between the witch and Sigismondo over the kitchen table as the witch kept up a stream of grumbling gibberish with a very occasional word that could be understood, while Sigismondo gave an approving hum as he fingered the herbs she proposed or sniffed at the pots of preserved ones. He murmured his comments: yarrow, good against fever, sweetened with honey; motherwort to allay nervous agitation; cinquefoil for her sore throat; and skullcap against hysteria. Benno gathered that the concoctions were just the thing for a girl who had been out all night, worn hose instead of a skirt, and was having difficulty in forgetting she had seen her brother's head cut off.

Benno was pleased that his master had the knowledge of herbs to check on what the witch was brewing; he would not have dreamt of asking where Sigismondo had learnt it all, any more than he would have asked how he came by the technique with a double-headed hand axe, which Benno had had occasion to admire. If Sigismondo had revealed an intimate knowledge of plainchant, falconry, logic, or embroidery, Benno would not have been surprised.

It did surprise him to learn that they were going to Colleverde the very next day.

"You're going to do what that Cardinal asked, go and tell him *he* is dead." Benno jerked his head towards the mound Sigismondo was inspecting. "Won't the physician he's sending tell him?"

"If he comes. His Eminence will have plenty to do in

Colleverde today; he may not think of hunting lodges until he has more leisure."

"This grave is just a precaution?"

Sigismondo touched the mossy memorial tablet of a past Giraldi in the niched wall and looked at a flattened grave a few paces away. "The Giraldi must have kept this place as a summer villa not so long ago." He entered the little chapel, Benno following, and bent his knee to the altar although it was bare. He stood looking round at the dim frescoes, the leaf-strewn floor, and a small jar of rosemary sprigs before a tablet in the wall.

"Someone, if not the physician, will be along sooner or later. If the Cardinal has to wait about at all after the wedding, he won't spend all his time praying; he'll remember. And it looks as though we shall have to wait here until the Lady Minerva is better."

Benno had bent his knee and muttered his customary prayer for the souls of his parents, neither of whom he had ever known as he had been abandoned hurriedly at birth. "Who d'you suppose brought the rosemary?"

"I expect it was the old woman Sybilla. Not Massimo, at a guess."

Benno was not surprised that his master had found out the witch's name, only that she had one at all. Somewhere in the building's several yards the guard dogs set up a mournful yowl. The real lord must have died Benno supposed some time after the present "Giraldi" was brought here, promoting the useful idea of a dead man living on. Benno shambled out into the garden after Sigismondo and stood beside him, gazing over the valley to the blue distance where the white walls of Colleverde spilled down the shallow hillside in the evening sun.

"You really going to see the Cardinal? I know he's a great man and a priest, but he looked a right snake to me. Aren't you going into the lion's mouth?"

"Where better to examine the lion's teeth than there? The Princess Oralia said that the Duke's eyes were shut. If she were speaking of some plot against her brother, which he didn't suspect, I have a better chance of opening Duke Ludovico's eyes to the danger if I know what it is. And if she meant another duke, then it's still useful to know. Dukes may not stand or fall together, but if one falls, it may pull another down."

"What are you going to do about the blind Lord if the Cardinal's men come when you're away?"

"Massimo knows what to do."

From the firm closing of Sigismondo's mouth, Benno knew that answer time was over.

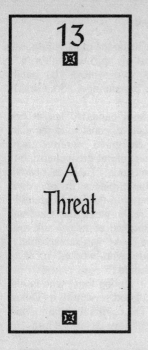

13

A Threat

THE ROOM WAS LARGE. THE OAK panelling shone with beeswax, the ceiling was of diapered plasterwork, and on the chimney breast were the Cardinal's arms in stone, surmounted by the hat with the tassels ranged down either side. This was, no doubt, an expensive compliment from his sister in her own palace. There was a whole shelf of books and scrolls; a chest in age-darkened wood; a stool or two; a carved table where the Cardinal sat in his tall carved chair; a tapestry of Susannah and the Elders, the exigencies of either weaving or design making Susannah's naked form more bulbous than voluptuous; a tall red-curtained bed; and a prie-dieu. A rich carpet covered the table.

If Benno, left with the horses in the courtyard of the Palazzo Corio, could have seen the Cardinal, his sister, and his nephew, all staring at Sigismondo, he might well have thought them a family of snakes. All three were pale, slender, distinguished, but they had not the type of countenance to inspire trust and affection. Torquato, a pace behind the Cardinal's shoulder, in his black robes, was the least impressive, and he kept his head a little bent in his uncle's presence, as though in deference.

All three had hooded lids, thin noses and mouths, and arched, disdainful eyebrows, and although the Princess Corio, in green silk damask this morning, resembled a cobra more strongly than did her brother, it was the Cardinal, spinning a gold paper knife under his hand on the table, who looked the more dangerous.

Dangerous men always need protection. Sigismondo had mounted the stairs beside one of the Cardinal's Guard. Two, equally huge, stood outside the door, and one had announced him. His Eminence seemed to have chosen the most villainous-looking men he could find to support his spiritual authority.

The Cardinal halted the knife's spin with a flat hand, weighed the blade, and pointed it at Sigismondo. "So, Giraldi being dead, you are out of a job."

The Princess Corio, straight-backed, hands folded at her waist as if to curb their desire to be active, considered the man before her—the broad shoulders, the grave secretive face. Surprisingly, she smiled. It was not a smile of great charm, but her eyes showed appreciation. She said: "There is always employment for such as he. I have places in my own household. . . . How long were you with the Lord Giraldi?"

Sigismondo's mouth opened to reply when the Cardinal leaned forward suddenly with a sibilance of heavy silk and narrowed his eyes. The likeness to a snake was remarkable.

"*Sigismondo* . . . the Sigismondo who worked for Ludovico of Rocca when His Duchess died?"

This was not a good place to admit, among those who might be conspiring against Rocca, being a good servant to its Duke, but there was hardly an alternative. The Cardinal certainly had his intelligencers in Rocca, who might have described him. He bowed acquiescence.

For an agent of Duke Ludovico to turn major-domo for the insignificant owner of a run-down villa might be the screen for a spy. Ludovico had lived on good terms with Nemora, but all States were capable of ambition and aggression; all States kept spies beyond their borders. The three pairs of eyes that regarded him had all simultaneously dropped their lids a little. The effect was not in the least comic.

"Your Eminence. I have worked for the Duke of Rocca in the matter of the Duchess. He then wished me to take a message to his sister at Montenero; and one at his court asked me if I would, on my way, stop at Fontecasta and see to the welfare of a relative of his." Sigismondo shrugged. "I would not have stopped so long if I had realised how near to death the Princess Oralia was. I would have hastened to Montenero. I meant to go there on my way to Rome to seek employment."

The mention of the Princess Oralia's death gave a heaviness to the silence that ensued. The additional news of her son's death at the hands of her husband must be strongly in the minds of anyone of influence at Nemora. It might not be general knowledge, but it would also be evident to those much less clever than these people regarding Sigismondo so closely, that with the bride missing, the wedding would lack a certain something. Still, word of the Lady Minerva's escape might have been so discreetly reported, or suppressed, that the forthcoming union between Nemora and Montenero might still seem possible and, in her enhanced position as heiress, even more desirable.

The Cardinal was the first to break the silence.

"You no longer work for the Duke?"

"I am a free agent, Eminence."

The word "agent" was a dangerous one in these precise circumstances. There was a short silence before the Princess Corio rustled her way to the window and glanced out. The move seemed designed to bring her nearer to Sigismondo, because she now turned to look him in the face. Today the cross on her bosom was one enamelled with flowers and set with table-cut diamonds that gleamed dully as she breathed. The scent released by her movement was of musk and sandalwood.

"You do not, now, go to Montenero?"

Sigismondo turned his head towards the Cardinal who, with his nephew, still watched with acute interest.

"They were talking at the gates just now of events at Montenero. As the Duke Ludovico's sister is dead—" And he shrugged once more. It seemed that this was the first he had heard of it; and obvious that he did not feel concerned.

"May she rest in peace," the Cardinal reminded them with a frown, signing himself with such deliberate formality that the others' automatic gesture finished before his did.

The Princess Corio, however, turned to practical matters.

"You have been, then, at Fontecasta some little time. Is it in much dilapidation?"

"It has been kept dry and in reasonable repair, Princess. I can inform you in detail. . . ."

"Giraldi's family shall have their price for the place," the Cardinal remarked, picking up his breviary. The lady, with her fingertips on Sigismondo's arm, drawing him with her, moved towards the door.

"What servants are there?"

"Two active men—one no longer young; the cook, an old foreign woman; an old kitchen servant whose sight is gone; and a page, who is ill."

"A page? Young?"

"Oh, a child, Princess."

"Poor thing! He must be brought here. I have some knowledge of remedies."

"We fear infection—"

"Puh!" She turned to her brother, who raised watchful eyes; her skirts' swirl released the musky scent once more, and her hands caught at the folds of cloth as if now they had prospect of an occupation. "Didn't I last year drive out the plague itself from my brother by keeping him between two blazing fires to burn away the bad air?"

The Cardinal coolly acknowledged it.

"You are to return here later today," and she tapped Sigismondo's arm, affirming her command, "and I will tell you what arrangements I have made for nursing the boy here."

Nothing in Sigismondo's face or bearing gave indication of the disaster that this was.

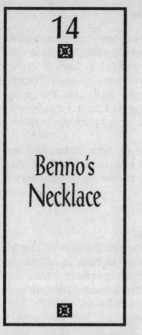

14

Benno's Necklace

BENNO WAS NOT IN THE COURT-yard. Sigismondo surveyed it: As one might have expected in any area ruled by the Princess Corio, it was well swept and ordered, and the people crossing it went briskly about their business. His horse, the big dun, and Benno's small grey were still tied to the rings by the watering trough. Perhaps it came to Sigismondo's mind that Benno, so unsuitable to such a neat and cleanly place, might have been swept out, but clamour and bustle came from the street, and Benno was fond of clamour and bustle.

Sigismondo at the courtyard gate glanced up and down the street, seeing nothing more remarkable than a man wheeling a cart loaded with cabbages, another selling caged larks, and two women with shawls over their caps gossiping at the corner. A cat, sunning itself on a windowsill opposite, arched its neck to look down at a little dog that limped along by the wall, a woolly, dirty little dog with one ear.

Biondello crossed the street to Sigismondo in a rapid limp, looked up at him, quivering, and whimpered. Sure of Sigismondo's attention, he limped quickly in the direction of the Cathedral square, looking back over his shoulder to ensure that Sigismondo was following.

Biondello's route took them out of the cobbled street and through the Cathedral square itself, crowded still with the faithful here to see the relics and with those who had collected to supply their need for food, drink, entertainment pious and secular, and the virtuous relief of giving alms. Once, losing sight of Biondello, Sigismondo followed by observing where beggars and pilgrims alike aimed their kicks.

Benno had attracted more than kicks. Seeing the dog flying

out of a doorway on someone's boot only to crouch and whimper on the step, Sigismondo went in under the arch with the Bishop's arms on the keystone, and found himself in the hall of the Bishop's Marshal. Tall windows allowed fleeting sunlight to shine on smoke-darkened walls, on the great chimneypiece with the Bishop's arms again, and on Benno, centre of a noisy group, his arms held, wearing a rope round his neck.

Sigismondo was greeted with joy, by both Benno and the group who, although now clad, were plainly the pilgrims who had been bathing at the holy well. Benno bore an extra layer of street dust, and his nose had bled.

"Here he is! We have our accuser!"

"See, we've caught your thief!"

"Where is your daughter, dear soul?"

This last was from the woman who, with her hair tied up in a cloth like a pudding, had been so helpful in splashing Sigismondo's "sick child" with the healing waters. Under the pilgrim's big hat, her head now sported a more extensive and ornate bag, and her face shone from exertion and triumph. She held the coil of rope from Benno's noose in a large determined fist. "Have you brought her to the Saint to be cured? This villain no longer had her dress."

She tugged the rope, and Benno would have lurched forward but for the Marshal's men who held him and who thoughtfully loosened the rope as Benno gagged.

"He's not got my clothes either," said the boy, jumping up and down with excitement. The whole group was in holiday mood, congratulating themselves and Sigismondo on a wholly satisfactory job about to be concluded.

The man in charge of concluding it was the Marshal, a small, twitchy man full of dyspeptic impatience. He spoke now, seizing his opportunity.

"Well then, no time to waste. You are the man from whom he stole, here are the witnesses, take him outside and string him up, usual proclamation on the fate of those who steal from pilgrims. Won't be the last today." He peered up at Sigismondo with the instant dislike of a short, insignificant man for a tall, impressive one—of a man in authority conscious that he has less of it than the man he speaks to. "What are you waiting for?" He thought of prodding Sigismondo in the chest but reconsidered it.

"I'm waiting for a reason why he should be hanged."

Sigismondo's calm voice halted their efforts to propel Benno towards the open door and the inviting gallows outside in the square. These had been erected two days ago opposite the Cathedral to show all visitors that Colleverde was ready to protect them. Only five people had been hanged so far; two of them, as the townsfolk liked to point out, pilgrims caught stealing from others.

"Reason? A reason? He stole a dress from you, and clothes from this boy—"

"I was forced to lend him a doublet," said a heavy voice. The Marshal flapped a hand.

"—clothes, I said, from this boy. Bishop's orders are, all pilgrims must be protected. Take him out."

The guard lounged forward to take the coil of rope from the red-faced woman, who struggled to keep it. Sigismondo stood immovable, in the way and holding the gaze of the irritable Marshal.

"But I have the dress back and have forgiven him its theft. Besides, he does not know what he has done; how can he be punished for actions he does not understand?" Sigismondo took Benno by the shoulders and turned him as if in display. Benno's unfocused eyes and hanging jaw did him credit. The Marshal, however, snorted.

"A half-witted thief is still a thief. Better he should take his wits to be mended in the next world. He'll soon learn in Hell fire what theft is. Take him away." He nodded to the guards and waved his hand at Sigismondo like a conjuror not sure of his ability to make something vanish. "You, sir: *You* may forgive him, but what of this boy? I am here not to play the priest but administer justice. Stand *aside*."

He found he could neither put Sigismondo aside nor prevent him from speaking again.

"Let's ask the Saint. Let her justice guide us on this holy day of joy. Come to the Cathedral and let us pray before the relics. Saint Bernardina will show us what we ought to do."

He had struck the right note. It appealed at once to the pilgrims, who cheered, clapped, and cried various versions of

his words, while the Marshal was clearly at a loss how to
enforce the Bishop's justice above that of the Saint. He made
several efforts to speak, but the woman with Benno's rope was
already towing her prisoner at a shambling run towards the
door. The boy whose clothes had been stolen was less
enthusiastic, sorry to have the hanging tediously put off until
the Saint should have given her blessing. The Marshal crossly
sent two guards with the party and turned in relief to a man
who had been found with his hand actually in someone's
purse—an uncomplicated matter of cutting it off before
hanging him. It appealed to the Marshal's sense of neatness that
the hand must be pinned to the man's chest before he was
strung up.

Inside the great depths of the Cathedral, the Bishop's Guards
were of powerful use in clearing the way. There was no service
going on at the moment except an echoing murmur of constant
prayer and the movements of the throng. Part of the floor space
was blocked by the lines of pilgrims getting to the relics the
hard way, by repeated prostrations. As some of them had been
measuring their length on the ground through the spring rains,
from their native villages, they not only looked barely human
under their penitential layers of dirt but had reached a
somnambulistic state, lulled by the smooth marble after so
many miles of dust, mud, and stones and by their repeated
prayers; even the butts of pikes nudging their ribs did not
interfere with the state that they had reached.

Sigismondo, apparently helping the woman to drag Benno
round their rising, falling, or recumbent forms, was actually
with an iron hand preventing her tugging from reaching
Benno's throat. Any trip over a penitent might throttle him
before he got to the gallows. Two priests came threading their
way among the kneeling crowd, brilliant in their ceremonial
green and gold in the Saint's honour, anxious that no improper
scene occur. One, seeing that the Bishop's Guards were
ushering the group, supposed that it must be a matter for their
master and led them all towards the comparatively clear space
at the altar rails. Beyond, in private meditation before the gold
arks of the reliquaries, knelt the Bishop of Colleverde himself.

The altar's triptych was closed, and in front of it had been
raised a picture of Saint Bernardina, standing on demons, the

altar candles lighting her gentle face and gleaming on her robes and halo.

The commotion of the pilgrims' passage, and the sight of Benno and his necklace, had aroused a certain interest in those worshippers who were not totally absorbed in prayer, which was the majority. Even the Bishop, after signing himself devoutly, turned with a face of mild curiosity to see what the stir was about.

He was a man normally distinguished by his mitre, but now, not officiating, he was without it. His sandy wisps of hair fringed a skullcap of purple silk as incongruously as the purple robes adorned his sloping shoulders. Slightly prominent eyes and an apprehensive twitching of the nose and lips brought to mind a rabbit rather than a bishop, but he was a good man whose only fault was liking his comforts; and Colleverde was fond of him, although annoyed sometimes when he lost a battle of wills with the Princess Corio. He seemed now apprehensive of some scandal, as he looked from the half-wit to the surrounding group, most of whom were attempting, respectfully and in subdued voices, to explain the situation. It was a relief to him when the tall man in black, with the shaven head, stepped forward and lifting his limp hand, bent to kiss his ring.

"Your Grace. We are here to submit ourselves to the saint. Here is a poor fool whom I have forgiven for theft"—the boy here muttered and was shushed by the others—"and we have brought him here to be pardoned by Saint Bernardina herself."

This was a programme the Bishop understood, although the tall man appeared a little overconfident of its outcome. Besides, it should not take long. Bishop Taddeo swept a hand towards the altar, as though making them free of the Saint's hospitality. He looked on with benevolence, clasping his hands over the comfortable sweep of his sash, as they sank to their knees. The guards, finding themselves conspicuously upright, and also very close to the relics, knelt down too. Sigismondo still warded off strangulation from Benno, gripping the rope as the woman holding it collapsed reverently and held up her hands, and the rope, towards the picture and the glittering reliquary.

The candle flames dipped and recovered in a vagrant gust of air, and the woman, suddenly dropping the rope, sat back on

her heels and gave a deep sobbing indrawn moan. A sound of
expectation came from two of her party in response, and she
flung up her arms with a plangent shriek and began to rock to
and fro, sobbing shrilly.

"*She moved!* Blessed Saint Bernardina! She smiled, she
nodded! I saw her bend her head! See how she smiles! She
pardons the thief, thanks be to God."

A loud murmur ran through the crowd as people who had not
seen or heard asked what was happening, and those who had
broke out in rejoicing cries. Bishop Taddeo, viewing the
throng, made a wise decision. He lifted his hands over Benno.

"Go free, my son. You are pardoned as our Lord pardoned
the thief on the cross on Good Friday. He has pardoned you
through the intercession of Saint Bernardina. Blessed be the
Saint that honours us so, and Our Lady, Mother of all
compassion."

One of the priests in gold and green stepped forward
promptly and struck up an *Ave*, joined wholeheartedly by the
crowd, the joyful sound spreading out into the square. News
spread rapidly through Colleverde that a miracle had occurred,
though there was controversy as to what kind.

The cause of this miracle, the repentant, simple-minded
thief, was being helped to his feet and relieved of his halter by
Sigismondo. The woman who had been so eager to have him
hanged was now embracing him, tears running down her red
face, pressing kisses on his scrubby beard, hugging him *forte et
dur*. Others of her party felt constrained to follow her example,
though the boy whose clothes had been stolen managed to
stumble and get in a sharp accidental kick on Benno's shin.

The woman who had begun the kissing was in no mood to
stop at her prospective victim, now that she had been graced by
the vision of Saint Bernardina. She turned from Benno to the
much more enjoyable business of kissing Sigismondo, reaching up to pull his head towards her. The Bishop, with prudent
awareness of the capabilities of the religious ecstatic, glided
out of reach. A happy sound of *Aves* filled the Cathedral.

As the woman reluctantly released Sigismondo and he raised
his head, he saw a man, who all this time had lain prostrate
towards the side of the altar, stir and rise. He was dressed in
unrelieved black of deepest mourning—of good quality but

nothing showing him to be of rank. Now he turned his face, sallow and deeply, almost savagely lined, with dark eyes glittering in dark sockets, and looked at the little group as though he found their antics distasteful. His glance of scorn lingered a moment on Sigismondo and then passed on, apparently with no recognition. Sigismondo had last seen him decapitating his wife's son. It was Prince Livio.

15

The Urgent Message

MASSIMO BURST INTO THE COURT-yard of the Palazzo Corio with a sense of urgency he could not, for all his caution, suppress. He happened to make his enquiry after Sigismondo to a page and not to a groom, and the page's training made him civil to this dusty and wild-eyed stranger. He went to find out. Massimo was too restless to sit down on the bench the page had indicated; he prowled the courtyard, watching a boy sweep up steaming horse dung left by Benno's grey before it and the dun had, a moment before, been led to the stables. He was passing below a window when he heard, stopping him in his tracks, the words "going tomorrow to Fontecasta."

"Where's that then?"

"Not far. That's where the old man died so very conveniently."

"Oh yes. Very convenient. After all these years."

"Someone will be asking questions about that."

Massimo did not hear this as a reference to the convenience for Cardinal Petrucci. He heard suspicion cast on a death he knew had not happened. When the page spoke to him, he turned a face that made the boy step back.

"The . . . the men you seek aren't here. They—" The page, about to add that the two would be coming back to the Palace that evening, was left staring as Massimo, without a word, plunged into the street. His need to find Sigismondo was doubled.

As he had not met Sigismondo on his way from the gate, he set off in the opposite direction, towards the great square. The two must surely have made for the Cathedral. Everyone must be wanting to go to the Cathedral because of the relics.

Massimo had rarely been to Colleverde, and he was used, when he did come there, to a somnolent little town. Now he was hurrying towards a sound of gala, and already the streets had many more people than he had thought to expect. He could hear religious chanting and a secular pipe and drum and the sound of a crowd. He emerged from the street and halted. Between him and the Cathedral washed a human sea coming and going, sitting in groups on the stones, eating; pressing towards the Cathedral and issuing from it; buying and selling, watching entertainers, goggling at the gibbet where five bodies dangled in admonition, and gaping at a house-front where some kind of entertainment was going on. The dwarves waited their turn while a religious play, performed by the cordwainers' guild, was enacted.

Massimo thrust his way forward to the twin-towered, be-niched golden stone face of the Cathedral. He had difficulty with the crowd and, when he arrived at the north tower door, imagining himself already looking round the congregation within and easily spotting Sigismondo's noticeable head, he was halted abruptly by the beadle regulating entry; after a moment he understood that a coin would let him in ahead of the rest, and he paid it.

He looked. He wandered among the kneeling and prostrate crowds, peered everywhere, but not even in side chapels could he see that head. At last he joined the crush of those leaving by the south tower door and found himself on the steps, bewildered, with all the square in front of him as empty of Sigismondo as the nave had been. He was pushed forward by a devout group aglow with happiness and stepped up on the base of a pillar, almost dislodging a beggar who sat there.

"Don't mind me, good sir. Just an afflicted cripple."

"Did you see—" Massimo peered down and, reassured that the affliction was not blindness, went on again, "two men come out of here, one tall and shaven headed, the other small and filthy?"

"I've seen hundreds, good sir. How was they dressed, then?" The cripple pulled aside a rag that the breeze had blown to cover his exceedingly messy stump of a leg and looked up again.

"Tall man in black—"

"Hundreds!"

"—small man with a beard in a greasy jerkin and stained hose—"

"Hundreds!"

Anguished, his eyes ceaselessly scanning the square, Massimo called to mind, "Maybe a small one-eared dog?"

"One-eared dog!"

"The dog!" Another man, with a complicated deformity, came nimbly round the pillar. At the foot of the shallow steps a blind beggar with a metal cup hung round his neck croaked "Dog!" in uncouth tones.

"That dog, good sir, would get into the church come what may."

"Thought Saint Bernardina'd give him another ear!"

"He got kicked out. Thrown out."

The blind man, mouthing and dribbling, mimed an impact, and the scattering of his coins broadcast.

"That's right, caught Nello and all but knocked him over. And tried again after that."

"Frantic, he was! Thought Saint Bernardina'd give him—"

"—another ear, right. And when they come out—"

"The two men?"

"Aren't I telling you? When they come out, this little woolly object didn't he spring right up to the little man's chest and kiss him like a Christian."

"Which way did they go?"

"Go? You should've seen him jump straight in the air, right up on the little man's—"

"Which way did they go?"

"And there was a miracle," Nello put in, overcoming his impediment with a great deal of saliva and effort. "Don't forget the miracle."

Massimo got out a coin and crouched before the one-legged man. He poised the coin and said: "Which. Way. Did. They. Go?"

The pair of bravos who earlier had sought for the Saint's attention as she entered the city, with the help of a child and a cripple, at this point jostled Massimo from his place. They came swaggering out from the Cathedral close behind a man in black whom they dogged through the crowd, glaring at anyone who looked as though he might interfere with their plans for the man they followed. The man himself moved on, oblivious, pale, wrapped in his own torment.

Massimo regained his place, and the beggar pointed. "Your men went across to the arcade there."

Massimo pressed the coin into the willing hand and turned. He was all but run down by four dwarves coming full tilt down the Cathedral steps in high excitement. They vanished through the crowd.

He headed for the arcade. What did folk do coming out from a religious duty? Food and wine, and here were food and wine shops and stalls along the arcade. It only increased his anxiety to realise there were so many.

Now wiser, he mentioned the little dog; or he mentioned it as soon as he could get any attention. A smiling, sweaty woman told him "Just a moment" and was gone. He heard the "just a moment" again and again. A stall holder remembered the dog, which had made a pass at an ell of sausage, but did not recall the man. He gestured at the crowds.

Further down the arcade, while Massimo chafed in a bakery, Sigismondo put second cups of wine on the table and sat down again beside Benno, who was cradling Biondello inside his shirt. Benno's mud-brown eyes shone with tears.

"I can't get over how she saved me. Blessed Saint Bernardina. I'll pray to her all my life. Wasn't it lucky that woman saw her? Of course, it wouldn't be *luck*, would it? I mean, the Saint would make her see."

Sigismondo suppressed the information that, failing such luck, he had been about to have a similar vision. He felt that the woman who had seen the Saint had been a far more appropriate and convincing means of saving Benno. Sigismondo had, in that moment, asked the Saint's pardon for his plan and accepted, with gratitude, her amendment of it. He did not doubt the reality of the pilgrim's vision. It was what he had also seen in the Cathedral that troubled him.

"We going back to the villa then? We left our horses at that Palace though. We have to go back, don't we?" He examined Biondello's hurt leg, a graze decorated with cobweb Benno had scraped from a corner. "I did wonder if they'd get around to hanging me before you turned up, but then if they did, I knew

you'd look after Biondello." He gave Biondello a piece of
bread dipped in the olive oil and watched fondly as he threw it
back in a gulp. "Who's a clever dog then? You knew who to
find. . . . Just think, aren't I lucky? I've seen the relics from
right up close, like I never thought I would. Never thought I'd
even get into Colleverde when we started, we was in such a
hurry to get away."

"We still are, but we can't go until I've seen the Princess
again. Let's hope she doesn't keep us long." He emptied the
wine jug into their cups and drank his down. "We'll go and
look at the clock."

Benno did not expect any explanation for this pressing idea
of time, but Sigismondo surprisingly hinted at it as he stood up.

"I've seen someone who might be as interested in our young
man as he was in his brother."

Benno's mouth fell open in the way natural to him, as he
transposed "our young man" into "the Lady Minerva" and got
the message. Above the noise of the crowd, a drum sounded
across the square.

"I have to hope that this person's mood has changed."
Sigismondo pulled his hood forward again and hummed
slightly in its depths. "He was in mourning and prostrate in
penance. The saints can work more than one miracle."

As they came out into the long shadows of late afternoon the
bell of the clock sounded. Sigismondo said, "We have a little
time after all."

The drum redoubled its speed and noise.

The dwarves were already staging the story of the miracle.
At the moment they were exclaiming: "Oh, see the holy spring!
Surely God sent this thing."

Dwarves playing the pilgrims grouped together, taking off
boots and doublets amid pointed reference to each other's need
for a cleansing dip. They had hung painted canvas across
below the stage, and by climbing down onto a lower plank they
could seem to be descending into a pool; one of them crying
"Nay I'll not wait these waters pure to try" scrambled down the
ladder until only his head showed, and from there he tossed bits
of clothing onto the staging. Meanwhile a skulking figure
watched from behind a scaffold pole and then came forward,
bent and high-stepping, snatched the clothing, and pelted away

across the stage to disappear at the other side. The rest of the cast, unable to chase after because of graphically mimed rough ground ("My naked feet do bleed, at many a stone and weed") gathered in hubbub. The bather emerged pulling down his shirt ("Alas my clothes are flown! Lend me now of thine own").

Benno, entranced by seeing himself portrayed, had stopped still, and Sigismondo, from either indulgence or interest, stayed by him. The dwarves decked their colleague in a variety of inappropriate garments ("Now by the blessed Clare, a skirt I *will* not wear!") and set off. A turn of the stage brought them immediately "to Colleverde." They pounced upon the thief and marched him, rope on neck and to a slow drum, amid a massacre of couplets, off the stage and, to the delight of the crowd parting before them, to the scaffold. The rope was flung towards the beam, the thief prayed *fortissimo*.

Rising, clearly and insecurely lifted from below, a figure in tinsel finery appeared in a long wig of tow beneath a flapping halo and stretched beneficent arms ("See now amid his fears he knows the Saint's holy mercy").

A dwarf on stilts was circulating with a collecting bag. Sigismondo contributed.

"Not fair, was it, leaving you out?" Benno demanded.

Sigismondo hummed. "I prefer it. The fewer who know what I do, the better." His attention seemed to have been caught by a flashing arc of knives, rising and falling above the crowd's heads near the far wall.

16

"The Devil! The Devil!"

MASSIMO, GOADED ON BY THE DIScovery at Fontecasta, continued to ask desperately whether anyone had seen the two men and the little dog. No, he heard; no and no. A woman finally remembered them going into the Cathedral, "before the miracle," she added.

He moved on. He was in need of a miracle of his own, which he felt only Sigismondo could provide. He stepped up on the rim of a street fountain to peer over the crowd, and his boot slipped. He swore and landed like a stork on one foot in the basin.

"Get out of our water with your foul feet!" a woman cried, swiping at his head with an end of wet cloth. His ear sang as he squelched off on his search.

He thought the people were becoming more and more disobliging. He could not know it was a result of the increased fury of his voice. What to him was the twentieth repetition of his demand was to each of them the first.

"Have *you* seen—" He was near the end of the arcade. The patron of the wine shop, a rotund man in a purple-stained apron, turned.

"Have you seen a couple of men, one tall and shaven-headed, the other—"

"With the little one-eared dog?"

"Yes, yes!"

"Why, bless you, they sat there at that table. Didn't stop long, mind. They've only just gone."

Massimo span round to go, but his arm was held in the grasp of a man used to heaving wine barrels.

"The shaven-headed man."

"Yes, yes?"

"He put his hood up. You can't go looking for that head of his no more."

He released the despairing Massimo, who ran out into the crowd. A hood, he thought, like half the men in Colleverde. Saint Bernardina, another miracle if you're in the way of it. Only just left; can't have gone far. He went on doggedly. There was applause from over by the scaffold, and after a moment a drum set up its beat. A dwarf on the extempore stage shouted through cupped hands. Massimo forged on.

He pulled at the sleeve of a tall, black-hooded man who turned a bearded face. Another, at some distance through the crowd, also proved to be a stranger. The crowd thickened, as if they pressed back to make way for something. Massimo was pushed against the foot of the scaffold. There were some people under it, so he ducked there too and hauled himself up to glare over the crowd, unaware that he was appearing as an extra in the second performance of *The Miracle*, unconscious even that his fuzzy hair was being brushed by the bare foot of a hanged man swinging overhead. The corpse had not worn shoes for long as the Colleverdese were averse to waste.

A howl greeted Massimo's appearance, which coincided with the elevation of "Saint Bernardina," come to save the thief from Hell. The players incorporated his sudden appearance with glee and skill. As Massimo shaded his eyes with his hand, a falsetto cried, "See, Satan seeks for sin, Our souls for to win!"

A flung stone caught Massimo on the ear, as the crowd shrieked appreciation of the Devil in their midst. Bewildered and furious, he ducked down and was seized by strangers' hands, pulled painfully over a bracer at the scaffold's foot, and met half a trodden-on pie full in the face. Jeering and yelling, they thrust him into the crowd, crying "The Devil! The Devil!" and he stumbled through a gauntlet of blows and kicks.

He tripped suddenly over the totally unexpected body of a prostrating pilgrim and went headlong, striking his brow. The pilgrim, rising and praying, prostrated himself anew towards the Cathedral. It was not his first accident. He was offering his bruises to Saint Bernardina; other people could do what they liked with theirs.

Within the next minute Massimo was almost robbed and half

stripped; but a kinder citizen found him and helped him across to the fountain. A stout man with a purple splash on his apron noticed him there, being doused with water and struggling to sit up.

"Poor soul! That pair he was looking for must have set on him," he said. "Here, fetch him in. He can sit on the bench, so, till he recovers."

"That's the bell going," someone remarked. Massimo had thought the sound was in his head and was relieved until the speaker went on: "If he's from outside the city, he's here for the night. That's the gates closing."

Massimo's master had stressed the urgency of finding Sigismondo. If Sigismondo could not be found, Massimo was on his own and must act.

"Which way is the Palazzo Corio?" he demanded.

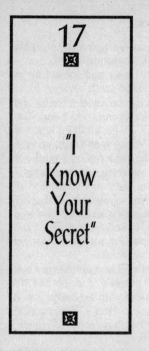

17

"I Know Your Secret"

THE KNIVES HAD CEASED TO FLASH by the time Sigismondo, with Benno in his wake, arrived. They found a circle of people also attracted by the display gathered round a young man who was telling fortunes.

In another city this might have been forbidden, but one of the complaints of the Princess Corio against Bishop Taddeo was that he was too lax; though in this he was only reflecting the Duke himself, known to be fashionably in favour of consulting the cards as well as the stars. The Marshal, in any case, was notorious for enforcing a rule one day and ignoring an infringement the next.

This fortune-teller's neck was hung with hair too gold to be natural, round features so beautiful that already some watching women had put their heads on one side with soft expressions that augured well for the young man's purse. He had laid out cards on a board put across a barrel and kept up a stream of patter in a light voice and an accent hard to place but far from the purest Tuscan.

His tunic was blue on the right, yellow on the left; a tambourine lay beside his hand on the board, but of his knives there was no sign, except for a rather uncomfortable impression that he could produce any, or all of them, without notice; and therefore, since he had proved he could send them where he wanted, to annoy him would be a mistake.

If a fallen angel had bothered to come to Colleverde to tell fortunes, he would have looked much like this.

"It's *Angelo!*" Benno clapped his hands, making the young man's eyes, so disconcertingly light in his pale face, glance up at him; but the patter did not falter nor did the face show any sign of recognition. A pretty girl in her Sunday best had

dragged her sweetheart forward to pay for a reading. Angelo
laid out the cards from the pack with conjuring speed.

"The Queen of Cups." He turned it over and looked up at
her, with a slight show of rather crooked teeth, strange in so
ravishingly regular a face. "That's for a honey-sweet nature and
fair display; and Judgement: a time for changes, fair one. You
may look to improve your fortunes." A speculative glance at
her fair-haired sweetheart made that young man flush, and the
next remark did not soothe him. "Ah, the King of Swords! A
dark-haired person will enjoy your company. And you, sir?"
The hand flashed out three cards again. "Seven of Cups. You're
going to see pleasure, sir; and the Seven of Swords, do I see?"
He mocked the young man into annoyance and then flattered
him until he was mollified. Then he flicked their money from
the board into his hands and dealt again for the impatient
matron fidgeting for her turn.

"The Empress! Why, lady, the card of a homemaker, a cook
to make mouths water, and to good purpose, for she can fill
them with good things. Deck your house with greenery, you'll
have good occasion for rejoicing soon. Here's Temperance,
though." He shook his golden head. "Don't try to do too much.
Give your husband a rest now and then."

The crowd loved this; the woman giggled and bit her lip. He
glanced round and saw that Sigismondo had arrived at the
front, Benno sliding into a place at his side. "And the Three of
Cups! The card of healing and enjoyment—lady, you have
suffered. The blessed relics will take away your pains, however
you came by them." His fingers did not so much pick up her
coins from the board as cause them to vanish. "And you, sir."

He threw a glance up at Sigismondo looming before him as
he dealt the cards, then lowered his eyes to the card he turned
up with a deft flick. "Ah. Six of Cups. Old acquaintance may
help with a new project." Sigismondo hummed in acquiescence
as the light eyes glanced up again; the gold head nodded at the
card. "Next . . . the Falling Tower." Benno stared at the card,
where a brick tower had, jammed into its top, a crowned cloud
raining gold discs. A man in blue plunged to obviously certain
death, helpless legs kicking. It seemed to Benno very ominous,
but Angelo's light voice went on without emphasis: "The
possibility of accident. Good sir, beware the unexpected." He

turned the last card: a woman in red robes, a book on her knee, and an odd hat on her head. "Ah. The High Priestess. Take care of your health, good sir; there is some danger to you. The cards do not lie." His fingers slid the coins from the board as he murmured what could have been, "Are they right?"

Sigismondo bent as if to inspect the cards for himself. "Hey, *now* he warns me! And I never knew she was married!" Only Benno could have heard the additional murmur, "Danger? So what's new, my beauty? Hang loose, we may want you," and Angelo showed his teeth in a genuine smile.

The first time Benno had met this man, thanks to an initial misunderstanding, he had nearly received one of the knives in the small of his back. Although they had parted the best of companions, and Angelo had used his knives effectively on their behalf, the small of Benno's back crawled in memory as they turned to walk away. The crowd, happy in the prophecies of trouble, as is general when the trouble is for others, watched them leave in sympathy. A woman, taking hold of Sigismondo's arm, begged him to go at once and ask the Saint for protection.

News of the Saint's intervention, the miracle in the Cathedral, had reached the Palazzo Corio by the time Sigismondo and Benno arrived. A miracle was thought excellent for Colleverde. It would improve business even when the relics were shifted to Nemora. Some contested that, as the miraculous picture of the Saint had been painted here, here it should stay; after all, it was the picture that had moved. The rest, although sympathetic to the idea, opined that Duke Grifone wasn't likely to leave it when he took the rest.

Someone suggested, to applause, that the Bishop might be in hot water with the Princess Corio for having allowed a miracle to take place when she wasn't there to see it.

The Princess Corio, however, was in excellent humour when Sigismondo was shown in. With her brother and nephew, she was still seated at table drinking wine after their feast and eating nuts and sweetmeats. A great fire, to warm the big barrel-vaulted room on this chill evening of early spring, burnt on the hearth under the carved stone of the Corio arms. The light of the flames, enhanced by wax candles upon the table, gave the red silk of the Cardinal's robes a glow of rubies and almost warmed the sharp-cut, clever face above. The Princess Corio was dressed in green-and-silver damask whose quilting imparted an impression of glittering scales as the light shifted on her long sleeve. Their nephew Torquato, in his usual black, looked angry as well as sly; it might be that Sigismondo's return had interrupted a family quarrel. As if to console himself, he had cornered a silver comfit dish and was popping into his mouth gobbets of candied rosewater that glittered with gold leaf; his aunt's cook had sent up *manus Christi* for the Cardinal's dessert.

The Princess Corio spoke.

"You have been to the Cathedral? What is this talk of a miracle?"

"The Saint was seen in her picture to smile and bow her head. The innocence of a thief was in question, and he was pardoned as we prayed."

"You were there?" The eyes of all three, again, were on him.

He bowed. "With many others, Princess. It was a pilgrim who had this vision."

"What clergy were present? The Bishop?" Her tone had sharpened.

"His Grace was praying."

"He should have sent to tell me. To tell us." She spoke almost as if to herself and tapped the table. The Cardinal, with a great rustle of silk, rose and warmed his hands an instant at the fire before turning.

"It is no matter. I shall question the pilgrim myself tomorrow. Did any share her vision?" It was a professional speaking. A miracle was a matter for Rome, should it prove genuine. Torquato had risen dutifully when his uncle did and stood, sucking his candy, studying their visitor out of the corner of his eye.

"No one said so, Your Eminence, at the time."

The Cardinal smiled faintly. "Ah, by tomorrow there may be several—too rapt to speak when it happened. Where's the thief?"

Sigismondo shrugged. "He vanished, Eminence."

"And, I dare say, won't be found again!" The lady's tone suggested that had she been there, she might have interpreted the Saint's message differently. A smile and a nod might as well mean approval of a hanging as of a pardon.

"We shall see. Before the Duke arrives tomorrow, there will be time to see to many things. For tonight, I shall go to my chamber, Sister, and do not wish my meditations to be disturbed." The Cardinal bent and kissed her on the brow, extended his hand towards Sigismondo, who came swiftly forward to kneel and kiss his ring, and passed, his skirts flowing behind him, to the double doors at the far end of the room, which were opened for him by two assiduous servants at the exact moment when he reached them. Without checking his pace, he went on into the room beyond. Candles already burnt on the desk there.

"I'll bid you goodnight, Nephew." The Princess checked Torquato as he was about to sit again. "I have things to discuss that need not trouble you."

Torquato's mouth tightened. Sigismondo had observed that an attempt to follow his uncle had been prevented by an upflung palm from the Cardinal, and now he was excluded from yet more of his family's business. He kissed his aunt's brow perfunctorily, inclined his head coldly to Sigismondo, and left with the last *manus Christi* from the dish as he passed the table on his way to another door.

His uncle's servants had left the study door and now came to clear the table, but the Princess dismissed them and, when they were gone, pointed to a large tapestry-covered stool opposite the chair she took at the fireside.

"But you'd like wine? Or fruit?" She indicated the dessert on the table. Sigismondo merely sat down, smiling, bland, put his hands on his knees, and waited.

The Princess picked up her own wine cup and looked into it without drinking, as though she saw the future there. If she did, it pleased her. Sigismondo had been aware from the moment he saw her this evening that her mood was totally different from the morning's. Something had happened to produce an elation, a sense of excitement and anticipation as strong as the musky scent that disturbed the air around her.

She drank and looked at him with glittering dark eyes.

"I know your secret, sir."

18

⌘

We Must Look to the Future

⌘

NOT A MUSCLE MOVED IN SIGIS-mondo's smiling face. "Indeed, Princess. Which secret is that?"

She flung back the head, swathed in silver gauze, pinned with emeralds, and laughed, clapping her hands so that the rings clashed.

"If only I had time to find out more! And this," she levelled a finger at him, "this is more the secret of the late Lord Giraldi than yours, I think."

Sigismondo raised his eyebrows and tilted his head to one side, the picture of polite bafflement. She wagged the finger.

"My physician has told me all." She laughed again. "Perhaps the old man's death was brought on by his exertions. Don't tell me, sir, the secret was so well kept that you did not *know* the page—the sick page you spoke of—was a girl?"

Sigismondo shrugged. "I did not attend her sickbed myself. An old woman waited on her."

"I had heard he was dead before; a rumour put about, I suppose, to keep away people who might pry into his way of life." She became suddenly severe. "Why was she not banished from the house when the Lord Giraldi made his last confession?"

"She was too sick to move, Princess."

She clapped her hands again, then levelled a finger at him. "You betray yourself, sir. You knew she should be removed from the house at such a time. You knew she was no page."

Sigismondo bowed his head, with a smile of complicity. "Impossible to deceive Your Highness."

"Well! It's of no importance now." Her hand fell on a folded paper on the table at her side, and her fingers smoothed the edge of it. "He's buried, and we may hope his Shulamite is forgiven him. Every man seeks consolation in this world." She glanced sharply at him. "Duke Ludovico, does he look for another duchess soon?"

"Princess, it is but a few weeks ago—"

"Yes, yes. I don't speak of private grief but of policy. A prince puts his state before all. If that weren't so, we in Nemora would not now be preparing to celebrate this union with Montenero."

She looked into the fire and smiled, a smile more to herself than to the man opposite. Her hand absently patted the paper. She turned her head towards him. "Did you think the wedding would be postponed? Prince Livio has assured us today that he will bring his daughter to Colleverde just the same, despite the terrible accident to his son."

Nothing in Sigismondo's gravity showed that he appreciated the euphemism that made a decapitation into what might be called a slip of the sword, or that he knew that the daughter Prince Livio spoke of bringing was not at the moment in his possession, and that it was curious indeed that she was still being called his daughter.

There was a brisk sound of rain upon the shutters.

"We have long yearned for such a union." She stood up, as if her mood could no longer bear inaction, but as he rose, she motioned him to be seated. She paced the room. The Cathedral clock sounded dully across the roofs.

"Now that the Prince Livio's son is dead . . ."

She said no more. Now that Prince Livio had no male heir—if he had no more sons by any second wife—the Lady Minerva was heiress, so that Astorre might expect to succeed to both Nemora and his wife's Montenero. "Of course, the wedding will not be celebrated as it would have been. Prince Livio is doubly in mourning."

"The accident—the Prince must be greatly distressed?"

The Princess returned to her place, picked up her cup, found it empty, and refilled it. "Crazed by grief for his wife. It's a fit that has come on him before." She touched her mouth with the embroidered linen napkin that lay on the table and picked up the paper from beside it. "He wasn't aware what he did when he ran from her deathbed. If the poor boy had not met him in that fatal moment! But the workings of Fate are so strange, are they not?"

"Indeed, Princess." Sigismondo wondered if she had heard how unluckily Fate had also worked on the Lord Eugenio. The letter from the Prince must have arrived very recently, but the foot of Rumour is faster than even the letters of princes.

"The Prince's astrologer had warned him of a bad conjunction between Mars and Venus, threatening his State, and alas! He lost his son . . ."

Sigismondo admired the impression of inadvertence given by this phrase.

"Yet we must look to the future. The world will pity him."

Sigismondo murmured what she might take for agreement, but it seemed that she was anxious for his opinion on the Duke Ludovico's attitude regarding so suddenly defunct a nephew. "Ludovico sends to say he cannot attend the wedding because of the recent death of his duchess. Now his sister, Oralia, is dead too, there will not be the same bond between Rocca and Montenero. Prince Livio is sure to regret that . . ."

"It seems he is forging a different bond, Princess." He spoke as her voice died away. Her glance was startled. Then she laughed.

"Yes indeed! The Princess of Nemora will—"

Sigismondo sniffed, twice, sharply, and her face expressed surprise. No manual for courtiers recommended sniffing as a form of civilised communication. Suddenly, without asking her leave, he rose and pointed.

From under the door of the Cardinal's room a wreath of smoke oozed out and moved thickly on the air. She could faintly hear a crackle and spit of fire. By the time she had, screaming, rung the bell that stood on the dining table, Sigismondo had reached the doors. They were locked. She ran, still screaming, towards him just as he kicked them open. She stopped in her tracks, staring without believing what she saw.

Her brother, lashed to his tall chair in the middle of the room, stared back across the gag that hid half his face. Flames enveloped him from foot to head, scarlet as his robes.

19

"We Need to Know These Secrets"

SIGISMONDO TURNED AT ONCE towards the bed, gripped the nearest curtain, and with powerful grasp wrenched it down. In the moments that this took, a grey-haired servant had run in—the Princess Corio staring as if at Medusa, hands to her mouth, screaming through her fingers—had snatched up a jug from somewhere, and hurled its contents at the dreadful fire. There was a hiss and a redoubled bluish fire. The jug had held wine.

Sigismondo flung the heavy folds of cloth over the Cardinal, swathed him in them, and beat at the flames. There was choking smoke, the reek of burnt flesh, oil, and cloth. Water hissed on the fire, servants beat out the flames that licked along the floor.

When at last the fire looked to be smothered, Sigismondo, whose formidable knife seemed to jump into his hand, cut the Cardinal free. They unwrapped the heavy curtain from his body.

When this was done, it was indeed only his body in the remnants of his robes that was there. His eyes, without lashes or brows, stared sightlessly. The Princess Corio, frantically giving orders for bandages, for egg white, oil, houseleek, peeled the remains of the gag away and with shaking fingers found that more linen had been stuffed into his mouth.

She was again for the moment in command. She had her brother carried to his bed and continued to demand haste with the remedies. Sigismondo said to her, "Princess, His Eminence is dead."

She fell silent, leaning over her brother, while the room filled with servants, some carrying bandages and jars, others staring, whispering, and sobbing.

Sigismondo stood back, glancing round the room. He saw
various small changes from when he had last been there.
Papers had been disturbed on the table, crumpled and scattered;
some might have been used to fuel the flames. On the desk was
a small coffer of burgundy velvet, which looked fit to contain
something precious, though rather large for jewellery. The bed
on which they had laid the Cardinal had been rumpled already,
the cover pulled back and a pillow halfway down, though this
had been hidden at first by the curtain Sigismondo had
wrenched away. On the far side of the room, a door in the
panelling was ajar.

The Princess ordered the servants away from the bed. As
they pressed back, they made way for the clerics entering,
Torquato among them. Sigismondo took a roll of linen bandage
from a retreating maid and ran water from the majolica cistern
hanging in the corner over a basin. He plunged his hands in and
soaked the bandages, keeping meanwhile a watchful eye on the
room. Wrapping his burnt left hand and right wrist, he listened
to the physician confirming death and to the exclamations of
horror and a promising onset of hysteria among the servants,
controlled at once by a practised voice starting a prayer. As
everyone in the bedroom and the room beyond sank to their
knees, Sigismondo slid through the panelling door.

A narrow flight of stairs led very steeply down to where a
lantern burned. Knife again in hand, he descended.

At the foot, a small lobby opened out; a man lay there prone,
hands beside his head. The outer door stood ajar. Sigismondo
stepped over the man and looked up and down the silent street.
It was inhabited only by moonlight, bright on the puddles of
the recent rain and on the fur of some small shadowy animal
eating busily in the gutter. He shut the door, dropped the heavy
bar across the sockets, and turned the key.

He crouched to see if the man lying there had anything to
say. His helpless weight on Sigismondo's arm had its own tale
to tell; if the man had anything to say, he lacked the means to
give it voice. The Cardinal's livery, dark red with his badge on
the chest, was now a darker red, and the badge was obliterated.
The man's throat had been cut clean across in a single,
professional slash. Sigismondo lowered the body gently to the
floor. There was a bench fixed to the wall. Under it, kicked into

the shadows, lay a pair of chopines the size of a woman's feet. The leather uppers were tooled in patterns and painted green and red; one lay on its side, the mud on the cork sole still soft to the touch.

As he mounted the stairs, the smell met him again, a nauseous miasma: burnt oil, burnt flesh, smoke, with the extra pungency of working clothes. As he came in, he saw that yard servants and grooms had crowded in on the prayers. Beyond the door others knelt, Benno at the forefront. By the bed, Torquato in a stole and the Cardinal's confessor were administering the last rites.

Sigismondo too knelt. He was beside the desk and, as he spoke the responses with the rest, he glanced under his lashes at the coffer on the Turkey carpet over the desk, at the burgundy velvet and finely worked brass hinges. Had the Cardinal been prepared to pay for something? Had he himself been paid? The prayers reminded the listeners that it was not with money that Cardinal Petrucci must now be making his account.

When the priests ceased their prayers for the moment, prayers to which groaning responses and smothered weeping provided a respectful burden, Sigismondo stood up, and the eyes of Princess Corio were at once upon him. She rose from her knees beside the bed with the threatening swiftness of a cobra and stood surveying the crowd, her mouth tight as if in disgust. Never before could such a rabble of underlings have penetrated to the Cardinal's sanctum. She opened her mouth to order them out when she saw that Sigismondo was threading his way towards her. She waited, saw his bow, and heard him murmur: "Princess, would it not be best that no one should leave the house as yet? News of this ought not to be spread until you have found out more. His Eminence knew his murderers. He was expecting their visit; Your Highness and I heard no cry, no struggle."

She gazed at his face and nodded. Her eyes stared, as if in reflection of her brother's: the beginning of shock. Still she was in command, although she shuddered. He said, "The porter at the private door below—he has been killed."

Again she nodded, as if it were no more than to be expected.

She put a hand on his sleeve, and once more the tremor went through her as she stared at the bed.

"It shall be done as you think right. I put the enquiry in your hands." Her eyes narrowed. "My brother shall be avenged. There are those who will avenge him. His murderers shall suffer his very fate; but not until they have screamed for the mercy of the fire." What she said was the more forceful for being delivered in almost a whisper. She folded her hands again at her waist, severely, as if controlling their desire to reach out, to claw, twist, torment the truth from anyone who could yield it. She had found, for the moment, the man to be her instrument in this.

Benno, kneeling with the rest, saw the Princess and his master go to the desk, and he watched Sigismondo try the lid of a coffer standing on it. It was not locked and swung open with the back of it towards those in the room. From the expression on the Princess's face, she was surprised at the contents. Even his master raised his eyebrows. He seemed to question the Princess, but she shrugged, put her hand in the coffer, and sifted what was in it thoughtfully. The sound of gold coins kissing one another is perhaps unique: Benno believed that was what he heard. If the coffer was full of them, there was enough to buy a couple of farms and have plenty left over to furnish a palace. Benno knew very little about cardinals. Possibly, coffers like that sat about for ornament. He did know about servants, and he supposed they were all too frightened of excommunication to have touched it.

The Princess snapped the lid down with decision and raised her finger to one of the servants leaving the room. She spoke in his ear; he picked up the coffer with an effort that made his jaw muscles set and, helped by another servant summoned by the Princess, carried it out, presumably to a strong room.

When the servants were all dismissed, Benno stood back against the wall, hoping to be invisible. He saw the Cardinal's nephew stalk out and other priests and clerks following the servants; he saw his master escort the Princess Corio out of the room of death and stand talking to her for a moment, low voiced, by the fire. As he parted from the Princess Sigismondo lifted a finger to Benno. Catching sight of him suddenly, she cried, "What's that creature?"

"My servant, Princess." A smile and a finger tapping the temple. "He will have been lost, wondering where I was."

Benno gave the Princess a bow and scrambled crablike from the room after Sigismondo. He was accustomed to being looked at by the gentry as if he had that moment inexplicably left a dungheap.

Sigismondo paused at the head of the staircase, surveying the departing throng of servants. Some were going to bed as ordered, others had work to finish. Two women in the Corio grey came up the stairs, one elderly in starched linen cap, wiping away tears with the back of her hand. The younger woman carried a pitcher of water and a basket full of linen and raw wool. The linen was rolled in bandages, and she carried folded towels over her shoulder. Sigismondo stood aside for them, and they went into the long room. Benno realised they were going to lay out the Cardinal. He didn't envy them. He rubbed his nose and spoke in a muted voice. "Somebody really hated him, didn't they? I mean, they could have just stabbed him."

He looked up at the dispassionate face of Sigismondo. "Wouldn't be anyone in the house, would it?"

"Mm . . . if it was, they came in from the street." Another pair was trudging up the stairs, carrying a hurdle on their shoulders. "There was a man who kept the street door to His Eminence's private stair. They will be going to fetch him. Whoever it was who came in by that door didn't choose to be recognised."

"Did they kill him for that gold then? In the coffer?"

"If they did, why leave it behind? The Princess knows nothing of the money, yet it's a small fortune. You, my Benno, might even call it a large one. . . . Perhaps someone paid for the pleasure of seeing His Eminence burn. Plenty of questions to ask."

Sigismondo looked down the great stair, speaking over his shoulder. "I'll start with the servants though. Every man, even a Cardinal, has a servant who knows nearly everything about him."

"You'll want Battista then," said Benno, "the Cardinal's body servant. He bosses everyone about, bad as the Princess, they say. Been with 's Eminence years and years. One of the grooms said Battista'd've been sacked a long while back, only he knew so many secrets."

"Good, Benno." Sigismondo gripped him by the shoulder. "Find this Battista. Say you ask by order of the Princess herself. We need to know a few of these secrets."

"We got a few of our own though, right?" Benno was innocently proud, thinking of the household at Fontecasta.

"We can hope so." Sigismondo turned and leant on the carved balustrade. "By the way, the Princess tells me that the marriage of Lord Astorre and Lady Minerva is not to be postponed, in spite of the mourning for her mother and brother."

Benno goggled. "But—"

Sigismondo's finger silenced him. "So we think. But it isn't difficult to get information from a man or woman under the lash; he may be confident of producing her in time." He raised the finger again as Benno began to speak. "And yes, I do have confidence in Massimo. If there is danger, then he follows my plan, and they will be safe this night. In the morning, when the gates open, we will bring them in."

"I thought you said," Benno was not reproachful, but the thinking he had been doing had upset him, "I thought you said he killed the boy because he *wasn't his son*; but they're twins, so she—I mean, she can't be—"

Sigismondo was smiling. "A lesson in policy. If you need a daughter to join your State to another's and you've no time to sire one, you must use what you haven't got. He has till Sunday; and this Friday we must keep to the matter in hand and leave him to his puzzles. The Princess is in the mood for flaying. . . . We'll start with this Battista."

20

"I'm Talking about Magicians"

If Battista were the man who knew the Cardinal's secrets, it was because he wasn't likely to part with any of them. His mouth took a downward turn in the bitter, wrinkled face, as if pulled by the weight of an invisible padlock.

"His Eminence? I have nothing to say about His Eminence. Who set you to question me?"

"The Princess ordered me to enquire into her brother's death. She wishes, as must all who loved His Eminence, to bring to justice the villains who did this thing."

Battista dipped his fingers into the bowl of goose grease a boy had just brought from the kitchens and anointed the blisters on his hands. A smear of oil-black smoke darkened the forehead under the cropped fringe of grey hair. Sigismondo, whose left hand and right wrist were still wrapped in linen newly soaked in cold water, waited. From long experience he knew that the art of questioning often lay in not asking questions. Silence will provoke what questions will suppress. After a few moments Battista grunted, from either irritation or the pain of his burns.

"They'll never catch them. With the city like this, full of pilgrims and strangers."

"The gates are shut for the night."

"And tomorrow?" A sneer looked very much at home on Battista's face. "Do you expect the Marshal to look into each load of cabbages for himself? There's ways of getting in and out of everywhere."

Sigismondo, without asking leave, stepped into the tiny room and sat on the stool. Battista shifted round to glare at him. They were almost touching; Sigismondo was not of negligible size, and the space off the Cardinal's chamber resembled a closet more than a room. It had a few shelves with folded clothes, a roll of bedding, cups and plates such as would serve a Cardinal, and on the lowest, wider shelf the bowl of goose grease, a jug of wine, an earthenware cup, and chestnuts scattered on a majolica plate of brilliant yellows and blues—a plate possibly rejected for better use because of the great crack that ran across it. Sigismondo guessed that it could have come by its crack from being hurled at Battista's head.

He reached out a hand and took a chestnut. People can be irritated into speaking, too.

"You have an idea, then, who these villains are."

"An idea? Who cares for an idea? His Eminence is dead."

Sigismondo ate the chestnut and reached for another, Battista just failing to block him by leaning against the shelf next to the plate. "Hey, but burning alive! Who'd do such a thing to a holy man?"

Sigismondo's voice was empty of sarcasm, but the remark won him a sharp glance from Battista.

"Who? Someone who'd seen another burn so."

Sigismondo slowly nodded, considering this. "A heretic?"

Battista snorted. "Heretics! It's in Spain they burn *them*. I'm talking of magicians. The black arts—" he stopped abruptly. He had noticed that he was talking.

"Mm-mm. The Cardinal burnt a magician?"

Battista turned his back and went on applying goose grease, his mouth drawn down sourly. He looked round swiftly as Sigismondo laughed.

"So the magician rises from his pyre like a phoenix and comes to burn the Cardinal. Keep that tale for the kitchen, or scare the grooms with it. Human hands bound His Eminence to that chair, gagged him, poured oil on him, and then set fire to it. Two pairs of human hands at the least."

"Of course it was. They couldn't save Antonello from the flames but they could avenge him."

"Antonello? That's the magician? No hand at magicking himself out of chains and flames into the sky then."

"He was a fool, whatever else—telling His Eminence he would die before midsummer."

Sigismondo shook his head slowly. The two looked at each other.

"Someone thought to help that prophecy to come true. Who could it be?"

"I don't know their names." Battista spread out his glistening hands and looked down at them. "Assassins. Bravos. Men said they were led by Achille Malvezzi, a friend to heretics."

"Why should such men wish to avenge Antonello?" Shifting comfortably, he leaned back against the wall. Battista pushed the majolica plate towards him with a forearm and delicately picked up a chestnut for himself. "Because he foretold success for Malvezzi and cured his son of a fever he was dying of."

"A physician too, this Antonello?"

"A magician, I tell you. He healed by spells. His Eminence fell sick a year or so ago, and his physicians could not cure him. Antonello was called upon—in secret, naturally. Certainly he cured His Eminence, but he made the mistake of doing more than he was asked for." Battista's sneer returned. "The fool. Nobody likes to hear of their death."

Sigismondo passed a hand thoughtfully over his bare scalp from nape to brow. "And these bravos—did they try to rescue Antonello before he was burnt?"

"Oh, they came too late. It was all mismanaged, and one of Malvezzi's men was caught and hanged."

"Yet another reason for revenge. Where did this take place?"

"In Bibbiena. And we passed through there bringing the relics from Rome only a week back." Battista paused, to give his words weight. "Someone stuck a piece of paper to the Bibbiena Cathedral's door with a knife; the message was *Hell flames wait for you, Petrucci*. His Eminence wasn't pleased."

Sigismondo hummed on a descending note, seeing again that clever, disdainful face before it was disfigured.

"And was there no other who would profit by your master's death? No one in household or family who hated him?"

"The nephew?" The sneer was very evident now. "That one has hopes of pushing God off His throne. Nothing His Eminence could do was enough for him. Was he to hand him his hat?"

"Surely with His Eminence's patronage he would have gone far?"

"It was not how *far* but how *soon*. He would not wait. Always at His Eminence for preferment."

Sigismondo wagged his head and rose as if to go, his presence filling the tiny room. Battista sidled away along the wall.

"And the woman? The one who was here tonight?"

"Woman?" Battista spoke, matter-of-factly. "His Eminence had retired for the night. No petitioner would have been permitted to see him."

Sigismondo's hum was deprecatory. "I don't speak of petitioners. In the case I speak of, if anyone asked favours, it might have been His Eminence."

Battista bristled. "He never had to ask a woman! They flung themselves at him!" He became aware of the moral deep water here and stopped. Sigismondo took up smoothly.

"Cardinals are still men. The world understands that. The Holy Father himself is a man." He put a finger on Battista's chest. "What do you know about the money?"

Battista stared. "Money? What money?"

"Was His Eminence going to pay anyone for their services tonight?"

Battista looked as though he might have scratched his head if his hands hadn't hurt. "If he was going to, he didn't tell me. Why?"

"Do you know of anyone who was going to render His Eminence a service tonight? A service worth payment of a coffer this size?" Sigismondo's hands indicated the invisible coffer. "Covered in wine-red velvet?"

"I know *nothing* of any money—of no such coffer. With much money, you say?" There was surprise and indignation; Battista expected to know of such things. "There was not a coffer like that on the journey. I would have known. On the journey, of course, we took much gold for the relics. That was not my affair; there were guards for that. But apart from such small sums as His Eminence keeps in his desk," Battista tapped the front of his tunic, leaving a greasy mark on its badge of the Cardinal's hat, "I have the key to the rest. His Eminence trusted me." It was now a desolate boast, perhaps not even true if the coffer were evidence to the contrary.

"The woman tonight. She had been here before?"

Battista hesitated. Sigismondo's proximity was overwhelming. He shrugged again, moved away as far as he could and put more grease on his fiery palm. "He saw her every time he came to Colleverde. She was his favourite."

"So you know who she is."

"A courtesan. Polissena. Very discreet."

"And the servant at the private door to the street—he had orders to let her in tonight?"

"His Eminence did not tell me every detail." From the resentment in Battista's face and voice, there might have been rivalry in this matter between him and the man whose throat had been slit.

Sigismondo bestowed a wide smile upon him and, from apparently nowhere, a gold coin that he slid delicately under the blistered hand on the shelf.

"I will inform the Princess how helpful you have been. I suppose she will find a place for you in her household."

Battista's downward mouth showed his opinion of this possibility, but he slid the coin into his purse with a mutter that might have been thanks. Sigismondo moved to the doorway and turned. "Have you been in His Eminence's service long?"

"Eleven years."

"An easy service?"

"He demanded the best, and he never kept a fool near him," Battista said, like a challenge. Sigismondo bent his head, acknowledging this self-estimate. His final question seemed casual enough.

"How did you come to throw wine on the fire?"

"You think I killed him? The water for his washing often stands there. I knew as I was throwing it that it was the wrong jug. I kill him? Where do you think I will go now? What shall I do without a master?"

He wrenched the leather curtain across the opening, shutting himself off. Sigismondo, pausing a moment, could hear the painful, choked sound of weeping. If Battista had thought he knew the secrets of the Cardinal's life, it did not appear that he knew the secret of his death.

21

"We've Got the Murderer!"

Sigismondo had raised his hand to knock at the door of Torquato's room when a commotion broke out downstairs. A few strides along the corridor brought him to the landing above the entrance hall. He looked down to see torches, servants, bustle. The Bishop was here.

As the Bishop's chief aims in this world were to lead a peaceful life and to avoid the Princess Corio, the present circumstances were a nightmare. With the Cardinal dead and, worse still, murdered in an unnecessarily ostentatious way, all responsibility for finding the murderers devolved on him as the senior ecclesiastic of Colleverde. This, of course, also meant that he was forced to come at the command of the Princess, to view the body (he was being led upstairs), to express his horror (which was considerable), to pray at the bedside (from which he withdrew as soon as he decently could), and to assure the Princess that his Marshal was already interrogating strangers in the inns and hostels—"all those who are not bona fide pilgrims with the proper *testimoniale* from their bishop."

"Suppose the perpetrators of this deed are posing as pilgrims?"

Within ten minutes of his arrival, she had made him feel incompetent; within fifteen, he was busy trying to suppress the un-Christian wish that, while they were about it, the murderers had included the Cardinal's sister in the bonfire.

"My brother will lie in state in the Cathedral."

The remains of the Cardinal had been laid out on his bed and prepared, to the best of their ability, by women of the Princess's household. The fire-scorched face, without lashes or eyebrows, gave the Bishop a very unpleasing idea of what he could *not* see and a more vivid idea of hell fire than he had hitherto entertained; the prayers he had uttered were fervent. It was hard to keep one's thoughts from speculation as to whether the Cardinal's soul was, at the moment, encountering any better fate than had his body. His Eminence had, it was to be supposed and feared, died without absolution; and he was known to be a worldly man.

A practical problem niggled: how it would be possible to present the remains in state.

"Of course. Of course. I will send people. All that is right shall be done, Princess. His Eminence shall receive all that Holy Mother Church can give. Masses are already being said for him in the Cathedral, for as soon as I heard—"

"Of course. The Holy Father himself must be informed at once."

"I shall send immediately to Rome."

Another voice slid into the conversation. "Would it not be best, Aunt, if *I* went to Nemora? The Duke should hear such terrible news from one of the family; from one who was in the house when it happened." Torquato sent a glance sidelong towards the Bishop as if to suggest that any message sent by him would be useless.

"I need you here. There will be plenty for you to do," said his aunt, before the Bishop could second the proposal. "You will help Signor Sigismondo to find the devils who killed your uncle."

Torquato's expression made it plain that he did not relish the role of dogsbody yet again.

"Is it wise, Aunt, to entrust this enquiry to a stranger?"

"He saved the Duke of Rocca from his enemies, Nephew."

"The enemies of Rocca! They are not the enemies of Nemora! And may he not have been sent to do this deed himself?"

"He was with me, you fool."

"There are agents who can be put on to do such things."

"He discovered the smoke, he beat out the flames with his own hands. Let me hear no more of this, Nephew. I have put him in charge of the matter."

The Bishop, during this family exchange, had listened in amiable bewilderment. "Sigismondo?"

The Princess lifted a hand and crooked a forefinger. The tall, broad-shouldered man in black with a shaven head who stepped from the throng at the door stirred recent memories in the Bishop. As the man knelt to kiss his ring, the Bishop exclaimed, "The miracle today! You were with the pilgrim who saw the Saint move. It was you who brought the thief for the Saint's judgement." The Bishop was pleased, both with himself for remembering—he was not good at faces, among other things he was not good at—and with the man himself for his action. A miracle would help all the unbelievers and backsliders in Colleverde.

"Never mind that," said the Princess. "He is the man you will order your Marshal to help."

"Ah yes." The Bishop knew his Marshal. He did not anticipate any pleasure in the collaboration. "And have you any idea, sir, who has done this terrible, terrible thing?"

"At present, Your Grace, it is not possible to say; but I do not doubt that, with God's help, we shall find them."

The Bishop was soothed by this quiet, powerful-looking man with the untroubled voice. "May God go with you and prosper your efforts, my son. The Devil will not prevail when we are armed by our Holy Mother Church."

Sigismondo went down on one knee again and bent his head. The Bishop responded with a blessing, while the Princess Corio, gripping her wrists, twitched with impatience at his side. When he had done, she took Torquato by the arm, which he plainly did not care for, and turned him towards Sigismondo, now on his feet again.

"Tell him all that you saw, Nephew. Even the slightest detail."

The Bishop was now anxious to be gone, hoping for a little rest before fresh harassment and further directions from the Princess. His consolation was that she seemed to place much of the responsibility on the tall stranger, and he prayed that the Saint would not extend her charity to those who burnt Cardinals as well as those who stole pilgrims' clothes. Christian charity must have its limits. Luckily it had not yet occurred to him that, with His Eminence dead, he himself would be responsible for conducting the wedding of Duke Grifone's son, under the Duke's eye as well as that of the Princess Corio.

While the lady escorted the Bishop to the door. Sigismondo seized what was probably the only chance of questioning the nephew without help from the aunt; he followed Torquato to his room. It was both study and bedroom, like the Cardinal's, though far smaller and less richly furnished. Several books were piled on the ledge above the desk, papers and scrolls were scattered upon it, and the small mat before it was more worn than the velvet on the prie-dieu in its corner under the crucifix on the wall. Opposite this and extending behind the bed was a tapestry of Hercules writhing in the fiery shirt of Nessus. Torquato stood beneath this without apparent consciousness of its appalling aptness; it was probably some time since he had noticed the thing. He looked at Sigismondo with no pleasure.

"I fear, sir, that my aunt has misled you in supposing that I have anything to contribute. I saw less than you did, indeed, coming in only at my aunt's outcry and seeing—only the—dreadful end."

"Were you in here, then, when the alarm was raised?"

"Of course." Torquato was clearly offended. "My uncle is . . . was not the only one with work to be done late at night." He gestured towards the desk. "I am preparing a report on the reception of the relics for Cardinal Zampata at Rome, who is enquiring into certain atheistical tendencies he has heard rumour of in Nemora." The explanation emphasized that Torquato's position enjoyed the confidence of the great.

"Do you think, Father, that His Eminence, your uncle, might have been victim of such freethinkers?"

"It may be so. My uncle had enemies—every great man makes enemies." He seemed to recollect something and glanced under his brows at Sigismondo. "My uncle did not pay attention to threats. There was one at Bibbiena on the way here." He frowned as the sound of prayers came insistently from the room next door. "Such a deed must stem from the Devil. What men could have dared to do it, in this Palace, with friends within call?"

"Someone who could obtain access; someone who knew of the private stair; someone whom His Eminence would not be surprised to see. Did many know of the private stair?"

Torquato shrugged slightly. "My uncle's affairs were very

much his own concern." He looked annoyed, as though they should have been his too.

"Certainly the woman knew," Sigismondo said, without giving the statement any importance. Torquato drew breath. He was too subtle to pretend, like Battista, that he did not know about his uncle and women, and far too sophisticated to excuse him.

"Did His Eminence receive intelligencers by way of his private stair?"

"Of course."

"Do you know if he meant to make payment to any tonight, Father?"

Torquato could only shake his head at this further evidence that his uncle did not confide in him. Yet his curiosity had been roused. "Why do you ask? Do you think the murder political?"

"Everything must be considered, Father. His Eminence, as you say, had enemies, as do all great men. He was about to effect an alliance of Nemora and Montenero; there must be some who don't wish it."

"But my uncle's death will alter nothing. Prince Livio—"

He stopped. Sigismondo was not going to hear how much knowledge Torquato might have gained from assiduous listening at doors and picking up scraps of conversation between his aunt and uncle. Perhaps his ear had caught, as had Sigismondo's, the soft flurry of black velvet skirts that preceded the Princess Corio, now suitably clad in mourning, who stood before them. She ignored her nephew and raised a crooked finger at Sigismondo.

Torquato, however, had a last card to play. He glided forward, adding black to black as he stood in his priest's gown before his aunt, looking sideways at his late interrogator.

"Have you thought, Aunt, that Signor Sigismondo may have been sent here by the Duke of Rocca? My uncle's death removes a powerful figure from the scene—it weakens the Duke of Nemora by taking his first counsellor. Is it not we who should be questioning *him*?"

The Princess's glance was speculative, as though she reconsidered the situation and the speaker. Perhaps, with her brother gone, it would be wise to promote her nearest male relative. Perhaps, even, some of the family brains had been inherited, and she should for once take heed of him. She looked from Torquato to Sigismondo with her hooded gaze, but her reply was unequivocal.

"He will answer with his life for the matter I have put in his charge. It is in his interest to find the murderers."

The hollow sound of the Cathedral clock came on the wind, striking midnight. The Princess spoke over the strokes. "Duke Grifone comes today, and he will expect to hear of progress in the matter. Pray, sir, that you can provide it." She paused, as Sigismondo bowed. "And now you may go to see what the messenger from the Marshal has to say."

Downstairs in the entrance hall, watched by an assortment of servants and Benno, the Marshal's man came instantly up to Sigismondo.

"We've got the murderer," he announced triumphantly.

Benno held one of the torches and trotted at Sigismondo's side, Biondello's head bobbing under his chin. The other torch, carried by the Marshal's man, went ahead. Both spluttered and stank of pitch. Shadows loomed and flickered over the fronts of houses up the street leading to the square, and the mud glistened.

"You don't think they have found him, do you?" Benno asked.

Sigismondo spoke from inside his hood. "It would be so *easy*, Benno. I've the feeling this is not going to be easy."

"Battista no use then?"

"He told of a recent threat to the Cardinal. Someone might have been avenging the death of one Antonello, whom His Eminence burnt at the stake for blasphemy and the black arts."

"But 's Eminence wouldn't just've sat there and let them get on with it, would he? Oh, you've come for your revenge. Would you like me to sit in this chair and not make a noise till you get the gag in?"

Sigismondo flung back his head and laughed, the hood sliding off and his bare head gleaming in the torchlight.

"Must've trusted whoever it was, right?"

"My Benno! You understand it exactly. Whoever came up that private stair was expected, or the Princess and I in the next room, Battista in his closet, Torquato in his room, all would have heard His Eminence being attacked."

"You'd think he'd call out, though, just before they got the gag on him."

"Suppose someone moves to stand behind you, you're talking to someone else, and you suspect neither?"

"I see." Benno was silent a minute. "But what about the gold, then? You find out any more about that?"

"No one seems to know how it got there. Fairy gold, Benno."

"Turn to dead leaves in the morning then. I reckon it's witchcraft." A thought struck Benno. "The witch at you know where—you don't think—they . . . none of them was fond of the Cardinal."

Sigismondo hummed. "That coffer would have broken a broomstick, Benno. And would they have been let in? We'll see if the Marshal's find has horns, then we'll know."

They were crossing the Cathedral square, their footsteps loud on the pavement; to this sound, the splutter of the torches, and the creak of the scaffolding was added a gentle splashing from the fountain whose water sparkled fierily in the torchlight. Sigismondo paused to wet the bandages round his hand and wrist again. "They feel bad?" Benno asked sympathetically.

"I was quick enough. They've almost stopped smarting."

There was disturbance on the Cathedral steps. Gowned figures argued in low urgent voices, one of the great doors of the Cathedral stood ajar behind them, and there was an echoing indeterminate sound within. Across the sloping expanse of shining stone, the door of the Marshal's offices stood wide open. Torches were stuck in the iron holders in the embrasure of the door, guards stood sleepily surveying the small party that approached, and, as they reached the door through which Benno had last come with a halter round his neck, a long, agonised cry from inside made even the guards start and look round and for a moment silenced the priests across the square. Sigismondo handed Benno's torch to one of the guards, to his annoyance.

"Come, Benno. The Marshal's got his man. Now he's getting his confession."

The big room with the Bishop's arms on the chimney held guards who stood round the walls, some with pikes in hand; they were watching three people in the centre: the Marshal himself, a clerk in black standing at a desk ready to write, and the back of a man with his arms tied behind him. His shoulders were hunched, partly in pain, partly because they were cramped up by a rope, which led high over the beam that traversed the room, tied to his upper arms. The Marshal was trying the strappado.

As Sigismondo strode forward, Benno stayed by the door from an inner conviction that the Marshal's temper would not be improved by the sight of him unchanged. He was made uneasy, as he stared at the scene, that there was something odd about the back of the man being tortured, and, as Sigismondo reached him, the man turned a face of knotted obduracy, streaked with blood from a cut over one eye.

It was Massimo.

22

Ready
for
Mischief

⊠

BENNO'S IMMEDIATE THOUGHT WAS: *He did it.* He recalled Massimo's distorted face after Petrucci had ridden from the villa, saying to Sigismondo, "*I would have killed him,*" Massimo and Gruchio digging the false grave for their master, having no doubt about whom they would prefer to put in it. Burning the Cardinal alive might not be a balanced return for the Lord Mirandola's gouged-out eyes, but Benno didn't feel Massimo would be niggardly where revenge was concerned; besides, it would remove a pressing danger from his master.

Of course, it didn't explain how the gold got there, but to Benno's mind, it explained why it stayed there. If Massimo had set the Cardinal on fire, he would have no thought for gold.

"I can vouch for this man." Sigismondo addressed the Marshal, who had risen from his chair and was fluttering his fingers on his chain of office, as if to reassure himself of authority. By his sour expression, he had been informed that the Bishop had permitted Sigismondo to take charge of an enquiry that should have been solely the Marshal's concern. "He lives at Fontecasta, some five miles from here, at the villa where I was major-domo to the late Lord Giraldi. He is no villain."

The Marshal's face was set in obstinacy as determined as Massimo's. He came forward, blinking. "He's your man. Look at his arm."

Sigismondo's knife parted the cords round Massimo's wrists. The Marshal's top lip drew down at this dramatic gesture that wasted good material. Sigismondo looked at the patch of skin between wrist and elbow, pink and raw with blisters. It accounted for the smell of goose fat.

"You see." The Marshal had come up. He prodded a blister with a triumphant finger; Massimo, wincing, directed a glare at him before turning his eyes back to Sigismondo like a trapped animal that cannot ask for help. The Marshal prodded again. "Burns. He pretends he got them on a *brazier!* He says he tripped over a pilgrim and fell on a brazier!" The Marshal snuffled with real enjoyment of the lie. "He was about to tell me how, in fact, he came by those burns when you arrived. *What are you about?*"

Sigismondo had undone the knot of the rope harnessing Massimo's shoulders, leaving him hunched with the pain in his joints and trying to rub or ease them without touching the blistered patch. "Mm-mm. I can't question a man who can't give me his full attention."

"But how can the truth be discovered without torture?" The Marshal was astonished at such unorthodox practices, but Sigismondo sat Massimo on a stool, to the resentment of the clerk who had been using it when he did not stand to his desk. Sigismondo, leaning back on the edge of the table, folded his arms and considered Massimo.

"Why were you in Colleverde tonight and not at Fontecasta?"

An impotent rage seemed to twist Massimo's features until he could not open his mouth against its tension. The Marshal, who had hurried to sit in his chair behind the table in evident fear that Sigismondo might usurp that place of authority, nodded and tutted at the silence that so clearly demonstrated the practical use of torture in interrogation. Finally Massimo got out: "I was looking for *you.*"

Sigismondo gravely nodded. "You were anxious to bring me the latest news about the sick girl."

Massimo looked apoplectic.

"Your late master's young mistress. You needn't have feared. The Princess Corio's physician reported to her that he had examined the girl—discovering, of course, that she was not a boy as your master had pretended. He found her fever to be slight. You were right to come and tell me. I think, as you do, that much of her illness is grief for the old man's death."

Benno could see that Massimo had been given a story, and he wondered if Massimo had taken it in. The Marshal had no time for any of this. He leant forward, his chain clacking against the table.

"Where did you spend last night?"

His tone accurately reflected his meaning, which was *Where are you going to tell me you spent last night, you liar?* Massimo glanced at Sigismondo, as though to check for permission to reply, and the Marshal slapped the table; but Sigismondo said, "Say."

"On the floor of a wineshop." The voice was grudging, hoarse.

"What wineshop?"

"I don't know. I'm a stranger here."

The Marshal flung back in his chair, with the thwarted frown of one whose next move would have been thumbscrews. Sigismondo, who had been gently massaging his chin with a forefinger, spoke. "Was the wineshop in the square? . . . Near the Cathedral?"

Massimo nodded to each question but winced as his shoulders hurt. "In the arcade."

"Would the man or woman who owns it know you again?"

The lines on Massimo's forehead pursued themselves into the fuzzy crown of hair. "He might. He got a girl to bring me something for the burns." He looked down at the glistening pir atch on his arm.

The burns from the brazier?"

"That's right. And I'd like to find that chestnut seller. Kicked me when I was down, he did. I'll get around to *him*, by all the saints." Massimo's ability for holding a grudge was one of the uninjured things about him. If the Marshal had the slightest inkling of the resentment cherished against Petrucci, Massimo would have finished the night partly dismembered and bloody and, such was the Marshal's zeal, minus the tongue that would not confess.

"Had the gates shut when you reached the wineshop?"

Massimo screwed up his already small eyes almost to the vanishing point. "Gates . . . they were saying about gates when I came round after this dint." He gestured with forced economy at the lump on his brow. "Saying they'd shut."

"You had the burns by then?"

Massimo visibly remembered not to shrug. He could see no importance in this crucial point of time.

"Lies!" The Marshal sprang up. "Now we have heard the story he means us to believe! Now it must be tested."

A disturbance at the door precluded Sigismondo's reply. Three guards, two pushing and one pulling, dragged a man through the door and hauled him round as he stumbled to face the Marshal.

"He was not in bed when we got there, Marshal! He was up and dressed and ready for mischief." The guard holding the man's arm gave him a delighted shake.

"You see, sir," the Marshal said to Sigismondo, pointing. "Where trouble is, a Jew's at the root of it."

The man looked back at them with eyes of melancholy dignity yet with humour in the curving mouth. His clothes were of rich cinnamon-coloured cloth edged with fur. The hands, which he now clasped before him as his arms were released, shone with heavy gold rings. He wore no star stitched to the cloth, no distinguishing hat: Duke Grifone was too much in debt to treat his Jews unkindly. There was, of course, always the risk that should his debts grow too heavy, it would be convenient to blame the Jews for some disastrous wrong—say, a missing child of respectable family or a visitation of plague—and then, by inciting a massacre, to clear all his debts at once.

The dark eyes understood such matters. He bent courteously towards the Marshal and included Sigismondo in his question by a glance.

"May I know why I have been disturbed on the Sabbath? How can anything for which I may be held responsible have happened in a city protected by holy relics?" His voice held no sarcasm, but a world of cynicism was in his glance.

The Marshal had bustled round the table to shake his fist up at the Jew's face. "It is your revenge, you accursed swine, on Saint Bernardina. I saw you writhing at the Mass you had to attend. The Bishop will have you hanged for this sacrilege! Hanged at the least!"

Irritatingly, the Jew did not withdraw from the Marshal's fist but looked beyond it at Sigismondo as if he sensed where the real power lay.

"Sacrilege? Good sir, what has happened?"

"Happened!" cried the Marshal, almost off his feet with indignation; but Sigismondo had straightened up from the table and inclined his head with the same courtesy he had been shown.

"A dreadful thing, sir. The Princess Corio, in whose house it happened, has asked me to enquire into the matter. Some hours ago, this very night, Cardinal Petrucci was murdered."

"Murdered?" The Jew raised his eyebrows and his voice.

"Murdered?" Massimo had uttered it in something reminiscent of a pig being slaughtered. Regardless of strained shoulder muscles, he clapped his hands together as if in gleeful applause, and Sigismondo, shaking his head, said: "Well may we pray, when such things happen. I must ask you, sir, how you spent this evening."

The Jew spread his hands. "As one spends the Sabbath. My family and I supped together, observing what it is the custom to observe—"

The Marshal uttered "Blasphemies!" under his breath.

"—we, none of us, left the house after dark."

"When did you last see Cardinal Petrucci?"

"At the Mass in celebration of the relics' arrival that our community was made to attend yesterday."

The Marshal cut in. "You spoke to him afterwards! I saw you speak to him!" He quivered like a terrier sighting a rat. "What did you say to him?"

"Sir, he spoke to me. He wished to see me on a question of money."

Sigismondo said, "He wished to borrow from you?" This would account for the gold on the Cardinal's desk, which the murderers had so inexplicably failed to steal.

"Not to borrow, sir. His Eminence wished, he said, shortly to lodge with me a large sum on which he could draw at need in the future."

Sigismondo silently shaped a whistle with his lips. The mysterious gold had been expected by the Cardinal. It was evidently a payment made to *him;* but for what?

"When was this to be, sir?"

"He spoke of today, but I told him I could do no business on the Sabbath. I would come to him before Prince Livio arrives on Sunday." He turned to the Marshal in polite interrogation. "He still comes, sir? They say the Prince's son is dead; perhaps mourning will put all these matters off."

The Marshal swelled with scorn and superior knowledge. "You know nothing, Jew. His Eminence himself told me, God rest his soul," he added with a faint look of surprise, as though he had only just realised that the Cardinal would have no more to say in this matter or any other, "when I waited on him by his command only a few hours ago, that nothing is changed. Duke Grifone and Lord Astorre arrive for the marriage this Saturday afternoon—today. And Prince Livio is coming at the same time, when I will have the streets to the East Gate cleared for the wedding party to proceed to the Cathedral." The Marshal became suddenly conscious that he was expatiating on his preparations to the silent attention of two suspicious characters— the Jew and Sigismondo—and concluded his speech by folding his arms and glaring at both of them.

"You must forgive me, Marshal, but there is little time before dawn and we have another suspect to question. I would suggest that you send Signor"—he questioned the Jew mutely, and was given the name—"Signor Ispano back to his house, where we know he may be found. The Duke may wish to question him himself when he comes."

The Marshal digested this. Duke Grifone's tender attitude towards his Jews was painfully known to him, and if there was anything the Marshal did not care to face, it was an angry Duke who would think no more of stringing up a marshal than the Marshal himself would of stringing up a thief. He reluctantly gestured at the guard holding the Jew's arm.

"Take him back." He turned on Massimo with venom. "Throw this one into the cells. We'll see what the Duke says to *you*."

Benno noticed that the guard who came forward actually forebore to take hold of Massimo's burnt arm, and he had the impression that Sigismondo's bearing had convinced more than the Marshal that it was wise to tread carefully in the matter. Duke Grifone was quite likely to leave the town with fresh heads nailed to its gates.

23

A Short Future

POLISSENA'S BLACK MAIDSERVANT, whom she naturally named Bianca, was not pleased to be woken from her catnap by a knocking at the door. She was certain her mistress expected no caller at this hour for the perfectly adequate reason that someone was with her already. Still, never offend customers: as she opened the judas window and peered out, she attempted to brisk her voice out of the grumpiness she felt.

"Who's there?"

The torch outside was held by a servant, who let its light illumine the face of the man who waited on the stairway. It was a strong, commanding face—someone to whom it might be sensible to be polite.

"By order of the Bishop's Marshal I am here to see your mistress Polissena."

The Bishop's Marshal was, by common consent, a fool, but he had the authority to be a dangerous fool. Bianca unbolted the door, wondering what absurdity of men was on foot, but confident that, whatever the Bishop might have in mind in the way of moral strictures, the Cardinal would cure him of it. Her mistress had the favour of the Cardinal and it followed that nothing in Colleverde could touch her. She opened the door.

"You'll have to wait. My mistress is engaged." The torch had been lodged in the iron bracket outside the door, and now the light of Bianca's lamp showed the stranger who, as he let his hood drop on his shoulders, was seen to have a shaven head. This did not surprise Bianca, who was accustomed to the clergy. She lit a candle that she left on the little table in the lobby and took herself away into the depth of the apartment to find out her mistress's pleasure.

Benno, left in the small lobby with Sigismondo, looked about him with intense interest. It was the first time he had been in the apartment of a courtesan, although back home in Rocca he'd had a famous one pointed out to him and rejoiced that you didn't pay to look. In a narrow niche to the left of the door stood a majolica vase with peacock feathers—purple, green, and gleaming in the flicker of the candle as if they'd been sprayed in gold. He wondered that she did not know peacocks were bad luck; except, he supposed, when you ate them.

The man who emerged into the lobby looked as if he had worse than indigestion. A pale young weed with a large nose and no chin, he was busy tying his points and continuing an argument under his breath. A furred cloak hung askew round his shoulders as if someone else had put it there. His complaining mutter was that he ought to have money back for this interruption. Failing this, he thought to vent his bad temper on the client for whom he was being turned out, but he noticed Sigismondo's face, and shoulders, and let himself out, still grumbling, but to himself softly.

Bianca's skirts brushed the doorway as she came back; she was annoyed to find that he had left no tip. She felt over the table's surface as if she could not believe it. "Some people have no manners. . . . You're to go in, sir, my lady says."

Benno, left alone with Bianca, smiled ingratiatingly and sank to his hunkers against the wall opposite the table. His imagination followed his master into the presence of the beautiful Polissena.

She was beautiful. Sigismondo had expected nothing else of the Cardinal's taste, and he stood for a moment after shutting the door, enjoying the picture she had carefully presented. The bed had a full tester fringed with scalloped silk and poised on delicate barley-sugar columns. On the bed, lounging on bolsters of ruby brocade and lit by several wax candles and the fire blazing on the wide hearth, was Polissena.

The curve of breast and of hip could be guessed but not clearly seen through the gauzy green silk robe she had put over her. Fair hair, which must have been damped in plaits to produce that crisp ripple, fell over white shoulders. The face was that of a wayward young cat, with slanting eyes and pointed chin. There were dimples in the cheeks, and the rouged mouth was pressed into a wicked smile. Herbs had just been thrown on the fire and filled the room with a dry sweetness, like lavender in the sun.

"Such haste, stranger! Are you commanded to bring me to the Bishop's Marshal just as I am? Or is he to follow you?"

"Very foolishly, he never thought to beg for such good fortune." He came forward, with the bow that had made Cardinal Petrucci look at him twice. "I am Sigismondo, at your service, lady. I have hopes that you may help me."

She pushed herself up on one straight arm and the green gauze, with discreet indiscretion, slid further from her left shoulder. The young cat was purring now. She put her head back a little.

"Help you, *Sigismondo?* Come and explain yourself more clearly." She patted the bed, and he stepped up on the bed platform and sank beside her with a smile that matched her own.

She put a hand out and rested it softly on his chest.

"What's this talk of the Bishop's Marshal? Nothing"—she prodded him with a yielding forefinger—"*nothing* will make me think you're employed by the Bishop's Marshal. That man could not employ a *flea* of his own power." Her finger on his chest felt the subterraneous, all-but-silent laugh.

She raised the finger to tap his mouth. "Truth, now. What has the Bishop's Marshal to do with your being here?"

"We are both under orders from the Princess Corio—"

Her eyes widened in mock awe. "*She* sent you here?"

"—to find the villains responsible for her brother's murder."

Her hand went back as if his lip had stung her. She sat bolt upright, losing her gauze robe without caring. "Her brother . . . ? The Cardinal? The *Cardinal . . . murdered?* But when?"

"It is possible," Sigismondo needed his eyes for her face, but he had excellent peripheral vision, "that it was shortly after you left him this evening." As he watched her, his hand played with the gauze that had shimmered across his thigh.

She was silent, watching him in return, white against the ruby brocade.

"You left your chopines."

She shrugged, a disturbing displacement. "And I suppose Nardo said he'd let me in."

"Difficult to say anything when your throat's been cut."

She took a sharp breath, and her eyes widened again. She looked away, a cat that needed to step carefully on another's territory. She took the gauze from his hands as though suddenly she was cold and held it to her throat.

"Battista told me you were expected. When did you leave His Eminence?"

"Did they cut his throat too?"

Sigismondo gave a short, reflective hum. "They lashed him to his chair and burnt him alive."

The gauze jumped to her mouth and was held there. He repeated, without emphasis, "When did you leave His Eminence?"

Her voice was shaking. She spoke through the gauze. "We heard the Cathedral clock, I don't know what hour it sounded. He told me at once to take my cloak and go. He was in a hurry."

"He was expecting someone."

"He didn't say so." She lowered the gauze and a trace of remembered indignation crept into her voice. "He called down to Nardo to see me out quick. . . . I was *hustled* out! I was in the street with Bianca and Pietro before I could ask for my chopines. Bianca wanted to go back, the streets were still wet, but I knew it would make trouble so I came home."

"You knew there'd be trouble?"

"He likes people to do as he says. *Quick* means *quick* and not go-back-and-make-a-fuss. Bianca can make a great fuss."

"So you saw no one arrive after you left?"

She looked at the fire. "There was no one in the street. No one on the way back at all except a drunk spewing in the gutter. I could have saved myself Pietro's pay; it was Bianca kicked the drunk out of the way." She paused and shivered. "Who would do such a thing as that? Burn him alive? They must have hated him."

"And you? Did you hate him?" The question, negligently put, roused her.

"Hate . . . ? He was one of my best clients! I looked forward to his visits to the city. He paid well."

"This evening: how did he pay you?"

"He took money from a drawer in his desk—a little drawer he has money in—just as usual."

"Was there a coffer, *this* size, on the desk?"

She looked a little surprised. "If there was, I saw none. Why? Have they robbed him as well?"

"Quite the contrary. They left gold there."

Her eyebrows rose; she made a face of disbelief. "Left what they could have taken? They must really be mad. But this was in his sister's house. Didn't he call out? How did no one hear?"

Sigismondo smiled, his lips curving so that she half smiled too. He shook his head. "I came here to ask questions, not to answer them. You'll hear it all in the marketplace tomorrow, with pretty embroideries. Tell me, did you see anything else about the room? Anything strange?"

She seemed to picture it in her mind, then shook her head. A dimple made a fleeting return to her cheek. "His Eminence engaged my whole attention." Her hand dropped the gauze and came to touch his thigh. "I am sorry he's dead. A good client whenever he came to the city; and a very attractive man. There are great men whose charm stops short of the sheets, but not his."

If this surprised Sigismondo, he did not show it. Instead, he picked up the hand on his thigh and, turning it over, examined the palm, tracing the lines with his thumb. The dimple deepened. She leaned forward to see.

"What's in my palm, sir? I've been told my Mount of Venus is very well formed. Do you see my future?"

He turned the hand over again abruptly. "Hey, a *short* future. Unless you tell me everything."

"But I have told you everything. What more can I tell you?" She dropped back against the bolsters, and her hair rippled over the gauze, veiling her again. "I'm not lying."

Sigismondo hummed. "You may have chosen to forget something. Who was in the street when you came out, as well as the drunk man in the gutter?"

She was startled. "What makes you think I saw anyone?"

"You looked away before you told me. You weren't remembering. You were *forgetting*." The amusement vanished. *"Who was it?"*

She started; and she was still tense, but she watched his mouth as she answered. "What will you do, Sigismondo, if I don't tell you?

"Hey, it's not what I will do. I remind you that the Bishop's Marshal is a conscientious man." He took her hand again and shook his head at it regretfully. "He won't stop at thumbscrews. And Duke Grifone arrives in a few hours. I've heard he's not at all a patient man."

She took her hand away, put her hair back behind her shoulders, and sat up straight, as if she needed to get more air into her lungs.

"It's of no consequence. I didn't mention him, I suppose, because I'm so used, now, to his being there. Tomaso Delmonte. He's been following me for months."

"A client?"

"But an awkward one. He wants to marry me." She pulled an amused, rueful face. "The old story. Giovanezza, a friend, you might say a colleague, she says it happens every so often. It's absurd. I told him, no one marries a courtesan, his family would disown him. . . . I've done everything to discourage him. He's become obsessed. Writes poems to me. He can't see reason. He's poured money at my feet, begged me to go away with him, to Rome, to France, anywhere."

"He has money, then, to pour?"

"Oh, he's rich. The family's rich, and he's the apple of his father's eye. I told him his father'd find the worm in the apple right away if I turned up. Tomaso would get his allowance cut off, and then how would we live, in Rome or France? *On my earnings?*"

"Did he follow you home tonight or stay?"

"I told him I would not have him following me; he was to do it no longer. And he didn't, for a wonder. I waited until we were at the street corner, not to make any fuss outside the Cardinal's door; particularly if he was expecting company. I was furious to find he'd followed me to the Palazzo Corio. The Cardinal hates gossip. When we turned the next corner, he was still standing where we'd left him."

"Not far from the Cardinal's private door."

"You can't think he—Tomaso wouldn't; he couldn't hurt a fly."

"I've known those who'd spare a fly and kill a man. Obsession makes monsters. Did His Eminence know Tomaso?"

"I doubt it. The Delmonte are rich merchants; he might

know Tomaso's father, but I don't see the Princess Corio inviting the family to meet her valuable brother. Why?"

Sigismondo laughed. "Another question? Because those who murdered the Cardinal were expected. Nardo already knew he was to let them in."

She smiled suddenly and brilliantly and lay back on the bolsters. "Not Tomaso then. I can't see Nardo letting him in after me." She giggled. "His Eminence was in a hurry too. No one's ever going to be in a hurry to meet Tomaso."

"That might not be true now."

A line appeared between the perfectly plucked brows. "You mean?"

"I mean that if Tomaso saw the person who was expected, he may look to join Nardo."

She sat up, concerned. "Oh! Can't you save him? Poor Tomaso." It might be his epitaph, kindly spoken, as for a pet dog.

"If the murderers thought he'd seen them, he's dead by now, and the Marshal's men combed all the streets round the Palazzo Corio. No dead bodies brought in. We can hope that Tomaso, deprived of sight of you and under your displeasure, went home at once. He may have had a poem in his head that he couldn't wait to write down."

She lay back again, laughing heartily, showing small, good teeth. "Those poems! I won't tell you what Bianca uses them for. I say to him it's a waste of expensive paper, but there's none so deaf as those that won't hear. But what are you going to do? Can I help you anymore?" She slid down on the bolsters and the green gauze slid further than she did. She extended her arms before her with a quiver like a cat stretching.

Sigismondo got up, put another branch on the dying fire, and, returning to the bed, poured a cup of wine from the ornate silver pitcher on the chest by the bed and offered it to her. She waved it back at him with a graceful gesture, and he drank, looking at her while the fire eagerly embraced the wood.

Since he had saved the Lady Minerva from leaving her head on the floor at Montenero, things had moved fast and the dangers had increased: he was responsible for the lives of several people, and these lives were to be under severe threat with the Duke's arrival this coming afternoon. However, all

that could be done had been done, and Sigismondo was not a
man to waste energy in anticipating trouble that, experience
had taught him, he could deal with when it turned up. The last
time he had slept had been at Fontecasta on Thursday night,
and he hoped to sleep again for a few hours before Saturday's
dawn. Meanwhile, there was Polissena.

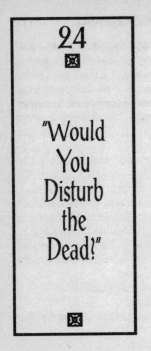

24

"Would You Disturb the Dead!"

BIANCA HAD APPROACHED BENNO cheerfully. She liked his air of being at ease and asking nothing, and he gave her a cordial grin. She was ready to spend time to her advantage.

When she came nearer, she halted. She looked him over, and a bubble of amusement broke irresistibly within her. She put her knuckles on her hips and leaned over, cramping her shoulders forward so that her dress fell away from her bosom. She said, "Would you like me?"

Benno took breath. No offer like this had ever come his way before, but he would take what luck sent him. Oddly enough, the thought of money did not cross his mind, perhaps because he was used to his lack of it being obvious to all the world. He said, "*Would* I!"

"Then you must do as I say. Absolutely. Understood?"

"I've to be here when my master comes out."

"I know my mistress, and I took a good eyeful of your master. She'll not let him go in a hurry, and a man with that mouth on him isn't going to say no to her either. He's got plenty of time for women, am I right?"

She shimmied a little. Benno's eyes missed nothing. He said, "What've I got to do?"

Straightening up, she whisked round, opened a door, and said, "In here."

Benno followed her. The small room was lit by a low fire and held a large tub and a pallet and a screen with a sheet draped over it. Bianca turned and with careful fingers undid his jerkin. He said, "Watch out," and she froze as Biondello's head erupted, nostrils working at the new smells of herbs and scent in the room.

"Dear God! I just thought you had a spare shirt in there or . . . He'll have fleas too, I dare say."

"Oh yes," Benno agreed, "he has."

"Take your clothes off."

Benno shed his jerkin, putting Biondello on the floor. After a brisk smell round, the dog sat by the fire and set to work biting at his flank.

"Come on. All of it."

"All of it?" Benno pulled his boots off, and Bianca set to work on his points. "Why all of it?"

"Because I say." She tweaked his shirt up over his head.

With his shirt came a shower of crusts, a greasy cloth bundle, a mouldy dried plum, half a dozen hazelnuts, a squashed dried fig, a lump of cheese, an onion and an apple. Galvanised, Biondello advanced, foraging. The nearest he had been able to get to these treasures so far had been by devotedly licking the shirt inside which they reposed.

"Hey—" As a crust disappeared, Benno reached for it.

"Hey," said Bianca and shed her dress.

Benno went towards her. She sidestepped and pointed to the tub.

"In there."

He looked. "It's got water in."

Still she pointed. Benno, puzzled but willing, stepped into the fragrant water up to his shins. It was tepid on the surface, warm below.

He had never seen a naked woman before in his life. At her command he sat down; she stepped into the tub opposite him and began to wash him.

He had often wondered why the gentry had baths from time to time, and now a seraphic smile spread in the midst of his beard.

In the next hour, with interruptions both practical—as when she leaned perilously out to reach wood to throw on the fire and when he prevented Biondello from joining their investigations—and erotic, Bianca washed him from head to foot. Benno's experience of girls had been against a wall or in stable straw. This leisurely business was as new to him as was the bath. He was entranced.

† † †

At Fontecasta it could almost have been a family party in the great kitchen. The fire blazed; the old woman crouched, picking over herbs by its light; the blind man sat on the high-backed settle listening to the girl read; the older man hunched on a bench in the shadows, dozing.

The Lord Mirandola was grateful for the Lady Minerva's reading. He was grateful because her flexible voice and her understanding of the Latin she read made an incalculable difference to his pleasure in listening. His former reader, dead these three years, had read in a measured chant, glad to get the words said without any trouble about their meaning.

He was grateful also because it distracted his mind. Massimo's absence meant that he had been shut in town for the night, and Mirandola feared that worse could have befallen him. The physician's discovery had appalled Mirandola. The girl had done her best to deceive. He had heard her speak exactly like an ailing and peevish boy, but by an unlucky stroke of Fortune, the physician's predilection was for beautiful young men, which had led him, not satisfied with the usual bloodletting and urine testing, to make an exploration fatal to both her modesty and her disguise. The wretched man would take word to Colleverde. To Mirandola, the presence of a girl here, with his own consciousness of his connection with the Princess, her mother, made it obvious who she was. He could not know that Sigismondo had denied to the Cardinal that he had been to Montenero so that there was no evident connection at all with the Princess Oralia. Now Sigismondo had not returned, had not responded to that urgent message. They must be in danger here at Fontecasta as soon as the town gates opened in the morning.

The girl paused. She said, "The dogs are barking a lot."

"They bark at the moon. They're not good watchdogs in that respect. They are always barking."

She was still dressed in her boy's gear, with the undoubted improvement that Sybilla had washed it all while she lay ill in bed. She was wrapped now in addition in a white filmy shawl her mother had sent Lord Mirandola, and her neck was swathed, at Sybilla's insistence, although her throat was no longer sore, in a scarlet kerchief against night air. Sybilla picked up an earthenware cup from the hearth and trundled over to present it to the girl, with a chiding grumble about "throat" and "voice."

"Drink it, my lady," Mirandola said, amused. She was drinking, and the old woman waiting for the cup, when Mirandola put out a warning hand. They looked at him, saw he was acutely listening, and were still, frozen in movement.

"In the orchard?" The harsh tone was muted. "Out there . . . digging."

They had a flambeau and a lantern. Two men dug, their picks clawing the earth; another held the horses outside the broken gate in the wall; while the fourth, furled in a cloak, waited, his eyes glinting. They were not troubled at the noise they made; the house, perhaps a hundred yards away, showed no light nor did the dogs' monotonous barking arouse anyone. Their flambeau's shape was echoed by the huge dark cypress beyond. Gnarled orchard trees crouched in the dark almost unseen. The digging men, whose breath steamed as they worked, glanced up now and then at the silent house. They dug, took up the shovel, and came upon broken stones.

A vast bird swept suddenly low over their heads with a whoosh of wings, and they ducked and paused, one man's pulse visible for a second in his throat.

"Get on."

They dug and threw up broken stones onto their spoil heap and the grass, and searched among the remainder. They took the lantern to make sure. Then they stood and looked, without words, at the watcher. The torchlight showed him grasping the cloak at his throat, and a swimming glitter of his gloves' gold embroidery betrayed how hard he breathed.

"No corpse?"

"Nothing, m' Lord. Just stones. We've reached the bottom."

They heard the ringing hiss as he drew his sword.

"Then he lives. Bring your picks. Give me that." Indeed, as the men scrambled from the grave, he seized the flambeau. "To the house!"

There had been the distant muffled barking all this time. Now suddenly it was nearer, and then in the open and approaching. There were two hounds, heavy and shaggy with eager jaws. A pick swung sideways caught one on the head, lifted him, and left him sprawled, twitching in the grass. The flambeau in the other's face sent him backward, yelping, as the torch's flare and the lantern's swinging light showed a man with a halberd, a stocky figure of challenge, who shouted: "What the devil are you about? Don't you know there are ghosts here? Would you disturb the dead?"

Gruchio, confident from successes in the past, had disregarded Sigismondo's emergency plan taught to the household; but he was not this time dealing with peasants already scared at the place's legend. Hardly could he realise this, and see what had become of the dogs, before his chest was pierced by a pickaxe.

The three waited a moment for a further attack; the burnt dog pawed at its muzzle and pushed it along the earth until the leader of the three flung the flambeau at it and sent it yelping into the distance. Then he pointed his sword towards the house.

Gruchio in his confidence had left the door open. The leader pushed it wide, and his henchmen held up the lantern swinging on its chain. They were looking along a short corridor. At the far end against a curtain stood a slender boy, motionless, a haze of fair curls round his head, his body half seen through a filmy shifting white substance, a scarlet gash separating his head from his body. The lantern swung, leaving dark; when it swung again, the passage stood empty.

With an animal howl, the leader of the three turned and staggered away. *"There are ghosts here!"* rang in his head. *"Would you disturb the dead?"*

The men behind him caught a glimpse of what he had seen—the filmy figure that vanished in the swing of the lantern—and, electrified by his howl, scattered in a rush for their horses. One man, running in the dark of a cloud over the moon, nearly fell into the empty grave; the other, failing to free his reins from the branch he had looped them on, carried the branch with him in his mad gallop from the scene. The man in charge of the horses, unnerved by the howl, had the start of them and led the rush into the dark.

The man with the sword staggered after them into the orchard and fell shuddering to the ground as they grappled with their horses. As the hoofbeats died on the wind he was left, thrashing in the grass like a landed fish, his fingers snatching at the clods of earth thrown up from the grave.

The moon came out from behind the cloud and shone down impartially on his struggles and on the other body, stretched not far from him, that would struggle no more.

25

⊠

The Devil in Colleverde

⊠

SATURDAY'S DAWN SAW ACTION, both at Fontecasta and at Colleverde.

Minerva, snatched away by Sybilla into the kitchen as she stood frozen in the light of the intruders' swinging lantern, had spent the night in the cellar, under a hidden and bolted trapdoor beneath the kitchen. She had slept very little. The face of Prince Livio, the man she had known as father for all her fourteen years, to whose caprices of affection and impatience, neglect and scorn and violence of temper she and everyone she knew had been subject all her life, the man she had last seen striking off her brother's head—this face was before her and would not let her rest. He had been staring at her. He had recognised her. He would come back. She could not imagine why he had not advanced with that sword and struck off her head then and there.

She fell into a doze before dawn, cold and cramped on the sacks of vegetables, and dreamt. She dreamt she stood there, hands to her neck, looking down at her own head on the floor. As she started awake her moan roused Sybilla, on a pile of sacks, nodding over a pitchfork clasped to her bosom with both arms. If anyone had succeeded in finding and opening the hidden trap, Sybilla, ready to sell dearly what was left of her life, would have given the first man down a chance to see his own liver.

In the gloom, Minerva could hardly see Mirandola, lying on an old trestle table, wrapped in a cloak, silent if not asleep. No stranger had entered the house, nor had Gruchio; they could only think him dead, and it would be foolish to venture out yet. No dogs had barked; Sigismondo and Massimo had not returned. They might both of them be dead in Colleverde.

Minerva knew what she must do. Her study of the classics had supplied many stories of great sacrifice, of men and women who risked their lives, and often lost them, for the sake of others. Here she was, named after the very Goddess of War, who wears a helmet and carries spear and shield. Wasn't the bravest title a woman could win from men that of Virago? She would be a Caterina Sforza. She would show the world that nothing could daunt her. She would ride into Colleverde herself and see if Sigismondo and Massimo were alive. If they were dead, she would ride to Rocca and ask her uncle Ludovico to rescue Mirandola.

She was the only one who could. *She* was the protector of an old woman and a blind man. Five days ago, in the vanished world at Montenero, when she had been the cherished only daughter of the Princess Oralia, an old woman and a blind man would have been of no more account to her than the blind beggars at the Palace gates. Now she was of their world. She had even grown fond of the old witch who had cured her fever; who pushed her about with streams of unintelligible scolding; who seemed like a figure out of the dim past, like some old nurse, chiding but comfortable; barely remembered.

As for Mirandola, touched as she was by his courtesy and his consideration, she suspected too that she owed him the filial duty she had paid to Prince Livio all these years. There was affection in his voice when he spoke to her; and why should her mother have gone to all that trouble to protect and care for a man whom she simply pitied? Minerva's first shock and disgust at her mother's confessed infidelity had changed. She felt herself to be the guardian of a romantic secret. At fourteen, it gave her the strength to go out and conquer dragons.

While Minerva was standing beside Sybilla in the dewy orchard looking down with horror at the body of Gruchio sprawled supine on the grass, Sigismondo was looking down at another supine body, that of Benno sprawled on Bianca's pallet.

When woken, he could have sworn he had been in Paradise. He lay, confusedly smiling up at his master, while Bianca dropped his clothes on his stomach and curtsied to Sigismondo. "Mm-mm. I see I owe you for the hospitality you extended to my man," he said and gave her twice what she had hoped for as a tip, as well. Some men are natural gentlemen and understand how to treat people without any hints.

The little one-eared dog crowded round the gentleman's ankles, wagging its tail in welcome. It was the richer, though she didn't know it yet, by a piece of fine cake bread she had put by for her mistress's breakfast.

"Be careful, sir," she warned Sigismondo, "how you go about in town. They're saying the Devil's come to Colleverde. You've heard the awful news about 's Eminence?"

"I came to bring it to your mistress. Benno has told you."

"What, did he know it? He never breathed word!"

"I imagine he had better things to occupy his mind. What is this about the Devil in Colleverde?"

Although Bianca was disappointed of the worst of her news, she luckily had more and, while Benno scrambled into his clothes, she stood with hands on hips and told.

"Pietro brought the news along with the water this morning. The town's full of it! It's all in revenge for the relics, you see: Satan against the Saint. As it's the Cardinal who brought the relics here, he was first to suffer. And how could he have gone up in flames like that right in the middle of his sister's house if it wasn't the Devil?"

"How is the Bishop's Marshal going to arrest the Devil?"

Bianca wagged her head vigorously. "Ah, that one will arrest anyone he can to look busy. And the Devil's not far to seek either." She leant forward, hands on thighs, and lowered her voice, glancing at Benno to ensure he too was listening to this particularly choice piece of news. "They say, they say that he comes from Fontecasta. In the guise of *a dead man.*"

She straightened and looked at them both while she rewound her coral silk turban, aware she had made an impression. Sigismondo was quite still, watching her, while Benno's face emerged from the shirt he was pulling over his head, with a look of horror.

"Oh yes indeed! A dead man! They're saying some people came in at the East Gate at dawn half demented and babbling on about an empty grave out at the villa there, where the ghosts are."

"Fontecasta." Sigismondo had folded his arms and was

stroking his lip with a forefinger. "How did they know there was an empty grave?"

Bianca shrugged. She was used to having men glance at her bosom when she did that, but these two still watched her face. "How do I know, sir? There are those who'll do forbidden things. They say dead bodies have great power. The Marshal has a guard on the gibbet at night or there'd be bits gone by morning. It stands to reason if relics of saints can do good, bits of them that weren't saints can do harm. Which is what some folks want to do. Burning His Eminence, now, that's a liberty only the Devil would dare to take."

She was unbolting the door and held it open. Up the stairwell came the cheerful noise of scavenging pigs in the courtyard.

"You tell the Bishop's Marshal, sir, he'd best take a look out there at Fontecasta."

When Benno reached the courtyard, Biondello cascading down the stairs at his heels, he burst out in a hot whisper: "What you going to do? Won't everyone know the blind lord's not dead? Will the Marshal go to Fontecasta then?"

He saw Sigismondo's face and stopped. At first being taken into Sigismondo's service he had been warned against questions. He was aware he had asked three in a row.

Sigismondo put a hand on his shoulder and looked into his eyes as if to gauge his steadiness.

"You must go to Fontecasta, Benno, before the Marshal can. Bring them all here to Colleverde." He frowned. "I was going to induce the Marshal to release Massimo so he could leave at dawn for Fontecasta—as soon as the gates open—but we've been forestalled. Let's hope Gruchio got them safe to the cellar in time."

"We'd have heard if they'd all had their throats cut though. Wouldn't we? Sounds like the witch frightened them again."

Sigismondo's face seemed to relax, and he cuffed Benno genially on the side of the head.

"Bianca's washed your wits as well. But things are moving faster than I thought. I woke with the Marshal's words in my head: *Prince Livio comes at the same time.* Why should the Cardinal send for the Marshal to the Palazzo to tell him nothing has changed? Suppose he meant that Duke Grifone and his son arrive today, as expected, and the Prince is coming *at the same time?*"

"Not on Sunday?"

"Not on Sunday. That means Prince Livio either expects to have the Lady Minerva in his hands by this afternoon, or he is bringing a substitute."

"If he's going to be in Colleverde any minute, isn't it dangerous for Lady Minerva and the others to come here? Duke Grifone would know the blind lord, wouldn't he? And if he meant him to be eaten by wolves, he's going to want to finish off the job, isn't he?"

"When you have two dangers, you juggle with them and see which is the lighter." Sigismondo's eyes had left Benno and seemed to be viewing something only he could see. "Hey, I must stay here, and you need help. Come."

Benno, baffled, trotted at Sigismondo's heels with the same faith that filled Biondello, trotting after them both. They reached the Cathedral square at once. Even though it was not yet full light, shopkeepers were calling across to one another, stalls were being set up, lamps burned here and there, a crowd with buckets surrounded the fountain, and a buzz of gossip clouded the air. Pilgrims were thronging into the Cathedral. On their platform, the dwarves rehearsed their new play, still being composed impromptu, of the Devil's visit to the Cardinal. They were arguing heatedly over the possible risks to the stage, and to the building behind it, of torches held below a gap in the planking to roast the Cardinal.

The dwarves were not the only entertainers practising. Not far from the despondently swinging bodies on the gibbet and their yawning guard, the rosy light of morning caught the flash of blades rising and falling in the air.

"Angelo," said Sigismondo, as the young man deftly caught the last knife and made it vanish after the others in some cache on his slender person, "we need you."

The clear grey eyes examined them. Benno looked no more and no less half-witted than usual; Sigismondo looked calm. Angelo had expected nothing else, but to ask for help at all indicated an emergency.

"It'll cost," Angelo said.

26

✠

Now
You
See
It,
Now
You
Don't

✠

ACTION AT FONTECASTA WAS ALSO in the nature of emergency. Minerva, brought up as a princess and accustomed to having her own way, inspired by the thought of heroism, prevailed over Mirandola's efforts to prevent her going. Sybilla, far from trying to prevent her, apparently thought of coming with her, and only the impossibility of taking Mirandola too or leaving him there alone made her stay.

Sybilla was very angry over the death of Gruchio, even though she had not seemed to like him much when he lived; perhaps her anger was directed at him for getting himself killed. It seemed to give her energy for burying him. She did not, very evidently, think it safe or prudent to leave him unburied. Her gestures, and her occasional clear word, explained that the terrible visitors might return, so Minerva helped to drag and maneuver the old man's body to the grave and, since they could not lower it, to roll it in. She had to turn her head aside as Sybilla vigorously tossed spadefuls of soil and stones onto the white hair and waxy bloodstained face below. Mirandola insisted on being taken out to the orchard graveyard to say a prayer, and Sybilla, when he had finished, crossed herself and swaying, launched into a loud nonsense singsong of her own before cleaning the spade. There were words Minerva thought she understood in the rubbish Sybilla uttered, but as it wasn't Latin or Italian and she knew only a little Greek, she supposed the old woman was making it up.

She was helped by Sybilla to saddle the better of the two nags in the stable, which was as well, for she stood looking at them with a sense that horses in general arrived better equipped for her use than with a halter, and that the harness that hung on the wall would not miraculously apply itself. Sybilla had tightened the girth by punching the horse in the belly and pulling the strap when it contracted in surprise. Minerva set off for Colleverde by the path the old woman pointed out, with chopping gestures with the edge of her hand forward and the actual word, "Direct."

At the same time, Angelo was hiring horses to take him to Fontecasta. Sigismondo had told him that there were enough horses at the villa to mount the blind man and Gruchio and that the girl could ride double behind one of them; the old woman, if she would not ride behind Gruchio, could use the donkey that was kept in the orchard. "You'll be dealing with some very obstinate characters," he warned. Angelo simply showed his teeth, as one might casually flash a knife. Benno, far from being offended that he wasn't trusted to go on his own to Fontecasta, was profoundly grateful for Angelo's company. If anyone besides his master could deal with a dead lord and a witch, Angelo could.

The path Minerva rode was narrow, stony, and winding among trees and huge rocks, more suitable for goats than horses. Sybilla's fist had not hit hard enough; the saddle began to slip. Lacking the padding of skirts, Minerva's thighs began to feel sore.

Then the horse went lame.

She dismounted, wishing she knew how far Colleverde actually was, and led the horse doggedly on. Now the next problem arose. She was wearing Gruchio's boots. The little slippers she'd had on when Sigismondo carried her off were useless for more than marble or polished wood floors. Sybilla had seen her need instantly when she first picked her way through the orchard and had dragged off Gruchio's boots to offer them. Minerva balked. Never, ever, could she put them on. Then she remembered that she was a heroine and got into them. Now, limping along as uncomfortably as the horse, she reflected that it was perhaps not a lucky thing to step into dead men's boots. The wool Sybilla had stuffed into them to help their fitting had bunched up painfully. She was beginning to feel light-headed after an almost sleepless night, and her urge towards heroism was at a low ebb. At the back of her mind, however, was the nightmare that her father—that Prince Livio would be bound to come back to the villa to look for her; and when he did, it would be far better to be at Colleverde.

At Colleverde the Bishop's Marshal, walking to and fro and twittering his fingers, was undecided what course to take over the rumours that now filled the town and were swelling the horrified gossip about the Cardinal's death. He lacked the imagination to be superstitious himself, but if no supernatural act had taken place at this villa out at Fontecasta, then someone had gone to some lengths to pretend that it had. They ought certainly to be punished for that. He could not investigate for himself, with his hands full here, primarily, of course, making sure that the preparations for the arrival of Duke Grifone were completed and trying to keep an eye on that extraordinary man of the Princess Corio's. He must try to trace the men who had originally spread the rumour about Fontecasta; he would certainly question them very closely if they could be found, but there was not even a decent description of them from the gatekeepers, rascals who had certainly been instrumental in spreading the rumours, as he had told them, and very likely, in spite of specious stories, they had let these men in before dawn as well, since they gave away that it was "too dark" to see them. The only thing to do was to send some of his own men, whom the saints knew he could definitely not spare, to Fontecasta to see if there really was an empty grave—for ghosts were not likely to show themselves by daylight—and to bring in anyone found at the villa for interrogation.

So it happened that the Marshal's men, not as free of superstition as he was and proportionately reluctant over their errand, took the main road out of Colleverde by the North Gate, the Nemora road by which Duke Grifone and his son were expected later in the day. They were not in any hurry, so, although they did not know it, there was no danger of their overtaking Angelo and Benno, who had set off by the same route half an hour at least before and who themselves also had no chance of meeting Minerva.

However, she might have been overtaken by them on their

return to Colleverde by her own route if she had not heard them coming. The short cut from the villa to the East Gate was a lonely path, and she had seen no one, so the sound of hooves alarmed her, presenting her at once with the face of Prince Livio. Perhaps he had returned to the villa, tortured Lord Mirandola and Sybilla until he found out where she had gone, and was pursuing her with drawn sword.

Luckily when she heard the hooves, she was not on the path but had descended the stony bank to a stream that ran under an uncertain-looking humpback bridge. Her aim had been two-fold: to water the horse and to bathe her blistered feet. She had got Gruchio's horrible boots off and had both feet blissfully in the water when she had to jump up and lead the horse further under the bridge where she crouched, holding its muzzle and hoping it would not whinny. It seemed too discouraged to try, but when she heard the hooves drum overhead and a voice speak in a flat foreign accent, she prayed, and it was some time before she dared come out from her shelter.

Angelo had had a little trouble with Sybilla but none at all from the blind lord who, when once he heard Benno's voice and understood Sigismondo had sent Angelo as escort, entrusted himself to them without a protest. He warned them he had not ridden for a long time; but without fear for his own safety, and deeply concerned for Minerva's, he was glad of the opportunity to follow her.

Sybilla, after glaring at Angelo as if she could sense every one of the knives he had concealed about his person, had agreed—as far as they could tell by the nods accompanying the gibberish—to come too. When, however, Lord Mirandola had explained Gruchio's inability to form one of the party and had been helped to the saddle, the old woman was missing. The blind lord was distressed when Angelo declared that she would have to fend for herself, that he had his instructions, and it was imperative for the blind lord to be moved to Colleverde as fast as possible. The old woman could take the donkey and follow them. Angelo was leaving and leaving now.

Benno mentioned that Lady Minerva was more at risk than the old woman, whom he reckoned well able to look after herself, and he volunteered that the path that he and Sigismondo had taken to town previously was probably quicker than the way they had come. Angelo, without a word, took Lord Mirandola's rein, kicked his own horse to a brisk walk, and started in the direction Benno pointed out.

Sybilla was engaged in fetching the goats picketed down the hillside. She intended to shut them up before she started, for goats were far too valuable to be left to wild beasts. One goat had dragged its picket, and she was going after it when the Marshal's men reached the villa. Rumour had obligingly provided the detail that the empty grave was outside the little chapel in the orchard at the back of the villa, and as all the gates and doors were open, they went through the house and found the new grave without any trouble at all.

Only it was not an empty grave. It was a full one.

Everyone's first feeling on discovering a freshly dug grave with a mound of earth over it was one of relief—the man who started the rumour of an empty one had started it out of an empty head, out of malice, had imagined the whole thing. They stood round it on the earth-strewn grass, silent.

"That's all right then."

There was another silence into which someone said: "The Marshal will want a full report. I mean, he won't be satisfied if we haven't looked. I don't want to traipse out here again."

Feeling reasonably cheerful, though not without a glance or two round at the villa and the chapel to check that no ghost actually encumbered the landscape, they took up the spade and picks leaning neatly against a nearby tree and, watched by an interested donkey tethered near the wall, began to clear the earth. The Marshal's enquiries in town had established that the Lord Giraldi had been buried here with proper rites some days ago, so they were not expecting anything daisy fresh. When they had dug down to cloth, and brushed away the rest, they had an unpleasant shock that sent them scrambling out of the pit.

There was no coffin, no shroud. The wax-pale face they stared at was not several days old. It looked, under the scattering of earth, to have been alive only a few hours ago. Someone pointed with trembling finger at the mouth of the corpse. Blood had oozed from the corners (as they might have expected if they had known that the man had taken the point of a pickaxe in his lung) as if he were one of the living dead.

Without stopping for consultation they flung aside the tools, ran for their horses, and flogged them all the way to Colleverde.

Sybilla heard them go as she emerged from the barn, where she had been shutting up the goats with food and water, and she came out into the orchard with her pitchfork to deal with any intruder she might find. It seriously annoyed her to see the open grave and all her good work in burying Gruchio undone. She propped the pitchfork near to hand against a tree, took up the spade, and, grunting curses at every shovelful, began all over again. Her imprecations, an undercurrent to the birdsong in the orchard, and an occasional comment from the donkey, were divided evenly between the intruders—idiots from the village, she supposed—and Gruchio, who was being as much of a burden to her in death as he had been in life. All the same, when she had finished and he was once more decently covered up, she gave him a burst of prayer before she carted pitchfork, spade, and the picks acquired overnight, to lock them up in the outbuilding.

After that, she went through the villa, locking or bolting every door and shutter fast. She collected a bag of food, put out the kitchen fire, locked the house door, and, hoisting her skirts, put the keys in her pocket. From the yard she picked up a good thick billet of wood and a rusty nail, which she took into the orchard where, watched apprehensively by the donkey, she used a stone to hammer the nail into one end of the wood.

She was ready for Colleverde.

An hour later the Bishop, after an argument with the Princess Corio, which he naturally failed to win, was himself on the road to Fontecasta with holy water and the Host. He was supposed, as he had pointed out, to be at the North Gate later to receive the Duke Grifone with all the honours of the city, but the Princess had insisted that feeling in Colleverde demanded that measures should be taken by the highest ecclesiastic there; and now that her brother had been murdered, this was unfortunately the Bishop. He must go out to this villa and exorcise whatever was there. Duke Grifone would be very angry if he heard that the Bishop had neglected his duty.

So the Bishop on his mule, with the Sacrament borne before him and, in the rear, servants prudently provided with a stake for the undead, set out at a trot, praying he would be back in time to greet the Duke.

At least he knew what to expect: an open house and an open grave.

27

Out
in
the
Open

THE NEWS OF THE CARDINAL'S death, as Sigismondo and Benno had already discovered, had spread round the city shortly after dawn. As with all bad news that does not directly involve oneself, it was received with relish and passed from doorstep to upper window, from shop to shop, and all round the fountain; by the time the rumour about the Devil coming from Fontecasta in person to barbecue the Cardinal was in circulation, various artists in gossip had had the chance to add details that would have surprised any actual eyewitness.

Those who had not been fond of Cardinal Petrucci, or were also of the anticlerical party, whispered that he had burst spontaneously into flames while engaged in sin, such as gambling or whoring or both. This was the earlier version, later to be superseded by the one featuring Satan cleaving the roof of the palace with a thunderbolt that scored a direct hit on a copulating Cardinal. The earlier version was the one heard by Iacomo Bardelli when he went to buy bread for his party at dawn.

Erupting into their lodgings with the news and the bread, he dashed his doublet to the floor with force and then jumped on it.

"He's dead! Petrucci's dead! *Burnt alive* last night in the Palazzo Corio." His vehemence set him off coughing.

His three friends—one at the table cutting a lump of cheese to go with the anticipated bread, the other two still struggling up from the straw on the floor—stared in horror. To judge by their faces, it was the worst news they had ever heard. It did not improve their mood at all when Iacomo went on to say that the Marshal's men were going through the town, questioning every single stranger, and taking up anyone who couldn't fully explain his presence. With the Duke expected in a few hours, there was a certain urgency in this roundup; after all, those who had burnt a Cardinal would not balk at a Duke.

They were galvanised into quitting the lodgings, without benefit of breakfast, in a bid for anonymity among the crowds on the streets. Iacomo could not bear to leave the tools of his trade, and while collecting them was himself collected—and carted off without them—by the Marshal's men. He found himself facing not only the Marshal, whom he disliked on sight, but also a tall shaven-headed man in fine black leather. He did not hector Iacomo as the Marshal did nor had he an unfriendly expression, yet he made Iacomo sure it would be in his interest not only to avoid delay in his answers but also to make them polite.

"Why are you in Colleverde?" After the acid carping voice of the Marshal, the stranger's voice was deep and impersonal.

"Why, to see the relics, like everyone else, sir. And the wedding, too, of course."

"You are a pilgrim? You have a letter from your Bishop?"

Iacomo hesitated. "Why, no. Me and my friends were just, as you might say, passing. On our way home," he added helpfully.

"Which is?"

"San Sevino."

The man in black had his arms folded. He now caressed his lips with a forefinger. "On your way home?" There was amusement in the voice, though not in the face.

"We were making a detour, naturally."

"Where had you been and why?" The Marshal was not to be left out of this interrogation, and his tone assumed that Iacomo would be unable to account for himself. Iacomo's answer, however, had been well rehearsed and came out very smoothly.

"We're two stone carvers, and two assistants, you see, and we've been working on the new transept of Berano Cathedral."

"You were turned away?" *For malpractices*, the Marshal's voice implied.

"Well, they laid us off, really—"

"Ha!"

"Someone came who'd been working at Nemora, for Duke

Grifone, and they wanted him and not us. I think he was cousin of someone; you know how these things are."

Sigismondo had stepped forward and taken Iacomo's hands, studying the broken knuckles and nails and, turning them over, the callused palms. Iacomo coughed nervously.

"Has Cardinal Petrucci ever employed you on work for him?"

"No such luck. We heard he paid well for his coat of arms at Nemora over the gateway of his palace there. Nice work, that."

Sigismondo nodded and stepped back to lean again on the Marshal's table.

"Were you born in San Sevino?"

"Born in—? Oh no, not in San Sevino."

Sigismondo studied the face before him as he had previously studied the hands. It was an open, frank face, weathered brown as one might expect, with lively dark eyes and a mouth that only just closed on more teeth than it seemed able to manage. Iacomo was evidently anxious to set the matter of his birthplace straight. "I was *born* in Bibbiena. Lovely city." He coughed vigorously, bringing a hand up to cover his mouth.

"Were you there recently?"

Iacomo, with lips parted, considered the advisability of being in Bibbiena recently, then Sigismondo added something that decided it.

"Were you there when they pinned the threat to the Cardinal's life on the Cathedral door?"

"Couldn't have been, sir. Haven't been in Bibbiena for ages." He looked at Sigismondo with a bright glance, like an eager dog wishing to anticipate and please. Sigismondo hummed, a sound that Iacomo could not interpret but that made the Marshal stir and restlessly kick his booted foot against the table stretcher. Thumbscrews would settle all this and obviate pointless conversation. There was so little time before Duke Grifone would be here demanding to know who had burnt his Cardinal. Also the Marshal wanted to be out on the streets inspecting the arrangements of the guard along the route; you could never trust deputies.

"Bring in Tomaso Delmonte."

The guard glanced at the Marshal before he obeyed, which greatly improved the Marshal's humour. Perhaps, too, they were about to see some action. Though it was still annoyingly mysterious to him why the man Sigismondo had used his men to arrest Delmonte, he had at least asked his permission to do so, and the Marshal was never averse to having his authority respected.

Tomaso Delmonte looked very young, more of a grown-up child than a man who wanted to marry a courtesan. He had a puppy's face, large eyed and plump cheeked, with a willfulness about frowning brows and mouth that argued it would be very hard for Polissena or anyone else to get him to give up his fantasy.

He was at the moment angry with the anger of a young man of good family and a rich father.

"What does this mean? Do you know who I am? You can't treat me like this! I'll have the law on you!"

"We *are* the law." The Marshal, delighted at the challenge, skipped from his chair to range himself alongside Sigismondo and folded his arms in unconscious imitation. He knew the Delmontes were rich, and he rejoiced in his own reputation as incorruptible. His predecessor had been famous for the inventiveness with which he accumulated bribes. This lad was in for a sad shock if he looked to buy special treatment.

Sigismondo indicated Iacomo. "Have you seen this man before?"

Tomaso, thrown by having his complaint ignored and being asked a simple question in a quiet voice, turned his attention to the working man who stared awkwardly back.

"How can I tell? Why?" It was the puppy's effort to assert itself. "Why d' you want to know?" He frowned at Iacomo as if he'd been asked to identify a turd. "Where would I have seen him anyway?"

Sigismondo helped him. "In the street at the back of the Palazzo Corio? Last night just after the Cathedral clock sounded the hour of ten?"

Tomaso looked, if anything, the more taken aback of the two. This priest-assassin had supernatural powers. God knew there was enough talk already of the Devil in Colleverde.

The Marshal rubbed his hands; one thing he recognised and really approved of was people at a loss.

"Who told you I was there? Was he spying on me?" Anger

came to Tomaso's rescue with the suspicion that his move-ments were being reported upon. No lovelorn young man who is not being successful cares to be observed dogging the steps of his loved one. He glanced at Iacomo, who was guiltily staring at his feet as if wishing they could carry him away. "I wouldn't notice *him* anywhere—unless I *stepped* in him."

Iacomo responded with an unexpected flare of anger. "You wouldn't notice *me*, would you?" He jettisoned natural caution in being rude to someone who could get him punished. Thumbs in belt and generous allowance of teeth bared, he leant from the hips to taunt: "All the world's supposed to notice *you*, poncing about the streets in your sable cloak—"

The deep voice attacked, making even the Marshal jump.

"And you were wearing your sable cloak last night?"

Tomaso actually stammered. "I . . . I might have been." He recovered. "And why not? It's not a crime to wear a sable cloak if one's out at night, is it? If it's a case of a fine for breaking a sumptuary law or something, my father will see to that. It's a fuss about nothing."

He tailed off into silence, because both Sigismondo and the Marshal were smiling.

"Got 'em! We've got the pair of them!" The Marshal turned his glee on Sigismondo. "They were both there, the two of them! They're in it together!" This new insight of his quite thrilled him. He gripped Sigismondo's arm. "I see it! They arrange to meet outside the back stair, the Delmonte boy knocks with some excuse or other—he'd expect his name will get him straight to His Eminence—gets this lout in to slit the porter's throat—you said there'd be an accomplice and here he is—and it's up the stair to burn the Cardinal."

Tomaso's face of horror was noticeably not matched by Iacomo. He had clapped a callused palm across his mouth as if afraid of what might get out to incriminate him further. The Marshal strutted across to the array of instruments hanging on the brick wall: huge iron pincers, an iron boot open to reveal its tempting spikes, another showing only the compressing screws, smaller pincers for teeth or nails, hammers imperfectly cleaned of blood, ropes and knotted cords neatly coiled on hooks, hooks by themselves of baffling potential. All these were presided over by a bull-necked shaven-headed man in

sweat-stained leather, like a gross parody of Sigismondo. This
man now stood up in jovial anticipation as the Marshal
approached.

The babble of protest from both Tomas and Iacomo was
interrupted by the entrance of two more guards escorting an
excited little man with a red beard. Behind them Benno slid
into the room and effaced himself by the wall. Red Beard
didn't wait for an explanation of his presence but pointed a
blunt forefinger at Iacomo, shouting: "That's him! Said he'd be
back this morning to clear the cellar, but oh no! And I'd
explained I needed it for the wine I was getting in from the
country first thing—with the city full and the wedding and all,
did he think I could go on storing his miserable bundles of
firewood?"

"Firewood?"

"A fire hazard, as I told him, with those barrels of oil he'd
crammed in as well. If you're going to fine anyone for
dumping them on the street, fine him! First thing in the
morning, I told him, they've got to be out, and I put them out."

He stopped, panting.

"Oil? Wood?" The Marshal was ready to embrace the little
man. "You see? " He turned to Sigismondo radiantly. "There
we have the evidence!"

Sigismondo, still lounging against the table, nodded.

"Evidence indeed, Marshal; but evidence that he may have
been *intending* to burn someone or something, not that he did."
He glanced at Iacomo, who had retreated from the accusation,
shaking his head, until he bumped into the guard standing
against the wall behind him. The torturer, confident that his
services were at last to be called upon, was busy opening up the
pair of thumbscrews the Marshal had indicated, with a low
grating sound as if the metal itself protested against what it was
called upon to do.

"I didn't do it. I didn't . . . That wood was for sale. I was
going to sell it and the oil, there's nothing against selling wood
and oil, is there?" Iacomo appealed frantically to the nearest
person, who happened to be Tomaso and who contrived to look
more antipathetic to the idea of selling anything than the son of
a merchant had any right to. "It's not my fault I didn't go back

there to collect the stuff, I was *arrested*. You have to believe me!"

"I don't see that we're under any obligation." Sigismondo had straightened up and unfolded his arms; his voice made no threat, but Iacomo, to the grate and jingle of the thumbscrews, was pitiably anxious to convince him.

"Why would I want to burn His Eminence? Why would I?"

"Because he burnt your family at San Sevino."

Benno, watching Iacomo's horror-struck face, could believe this was true and wondered how his master had known. The deep voice went on: "This very day, a year ago, His Eminence burnt the rebels at San Sevino, in the tower where they had taken refuge. Your fondness for anniversaries, Iacomo, made you miss the chance. That wood and oil was meant for tonight, for the Palazzo Corio. You meant to burn the whole place down."

The Marshal was listening with open mouth. Tomaso recoiled as if Iacomo carried the plague. The torturer grinned in happy anticipation and bounced the thumbscrews on his thigh, and Iacomo began to weep, putting up his calloused hands to cover his eyes.

"My wife and baby! He had no mercy . . ."

"Villain!" The Marshal was rising on the balls of his feet, like a man limbering up for a fight. "They deserved to die! Rebels deserve to burn! And you too shall die, the Duke will—"

"By your leave, Marshal." Sigismondo had all eyes turned to him as to the centre of authority. "I am responsible to the Duke for this man. He must be put in the cells to await his coming, nor must he be put to the question until the Duke has seen him."

The Marshal considered this. The Duke had a well-deserved reputation for inventing his own tortures, and it was possible that he would be annoyed to be deprived of a chance to exercise his ingenuity. Reluctantly, the Marshal gestured to the guards to lead away the blubbering Iacomo. Benno felt his own eyes prickle as he watched him go. You couldn't help admiring him; he'd meant to make a good job of it, burning down the whole Palace. Benno had just realised this would probably

have included himself and his master when there was another
interruption.

Outside the doorway the guards had raised crossed pikes
instantly out of the path of the man who entered, and the
Marshal, turning in frustration at being thwarted of thumbscrews, changed expression at the sight of the livery. It was
perfectly evident from whose patronage the Marshal had the
confidence to insult the sons of rich families.

"The Princess Corio sends for Signor Sigismondo. She
wishes to see him now." There was but the faintest emphasis on
now, but Sigismondo inclined his head in respect.

"Pray tell the Princess I am on my way. Marshal, a word."
He bent to speak in the Marshal's ear: "As for these men: fear
may achieve more than pain. They know they have *you* to deal
with. I shall tell the Princess of the skill with which you are
handling this matter." He went on aloud: "You are right. These
men should wait in your cells to think of their fate."

He left the beaming Marshal giving directions that Tomaso
and Iacomo were to be cast in irons into the deepest cells, a
concession for which they did not seem to be sufficiently
grateful.

Leaving the Marshal's headquarters, Benno hurried to keep
up with Sigismondo, who put a hand on his shoulder as they
walked along.

"Mm. What's gone wrong?"

Benno muttered the answer towards his master's bent head.
The blind lord had been brought to town according to orders;
the old woman was following; but Gruchio was dead—killed
by the people who came last night and dug up the grave; and
the Lady Minerva had already left for Colleverde, alone, before
he and Angelo reached Fontecasta.

"Which way did she take?"

"The shortest, the lord said; and we came back that way and
didn't see her. She must have made good time. She came to
find you or Massimo. I thought you might have found her
already."

Sigismondo made no comment on this faith in his powers
but walked on through the crowd in the great square. It was all
the more populous now, swollen by those who had come to see
the remains of the Cardinal—and found themselves cheated of

the sight because the Princess, disgusted by the gawping crowds first thing in the morning, had changed her mind and commanded that the catafalque be transferred to the Bishop's private chapel. There were also those who had not yet seen the relics or who wanted to see them again, and some who had gathered to watch the dwarves' enactment of last night's tragedy.

Some voiced indignation that the relics had not saved the Cardinal, others felt an obscure triumph that the Devil had taken the challenge so keenly as to come to Colleverde himself. All looked forward to watching the entrance of Duke Grifone from Nemora later in the day. There was certain ghoulish speculation, fended round with averting prayers, whether the Duke might not be the next victim of Satan's wrath. Great men must earn their keep.

As Sigismondo and Benno forged through towards the street honoured by the Palazzo Corio, they saw above the heads of the crowd the flash of circling knives. By the time they reached the spot, a ring of onlookers had formed round the young man with golden hair.

Benno stopped following to stare. Angelo's act had changed just a little: he was inviting bystanders to have their cards chosen by his assistant as Destiny decreed. The assistant had silvered, dusty black hair curling to his shoulders under the peasant's straw hat, a coarse tunic hanging to his knees, his legs and feet tied in rags. As he turned scarred sockets instead of eyes on the crowd, Benno's was the loudest gasp.

Preventing anything more, Sigismondo murmured: "Angelo's doing what I asked. When you want to hide something, put it out in the open, where no one expects to see it."

28

Fortune Smiles, Eventually

THE WEDDING PARTY THAT WOUND along the road from Nemora to Colleverde had one or two resemblances to the late Cardinal's procession from Rome escorting the relics. The amount of dust kicked up was almost equal, and there were plenty of people from the farms and villages to stare at the cavalcade. Caps were doffed, people knelt, children were held up for a better view. On the other hand, there was decidedly less enthusiasm.

Whatever you might hope for from a saint, relics were certain proof that they were dead; but Duke Grifone was alive, in spite of optimistic rumour, and live dukes introduce an element of unpredictability. They can be pleased, and you might get your tax remitted or a new church built at their expense; or they can be displeased, with spectacularly grim results as at San Sevino.

The recent news about the Prince of Montenero illustrated this; if rulers lost their tempers, others round them could lose their heads. The cheers for the Duke and his son that echoed along the route were all the heartier for the knowledge that he was only passing through. Opinion was divided as to his likely mood: would it be rage at having his chief counsellor burnt alive, or good humour because he was on his way to celebrate a wedding, the alliance between Nemora and Montenero? This also provided a bonus since the unfortunate event at Montenero so recently—the likelihood that the Lord Astorre would in the end gain the principality of Montenero. Might not a good mood be expected?

Even his son was not sure. Summoned to ride at his father's side, Lord Astorre was conscious as always of a nervousness in his presence. Under the black velvet hat, sewn with a balas ruby the size of a gull's egg, the Duke's profile was bleak. It was a neat, battered face that he turned to his son, the good features—short curved nose, thin mouth—hammered as though by a sculptor keen to personify Grifone's sign of the Ram, and not unlike the sign recently painted on the great ceiling of his audience hall at the Nemora Palace. Even the curls of hair escaping from under the hat had the artificial look of rings of silver beaten out at a jeweller's bench, while the eyes turned on Astorre might have been dark crystals for all the expression they held. Those who studied the Duke's face hoping for signs of terminal illness had to concede that, although his hair was early white for a man still in his forties, and the lines on his face could have been scored with a knife, the general impression was still one of contained energy.

How that energy might manifest kept most people about him constantly alert and now troubled his son: "What are you going to do about the matter of the Cardinal, sir?"

The dark crystals gleamed. "Bury him. What's left of him. Roast the villains who roasted him."

"Is it known who they are?"

"I'll know soon." The Duke's hands on the scarlet reins were confident. "No one defies me for long."

"Is it private revenge, do you suppose, or someone plotting against you, sir?"

"Who kills my counsellor aims at me. There are traitors without number, as you'll find out one day. Petrucci was useful to me, over and over, sniffing out traitors and dealing with them." He laughed suddenly. "Remember San Sevino last year? It's the very day, Saint Bernardina's Day, that Petrucci crammed that crowd of rebels into the tower there and cooked the lot." He laughed again as he thought of it, then his face altered in a flash, becoming fierce. "I'll miss that man. He watched my interests as no one else has done. But for him I'd still be the dupe of that hypocrite Mirandola—"

Astorre spoke up bravely. "He was a good governor to me—and kind." Had it not been forbidden to speak of Mirandola at court, Astorre would have taken every opportunity of defending the man he still remembered with affection. The Duke snorted.

"Kind? Of course he was kind. Don't expect traitors to wear

a placard proclaiming their treachery, to behave disagreeably so that you can guess they hate you. My father trusted that man: called him his eyes. The Duke's eyes! I shut them for him!" He screwed up his own eyes in pure pleasure. "It was a kindness too—saved him the sight of the wolves as they came to dine." He leaned to slap a hand on Astorre's thigh, making his horse start and sidle. "Never hesitate to get rid of your enemies, my son, for they won't wait for you."

Not for the first time Astorre wondered if he would ever acquire his father's taste for political manoeuvre. He could see that it made a life in power a perpetually interesting one, but the perpetuation rested, dismayingly, on the detection and destruction of those, often seemingly innocent and even delightful, who wanted to remove you. He did not think he would ever come to enjoy watching torture and executions. He would always, as he had to now and then, simply endure the necessary spectacle. However, it was as impossible to admit that as it would be to say he didn't enjoy the pleasures of the hunt, which he emphatically did. His father, now, would certainly watch the gralloching of a traitor with as much equanimity as that of a deer; and it had to be admitted, people were a lower security risk without their entrails.

This line of thought led him to his future father-in-law.

"Is it known, sir, if the Prince Livio suspected his son of conspiring against him?" Rebellion in the family bosom was no novelty whatever to a ruler, but Astorre, as he spoke, was happily conscious that his father trusted him—and with reason.

"His letter spoke only of his grief." The Duke snorted again. "To add grief for his son to grief for his wife is a fool's trick. Livio's no fool; he didn't kill the boy out of grief. No, they say he has the falling sickness, although the fits come only rarely. I've asked physicians. The opinion is that the girl will not inherit it. Nor will your children." He gave his son a grin as affectionate as it was wolfish. "Never fear you'll spend your wedding night on the floor with a bride that chews the rushes."

Astorre remembered Minerva as an extremely pretty little girl with a pointed face almost lost in clouds of silver-gilt hair, who had scarcely looked up once during the betrothal ceremony to his brother nearly eight years ago. When fever carried off Ercole, his father had mourned him with passion and then announced that the alliance with Montenero would survive at all costs; so it led to the road they were now taking. Prince Livio must feel the same, or the death of his son, for no matter what reason, must otherwise have postponed these ceremonies.

"Look." The Duke pointed to the view before them as they breasted the hill. Colleverde in its walls shone in the spring sun. "Not long now. Our people have got the pavilion up, I see."

They paused before entering Colleverde—to have the road's dust brushed from their clothes, to change to the staid processional horses, to relieve nature—with a dusty journey behind them and a slow procession through the city to come.

The last stage of the journey was completed almost in silence. Grifone was reflecting with satisfaction that now that Livio's son was dead, the girl was his heiress: if Livio did not contrive to marry and get another son before one of his fits or an unlucky encounter carried him off, Astorre would in the course of time add Montenero to Nemora. Grifone, who had a habit of falling ill with a rapidity and severity that terrified his doctors and excited his enemies, recovered from these illnesses with similar rapidity, but one could not count on this happening forever. He hoped that Astorre would have the strength to hold on to Nemora when he was gone, let alone acquire Montenero. The boy needed good counsellors—he could not afford the loss of Petrucci.

One thing was certain. He would not leave Colleverde until he had found and very thoroughly punished whoever was responsible for that loss. No use delegating such a thing to Bishop Taddeo. That man couldn't bring a boiled egg to justice.

Astorre was silent because he was thinking about Minerva. He hoped she had grown up just as pretty. He hoped she wouldn't be too distressed at marrying so soon after her mother's death and the extraordinary killing of her brother. How strange it must be to have a twin, to see someone so like you, not you, not even your own sex—and then to lose him so suddenly and at your own father's hand. Astorre imagined that Minerva might be quite glad to leave Prince Livio and, although he was aware that his own father frightened people, the Duke would never harm his family; and that was what she would be within only a few hours. Minerva would find consolation and support; he was determined on that.

Astorre's horse broke into a trot as he unconsciously urged it forward, and the Duke's stallion, not to be outdone, matched the pace.

If those outside the walls of Colleverde were preparing to be received, those inside the walls were in a frenzy of preparing to receive. The construction of the triumphal arch at the North Gate had actually been finished the night before, a week later than promised, allowing almost no time for the rehearsing of Fortune's descent from its top to offer the Duke a laurel wreath. Fortune, a girl of noble proportions, was raising objections on the grounds of vertigo and of the fragility of the arch, and a fear that the machinery that lowered her would stall in midair, as it had done at the first tryout.

Besides, she did not want to wear Fortune's wig, which by tradition had hair only in the front and was bald at the back. It was pointed out to her that she had known about the wig from the beginning, and in any case no one was going to look at the back of her head when they had a live Duke to stare at. That her behaviour demonstrated her aptness for the role of fickle Fortune did not appease the director of the pageantry, who was a Florentine and very expensive. The Merchants' Guild intended to impress the Duke with their loyalty—a precaution they felt well justified—and were paying for him. The girl playing Fortune happened to be the mistress of one of the richer merchants, so it was impolitic to suggest a substitute. The director was in despair.

His despair had not been alleviated by the information, delivered late yesterday, that Prince Livio, whose entry to the city had been planned for tomorrow, was now coming in by the East Gate *today*, and planned to arrive either just after, or simultaneously with, Duke Grifone. The Florentine had dispatched his assistant to meet the cavalcade and to suggest to the officer in command, with proper tact and humility, that the best effect would be gained by an entry *after* the Duke's, when people's attention would be free; but he had long experience of dealing with princes, and he was not sanguine. A prince with true theatrical sense was rare. The Florentine, hard at work bringing all the preparations a day forward, had been forced to suppress a very fine tableau of the Death of Absalom after news arrived of the death of Prince Livio's son. A fight between the Archangel Michael and the Devil had been substituted—always a favourite with the crowd. The company of dwarf actors was proving absolutely invaluable. They were not only accomplished as actors but were already well supplied with horns, tails, masks, and pitchforks. There was a problem, as usual. Although they got on reasonably well with each other as a company, the man playing the Archangel Michael had made some jovial remarks about their suitability for their roles as devils and had subsequently complained of their clumsiness with the pitchforks.

The director was aware of the theological point that the rebel angels fighting the Archangel ought still to look like angels at that time, being transformed to devils only on their banishment to Hell, but he was staging these scenes partly for the crowd, whose theology was markedly weaker than their love of the grotesque, a love long ago accepted and exploited by the dwarves. The Prince would be unlikely to object—rebels ought not to appear as angels. A good fight always went down splendidly and, to please the bride, he had a chariot with Bacchus and Ariadne drawn by panthers. The panthers were actually hunting cheetahs the late Cardinal had procured on loan for him, and of course there was no question of making these delicate and nervous creatures do any work; the chariot was to be pushed from behind by a crowd of satyrs, and the garlands that appeared to link it to the cheetahs were to be held securely by their handlers to prevent any bolting; though at rehearsals the cheetahs had shown more of a tendency to sit on their haunches looking superior.

In the end, Fortune literally smiled upon the Florentine and ascended the arch, carrying her wreath. This was due less to his flattery than to Fame, Hope, Boldness, and Penitence, each assigned a lower place on the arch on carefully constructed platforms, each showing generous concern for Fortune's vertigo to the extent of offering to learn her speech *prestissime* and take her place. The director hastened along the processional route kept clear by the Bishop's and Cardinal's guards to make sure that his Bacchus was all right. Bacchus was a tall, slight youth, rather weighed down by the leopard skin that made him resemble a spare cheetah. As the director reached him, he heard the burst of cheering from the North Gate that marked the entry of the Duke.

The processional route had also been used by a tall man in black, known to the guards, as a means of reaching the North Gate just as the Duke entered. When the cheering had subsided and Fortune had begun her monotonous chant, Sigismondo had his way barred, as he had expected, by the Duke's own guards, who were disinclined to let a stranger reach the stirrup of their lord. Something changed their minds, however. The Duke, who sat looking as patiently superior as any cheetah, half listening to the speech and half assessing the present appearance of Colleverde with a view to future taxes, was relieved to have his attention distracted, although he kept his eyes steadily on Fortune.

"Who is it?"

His Master of Horse respectfully bowed over the saddle of the horse he had edged alongside. "Your Grace, a messenger from the Duke of Rocca. He says it is urgent."

Sigismondo held up for the Duke's brief glance a scroll with the heavy seal of Rocca dangling on the red silk ribbon.

29

※

Real Trouble Is What's Planned

※

HALF AN HOUR BEFORE, THE GREAT square of Colleverde had not been quite so crowded as to preclude free movement. People could make their way to and fro, gossiping and buying from stalls. One enterprising trader was doing lightning business in little pieces of wax that he swore were from the tapers burning before the picture of the Saint, the picture that had miraculously smiled and nodded when forgiving the thief. A rival had begun to sell single silk threads, stuck to scraps of black cloth to set them off, declaring them to be threads from the banner that hung behind the Saint's picture. Buyers ignored the cynics who whispered that the only true miracle lay in obtaining such articles for sale under the noses of priests aware of their value.

Such cynics naturally did not patronise the fortune-teller who had taken up a pitch in the arcade down the side of the square. It was here Sigismondo found them: Angelo in his particoloured tunic of blue and yellow, a cap of slightly rubbed blue velvet on his gold hair today; and Mirandola, noble face held slightly upward after the manner of the blind, still in his sacking tunic and peasant's straw hat, eagerly watched whenever he took a card from the pack. Angelo's eyes flicked to Sigismondo as he came to stand behind a gaunt woman with a pilgrim's staff.

"In good time, noble sir; you come in good time for your reading." Angelo took the coins from an elderly man who had just heard his fortune and conjured them out of sight while his gaze swept the crowd. "A private reading, masters, for which he will pay me in gold."

Sigismondo, knowing from this that Angelo had information

to be paid for, produced the coin and was beckoned aside behind a ragged curtain.

Therefore by chance Benno, emerging from the Cathedral for the third time that day after yet another search for the Lady Minerva, coming out of the great cave with its dark chapels and dazzling banks of candles and ceaselessly moving crowd, found his eye drawn toward the smooth scalp—his master emerging from Angelo's booth, straightening to his proper height, his shoulder brushed by the curtain.

Benno tacked rapidly through the square's crowd, who were now seriously thinking of lining the processional route but had diverse opinions on points of vantage. They forged resolutely in different directions, mostly across his path. A large man wearing a cloak proper to his size stopped suddenly, and Benno was in among the folds of it when he was extracted by a long arm that turned him round face-to-face with Sigismondo.

"You haven't been lucky, I see, my poor Benno. But I have," and the capable hand on the back of his head propelled him through the group approaching, which opened as by magic and made way at sight of Sigismondo. "In here."

"Here" was a doorway instantly vacated by an offended cat that left behind a strong indication that it regarded the doorway as its territory. Benno looked up hopefully. "Where you put her then?"

"No sign of the missing lady, Benno. We must expect to see her soon though."

"You know where she is?"

"The Prince is bringing her to be married, so he says."

Benno's mouth sagged. "You mean he's *got her?* When they said the wedding party was still coming, I thought—"

"We don't know he's got her." Sigismondo's eyes still scanned the crowd. "He may think she's dead. If he hasn't found out about me and the letter to the Princess, or if he doesn't connect me with her disappearance, then he may well think that an unprotected girl fleeing at random into streets she knows nothing of, or even beyond those streets . . ." Sigismondo did not trouble to go on, and Benno thought of the wolves on the hills outside Nemora for whom Duke Grifone had so considerately left the blinded Mirandola.

"But if he thinks she's dead, who's he bringing to be

married? Does he think they won't know what she looks like here? Isn't there always portraits sent beforehand?"

"Certainly they'll know what she looks like. It will be his little surprise as well as theirs."

Benno gaped again. "But someone important like the Lord Astorre, he's like a prince. He isn't going to marry just anyone. I mean, if it isn't her, he isn't going to say, 'Yes, very nice, you'll do instead.' I mean, there'll be real trouble."

"I believe real trouble is what's planned. Angelo tells me of a doctor asking what the cards foretell for him today."

Benno knew from his master's tone that this meant more than it seemed. "The doctor had been seeing ghosts. Not of his patients, because yesterday he wasn't a doctor."

"Wasn't . . . You don't get to learn all the doctor stuff overnight."

"Depends, Benno, on whether you can lay hands on a doctor's cap and gown. Angelo described him and his two followers; one very noticeable with a blue face, such as you get from a gunpowder accident. And the ghosts they saw, I believe, were at Fontecasta."

Benno nearly sat down on a pig that had put its snout between his ankles to snap up half a turnip discarded on the doorstep.

"Fontecasta!"

"Yesterday, before he was a doctor, he came to ask Angelo about the success of a dangerous venture. He said it had been forecast already the venture would succeed only if all debts had been paid; an astrologer had said this. Today, he said debts had been repaid, but there had been bad omens, and would the enterprise succeed after all?"

"But if he went to Fontecasta, *why'd* he dig up the grave? Did he want bits to put in his potions, like Bianca said? Or you think someone's trying to see if the blind lord's really dead?"

"So who is it who wants to know if he's really dead?" Sigismondo asked.

Benno thought for a moment. "Well, the Cardinal might have, but he knew the blind lord was dead because you'd told him, and he didn't know the lord at the villa was the same one meant to be eaten by wolves, right?"

"You forget the Cardinal himself was dead by the time the

grave was dug up. Prince Livio had had time to torture his wife's attendants by then. He was in Colleverde yesterday. I saw him in the Cathedral."

Benno's fingers covered his mouth, and he stared.

"The *Prince*—you mean the Prince was at Fontecasta looking to see—?"

"If his wife's lover was in fact dead. He wouldn't believe you'd send to a place several times a year with money and messages because you just fancy a man's eyes. And I doubt the Prince knew he hadn't any."

"He thought it was Lord *Giraldi?*" Benno made a dive to prevent Biondello from following a child eating a chunk of salami carried temptingly near the ground. When he stood up, he was aware that his master's attention had left him. Even over the rising excitement of the crowd, the sudden clamour on the steps of the Cathedral made itself heard.

Two boys were struggling with each other, one of them also belaboured by an old woman who was pummeling his back as he fought and kicking his legs as energetically as her skirts would let her. A Bishop's guard, there to clear the wide centre steps for the Duke's party, came across to intervene, was ignominiously thrust off balance by the old woman, and sat down on the collecting cup of one of the beggars. The old woman was shrieking gibberish as she punched the boy, and, with a shock, Benno recognised all three.

Sigismondo was already cleaving a way through the crowd. Benno in his wake collected a few retaliatory shoves and was hoping Biondello would have the sense to follow. Once at the steps, Sigismondo strode over the beggar groping for his coins and, taking both boys by the shoulders, pulled them apart. The old woman, cheered on by the crowd, was now punching the guard. He had regained his feet but not his dignity and was making an effort to arrest her.

"He's wearing my clothes! That's *my clothes* he's got on!" The boy, hanging in Sigismondo's restraining grasp, was scarlet with rage and bleeding copiously from the nose. Benno, with a skill he had never lost, effaced himself behind a priest. The boy had been cheated of seeing Benno hanged, and whether or not publicly pardoned by the saint, Benno was aware that hangings vied with miracles in popularity and were far more easily come by; he judged it better not to remind anyone that he still lived.

He was deeply relieved to see the Lady Minerva, her hair stuffed well out of sight, her tunic's wool embroidery spattered with the boy's blood, and the neckband of her shirt almost torn off, but triumphant. For one unaccustomed to soiling her hands with peasants, she had made a spectacular start.

"Hey, this is no way to behave!" Sigismondo addressed the peasant in question. "I gave you good money for those clothes, have you forgotten?" He administered a slight shake. "And this youth has no doubt paid good money for the gear. Don't call 'thief' before you know the truth. Young sir," he turned to Minerva, "come with me, and I'll stand you a cup of wine. We've time before the Duke arrives: There are three arches, a wagon, and six speeches between him and the Cathedral. Come."

The boy withdrew, scowling and putting out his tongue at Minerva. She, Minerva, passed him with her nose in the air. She had given Sigismondo a radiant smile, and Benno could read relief in it. No fun to be on your own in a city you didn't know, though she did seem to have found Sybilla or to have been found by her. The guard, giving up all idea of arresting anyone, had gone back to his post, making the sign against the evil eye; he hoped the old witch was too daft to put a curse on him or that the influence of the relics would counteract it if she had.

The crowd had enjoyed this, staged so conveniently where they could watch it all. They were sorry to see the actors disperse, and it pleased them when the tall man with the shaven head, one hand on the shoulder of the boy he had rescued, waved the other to a girl on the flower-hung balcony of a house next to the Cathedral. Some of the Colleverdese were able to explain to strangers near them that the house, though it might be described as private, would admit those with plenty of money, and that the girl was known as the prettiest in the town. She was waving back. Clearly the tall man, whether or not a Carthusian monk in disguise, either was known to her or shortly would be. He was certainly leading the youth into temptation. He and the boy, dogged by the old woman and followed at a slight distance by a vague lackwit and a one-eared dog, made their way to the alley along the side of the Cathedral and disappeared through an arch into the courtyard. Lewd advice to the boy was shouted after them, but no one thought it necessary to advise the man.

Minerva was indeed relieved to see Sigismondo. She had limped into Colleverde with her lame horse an hour or so before and solved the question of what to do with the animal by seeing someone in the yard of a hostelry giving directions about the care of his horse. The hostler, unimpressed by Minerva's workaday clothes, became respectful when she spoke. Her accent was that of the nobility and her manner effortlessly superior. There was nothing wrong either with the colour of her money

Easier in her mind she went out into the streets and, catching the general anticipation, felt for the first time a rising excitement instead of anxiety. There were a lot of people about, none of whom paid her any attention. Accustomed to being the focus of eyes, the special concern of a group of attendants whose sole duty was her welfare, she found this neglect of her very reassuring. In such a crowd, Prince Livio would never find her. The nightmare of her brother's death had receded in her mind among the dreamlike confusion and pelting impressions of recent days. She could even remember now how her brother had often cruelly teased her, had tormented her pet dogs, pulled her hair till she screamed, and over and over told her in triumph that he, the younger by some quarter hour, would by virtue of his sex inherit Montenero. He'd had a favourite old chamberlain dismissed, had threatened her with a nunnery when he should succeed their father—

Their father? He would have been bringing her to Colleverde tomorrow, riding with her brother and the immense train of the dowry for the days of festivity. Who would marry Lord Astorre now? What would become of her?

But she must find the Cathedral. Lord Mirandola had insisted on her taking money—"It came from your mother, remember"—and she must have Masses said, for her mother, for her poor brother. She would pray too for the safety of Lord Mirandola. Every moment of the time she had spent in his company made her more inclined to think that, if she sought a father, she would not have far to go.

The streets seemed to converge on the Cathedral. She saw its towers shining in the sun. The great clock spoke. She thought someone among the buzz of the crowd talked of the wedding. It must be disappointing for everyone that it wasn't to take place. She went into the candle-starred dimness of the Cathedral and was instantly rebuked for not taking off her cap. It was to be hoped no one here would recognise her without it, but it seemed that all the world was preoccupied. It took her a while to find a priest not too busy to attend to her. The side chapel had been small and dusty, but the Mass, for which she had to part with a surprising amount of money, had been soothing. Then she had prayed, from a dark corner, to the Saint. Some old women in front of her were praying for another miracle—it seemed there had been one yesterday. Minerva fixed her eyes on the Saint's picture. She would have liked a sign that her mother's sins were forgiven and that she herself and her father—the Lord Mirandola—were going to be safe.

Her confidence in their ultimate safety returned to her with the appearance of Sigismondo. Telling him, as they climbed the stairs in an unknown house, about the dreadful vision of Prince Livio last night at the villa, she was surprised how pleasant it was to give up responsibility, to be swept along again by mysterious events, such as being introduced to an extremely pretty girl in a low-cut dress of orange velvet.

"Polissena." Sigismondo presented the girl to Minerva. "She will look after you." As Minerva went ahead into the strange, luxurious room, she heard him murmuring and looked back. The shaven head was bent close to the crimped golden waterfall of Polissena's hair. He spoke with a bubble of laughter, and Polissena's eyes widened to look inquisitively at Minerva as she replied. He was giving her money. The words "Your best, mind," were clear. He turned to Minerva. "With your pardon, I must go. We'll meet within the hour."

He was gone before she could ask for explanation, and she was left with Polissena—and Sybilla, who stood in the middle of the room, revolving to see everything and muttering *po-po-po* with an unfathomable expression on her face. Polissena came up to Minerva and, curtseying, took off the shabby cap. Released, a cloud of hair spread out round Minerva's head and neck. The maidservant, standing arms akimbo, waiting for some action, exclaimed. Polissena lifted the ringlets with an admiring word. "Pearls! Pearls, I think, and silver gauze flowers. Bianca, my silver brocade."

Duke Grifone could guess, from the creaking of a pulley that gave an undertone to Fortune's last sentences, and from the equally recognisable sound of a peroration, that he was now to be the recipient of the laurel wreath whose trembling in Fortune's hands had betrayed her nerves. The thing would have to go over his hat and would probably obscure the balas ruby for which he had paid a city's revenues. On the other hand, he was not going to bare his head. The gesture would lack dignity and the ruby had been bought to impress. He maintained his smile and ran over in his head the brief Latin speech of thanks. He was disturbed; someone in this city hated him enough to burn his chief counsellor and representative, and now this shaven-headed messenger from Rocca standing at his stirrup was telling him of worse. How much was he to be trusted? Grifone had no treaty with Ludovico of Rocca, but Astorre was about to marry his niece.

The machinery worked perfectly. Fortune descended on her garlanded cloud towards the Duke and successfully deposited the wreath without crushing his hat over his eyes, obscuring the ruby, or herself falling forward and toppling him off his horse. Well rehearsed, he thought. A trumpet blew, too soon, interrupting his speech of thanks; the cortège moved slowly onward, to meet the Bishop, the mayor of Colleverde with its keys on the blue velvet cushion, the circle of dignitaries. The shaven head was no longer at the Duke's side; the man had vanished into the crowd before the Duke had an opportunity to read the letter, Sigismondo's passport to the Duke's attention with its seal of Rocca.

Riding forward, the Duke raised it and glanced at the superscription. Now, if Ludovico of Rocca echoed his messenger's warning:

To my beloved sister Oralia, he read.

30

⊠

"Father"

⊠

ONE OF THE REASONS THAT THE original programme for the wedding procession had been scheduled for Sunday rather than Saturday was to allow proper attention to be given to both the sovereigns attending. However, Prince Livio's astrologer, in the attempt, it was understood, to avoid the influence of the unlucky star that had presided over the deaths of his wife and son, had hastily recast the auguries for the ceremony. He decreed the best way to escape further misfortune would be to bring the ceremony forward by a day, catching the malign star off guard, as it were.

Now, therefore, the entrance into Colleverde of the Prince Livio at the East Gate was timed to succeed that of Duke Grifone at the North; but the Prince, it had been mutually decided, would forego some of the honours planned. Between pleasing a foreign Prince and the Duke who settled your taxes, the Colleverdese had little hesitation; the Florentine master of ceremonies had received precise instructions as to that. As Sigismondo had said, there were three arches, a pageant wagon, and six speeches before the Duke could reach the Bishop's Palace; while Prince Livio and the bride got one arch, the Chariot of Bacchus, the battle of Michael and the devils, and but one speech, and that in the vernacular. All would be made up for to the Montenerans at the wedding feast that night, however, when the planets were to make an appearance to bless the couple on a machine that, with any luck, would revolve.

This, of course, the crowds would miss, but they were not complaining. They had not got over the thrill of having the Devil come to burn their Cardinal for bringing the holy relics to Colleverde, and there had been the miracle the day before.

There was always the hope that something even more exceptional would happen today.

There was an immediate disappointment, though, that the bride was so heavily veiled. Women in the crowd excused her; she was in mourning, it was proper for a bride to be veiled before the ceremony; but not every bride was so very thoroughly veiled that her features could not even be guessed at.

Prince Livio's features—perfectly visible under a hat of black velvet dagged with gold, nicely compromising between mourning and festivity—were studied with enormous curiosity. Rumour having embroidered fact, he was now said to have slaughtered his wife on her deathbed in a fit and then, maddened by guilt, have run amok, killing anyone who got in his path.

The Prince was generally agreed to look the kind of man who could have done what rumour said. Some voiced the opinion that he was mad and piously hoped the strain would not descend through his daughter and infect the line of their own Duke. Many commented that he was so unsure of his own health that he had brought his physician with him, in cap and furred gown, pacing slowly by the Prince's horse. A murmur ran through the crowd that the Prince might have a fit at any minute, and, while most of the crowd hoped that he would, those nearest were glad of the Bishop's Guard with their pikes who lined the route.

The Duke was to arrive first at the Bishop's Palace, escorted by the Bishop, and there with his son receive the bride and her father. Three arches, a triumphal wagon, and six speeches after he had entered Colleverde, the Duke arrived, still wearing his laurel wreath over his hat and looking reasonably fresh. He acknowledged the cheers with a raised hand and went up the steps of the Palace with a turn of speed that was remarked upon. The laurel wreath was thought becoming, and the ruby grew in size with every comment. Lord Astorre's looks made the women dote. They settled to wait for the arrival of Prince Livio.

The Prince was judged not to appreciate the trouble that had been gone to on his account. While the crowd vociferously applauded the youth impersonating Bacchus, who had leant from his chariot to offer gilt-ribboned bunches of grapes to the bride, the Prince had snatched them from him and thrown them carelessly into his daughter's lap. The grapes were of glass, and, like everything Venetian, expensive. It was a mercy they were not broken. The bride held desperately to her veils in the breeze that swept the square. She seemed to care nothing for the entertainment, for she kept her head down. The cheetahs, despite the clapping, the shouts, and the Prince's abrupt movement, ignored everybody.

The crowd, unimpressed by Prince Livio's demeanour, were still more disgusted when he came to the wagon where the battle of Saint Michael and the devils was to be fought: he glanced at it and rode straight on, forcing his entourage and the whole procession to move forward. After this, people were only a little soothed by the number of baggage litters and pack mules in handsome caparisons, carrying the Princess's dowry.

In the Bishop's Palace, more preparations went forward. The Duke was giving swift, peremptory orders, one of which was to find a tall shaven-headed man dressed in black. No one succeeded in this because no one thought to look in the tiring-room where the Princess was to make ready, just outside the audience chamber where the betrothal was to be ratified. In the chamber, carved chairs for the Duke, the Prince, the Bishop, and the bridal pair were ranged at one end on a dais before the Bishop's best tapestry, and along the walls stood men from the Bishop's Guard. The stairs up to the chamber were lined by the Cardinal's Guard, who had insisted to the Bishop's Marshal that their dead master, who would of course have officiated at the ceremony, had ordered them to be there and that his unfortunate permanent absence in no way changed this. The Marshal had blustered to begin with, but he was in the habit of being overruled, and the Captain of the Cardinal's Guard had a face that lent a particular potency to his demand, being composed to a great extent of scar tissue.

One side of the chamber had three long windows leading onto the balcony that overlooked the piazza. The bridal pair were to go out there after the contract had been signed and show themselves to the crowd before crossing the little closed bridge from Palace to Cathedral to hear Mass before the relics. A table near the windows was surrounded with lawyers, self-important in black caps and gowns, fussing with the papers, arguing over their arrangement and the placing of the seals and the taper and the certificate of marriage, which was beautifully illuminated and had a picture of the couple holding hands in front of some classical architecture and a spring landscape of fields, trees, and allegorical animals. The arms of Nemora and Montenero had been carefully painted in large gold-rimmed shields beneath. All that was lacking were the signatures and seals.

Duke Grifone had taken his place on the most decorated chair, on a small platform of its own in the centre of the dais. Looking about him intently, he found that a chair had been set for the Princess Corio, to whom he had already sent a letter, condoling with her on her brother's death and informing her that, as she would not be present at this ceremony on account of mourning, he would himself call on her at the Palazzo Corio later that day. He instructed that the chair be removed. He took off his laurel wreath, handed it to a page together with his hat to be dusted, and wondered where the messenger from Rocca had got to.

If he had stepped across the room, opened one of the long windows, and looked out, he would have seen him.

After the Duke had disappeared into the Palace and Prince Livio had been treated to his arch and the Chariot of Bacchus, there was a tidal surge of the crowd. By the time the Prince had dismounted before the Palace and helped the bride from her litter, taking care that her veils and therefore her modesty should not be ruffled, the mass of the crowd was before the Bishops Palace. The Prince extended an impatient hand to the proffered arm of his doctor and appeared to need his assistance.

Two people were already on the balcony, but neither of them looked bridal. Both were in black; one had a shaven head and the other a leather hood. The latter had been standing at one end of the balcony for some time. The crowd decided that he was a trumpeter waiting to give a fanfare, but his trumpet must be at his feet, out of sight behind the flag-hung balustrade. This would account for his keeping himself out of sight of those inside the Palace yet being anxious to monitor what went on there so as to be ready. He had not been aware of the shaven-headed man's emerging from a small end door just behind him, because his attention was on the window he was peeking in at.

What happened was so sudden and so odd that the crowd disagreed about it immediately. The man in the leather hood dropped forward as though he had been tripped, or was perhaps reaching for the trumpet. The other caught him as he fell and helped him to the ground. He lay there apparently at ease while the man with the bare scalp stood up, talking to him in a friendly way, put on the leather hood, and took up the same position by the window. The crowd was baffled. As they stared, the man now in the hood turned and gave them a genial salute before addressing himself to watching through the windows. This dissipated, to some degree, the unease that had been spreading among them.

Prince Livio would have had a proper reception from the Duke at the gates of Colleverde if he had kept to the original plan and arrived the next day. Now he had to put up with second best in the person of the Bishop. Duke Grifone was not going to wait about on the Palace steps, so it devolved on their host to welcome the Prince at the foot of the great stair leading to the audience chamber where the contract was to be signed. The bride was hurried on up to the tiring-room off the great chamber, where she could arrange her hair and dress after the procession.

Prince Livio, finding the Bishop even more tedious than he normally found bishops, made little attempt to give even a civil attention to the Latin compliments so carefully prepared by Bishop Taddeo but watched with impatience his daughter's difficulties with her long enveloping veils on the steep stairs. The Bishop, thrown by the Prince's suddenly returning his attention to him when the group disappeared above, faltered under the burning gaze. He felt tension in the man before him and remembered all at once that this was the man who had killed his own son. He might now be at the Devil's command to do other appalling deeds. Satan had been at work that day at Fontecasta, locking doors and covering the terrible grave of the undead. He swallowed as he met the Prince's eyes, lost his place, and went on from a paragraph back, assuring the Prince once more of his resemblance to the noble Julius Caesar and wondering now if the end of the noble Julius made the comparison infelicitous.

By the time that the Prince had heard out and replied to the Bishop and been escorted up the stairs between the ranks of the Cardinal's Guard, the bride was ready. Had the crowd known it, the arrival on the balcony of the man with the shaven head had been a sign of this. Shortly after he appeared he had swung open the window through which he had been peering and slid inside.

In the great chamber, the girl swathed in her veils stepped to the Prince's side to be led up and presented to Duke Grifone, already descending from the dais to receive them. The Prince, however, found it necessary to lean on the arm of his doctor, who thus would have to accompany him towards the Duke.

At his other side, and ahead of the proper time, the girl threw back her veiling.

"Father."

She should not speak either. He turned.

The Prince's eyes fixed on Minerva's face.

31

❂

Who Was the Enemy?

❂

BENNO HAD BEEN AMAZED AT THE ease with which Polissena had led them into the Bishop's Palace, through empty side lanes behind the Cathedral and in at a back door where the servants seemed to know her. She went up some back stairs to a room equipped with screens, a commode, a table covered with a blue silk cloth and on it an embroidered pincushion and a silver comb and mirror. He had anticipated soldiers barring their way, awkward questions. He feared that Sigismondo, by leaving him with the Lady Minerva, had made him responsible for her safety, and, although his master's plan had not been revealed to him, he had enough idea of it to be very much alarmed. He wished fervently that Angelo were at hand instead of protecting the blind lord out there somewhere—if you could call exposing him to everyone's gaze protecting. Benno sighed. His master was not one to wait for things to happen, he invited them.

The invitation was bearing fruit. Benno had been hugely relieved to see Sigismondo come into the tiring-room, smiling at them standing there, the Lady Minerva in Polissena's silver brocade, with Sybilla muttering as she twitched at the skirt to make it hang straight. She had a proprietary air about the lady that was of a piece with all her oddness. Sigismondo raised a finger to his lips and stepped aside as the door opened again and a heavily veiled girl struggled in, trying to manage her skirts and stop those behind from treading on them. Sigismondo closed the door sharply after her two attendants were in, and stood by while all three gazed in stupefaction at the Lady Minerva. The veiled girl tried to curtsey, burst into tears, and was helped up and warned to silence by Sigismondo. She managed to breathe, "Thank God you're found, my lady!"

Polissena, at a gesture from Sigismondo, was rapidly unpinning the coronet of flowers and jewels that held the veils to the girl's head while she hung, weeping and half fainting, on Sigismondo's arm. The Lady Minerva bent her head to have the lawn and coronet arranged on her; Sybilla's fingers were as deft as Polissena's.

Sigismondo, settling the tearful impostor on the window seat of a shuttered window, leant to say a word to the rightful bride. Benno caught, "when I show," then his master slipped out of another door, which gave a glimpse of a balcony before he shut it.

Polissena let herself out and was gone. The Lady Minerva, followed by the two dazed and thankful attendants, went, like a Princess's daughter, pacing into the audience chamber beyond. Sybilla bundled after, and Benno, cramming himself against the wall by the door, saw the Duke rising from his chair in front of the tapestry, the Bishop turned to face the bride, the lawyers behind their table outlined against the window, and another window opening beyond them letting in the sea sound of the crowd and, like a shadow, Sigismondo. Then the Lady Minerva flung back her veils in a big gesture that sent wings of gauze to obscure Benno's view. Through the gauze he saw the pale face and staring eyes of Prince Livio as he turned.

Here Biondello, whose genius for the evasion of danger had preserved him from becoming puppy pie in his native village, sprang instantly from Benno's shirt and flew back into the tiring room.

Prince Livio had turned slightly aside as though twitched by an invisible hand and stood as if the Lady Minerva had Gorgon-like struck him to stone, while all else erupted around him. His doctor, anonymous hitherto in the cap and gown that marked him professionally, came to startling life. Abandoning his patient at the very moment he needed care, the man launched himself up the room at Duke Grifone; he might have been imploring help but for the stiletto glittering in his hand.

Benno gasped but found his view blocked by Minerva, whom Sigismondo was thrusting into his arms.

"Get her back in there and keep the door."

The attendant women scrambled past as Lady Minerva was borne back into the tiring room, more by Sigismondo's push than by her own volition. Benno, putting himself in front of her in the doorway, knife in hand, could see why Sigismondo wanted her out of it.

The deadly doctor had met the Duke's sword, to his grave disadvantage. A thrust, and he joined the Bishop, who was sprawled in a welter of his robes on the floor, having, Benno supposed, bravely got in the way as the doctor attacked the Duke. Now, his mitre off, he was pinned down by the doctor's body, which bloodied the episcopal gold and white.

Over him swung Grifone's sword, clashing with that of Prince Livio, who, jerked from his trance of surprise into furious life, attacked the Duke with a wild energy. The room seemed suddenly full of fighting men. Men in the Duke's colours, black and white, were wielding pikes against Prince Livio's attendants and, in the confusion, men of the Cardinal's Guard who had flowed into the chamber from the stairs.

Benno, craning to see where his master had got to, was hardly aware of the Lady Minerva scrabbling at his shoulders in an effort to see what was going on. He could hear sobbing and keening from the bridesmaids and excited comments from the lady, rendered incomprehensible by the tramp and clash and shouts in the crowded room. He caught a glimpse of Sigismondo, axe in his left hand, sword rising and falling in dreadful flashes, his face grave and concentrated as ever. A man in the Duke's colours came reeling backward and fell at Benno's feet. Over him Benno saw Sybilla, cap off and white hair on end, pick up a halberd the man had dropped and, wielding it like a flail, knock over a man in the throng and, on a backstroke, the just risen Bishop.

Past two staggering men who seemed to have lost their weapons and been reduced to trying to strangle each other, one of whom had the pockmarked face of the doctor's assistant, Benno got sight of the upper part of the room again. The Duke was hard-pressed still by the Prince, and Benno wondered that Sigismondo had not come to his rescue, when he saw why: a knot of Livio's men, one with a pike that could well outreach a sword, surrounded Sigismondo with his back to the window. Beside him fought the Lord Astorre, whom Benno recognised from his likeness to the Duke and his bridegroom silk and brocade. The young man was barely holding his own against an enormous man with sword to match; Benno, just as he took this in, was precipitated forward by a violent push on his back. He recovered, to see the silver brocade skirts of the Lady Minerva whisk through a gap in the fighters. He scrambled up from all fours to follow her, when the men strangling each other collapsed in a writhing muddle towards him, bringing him down again. Over them he saw the Lady Minerva reach the table by the windows, where green cloth was billowing as the lawyers beneath it struggled for the safest place. She seized an inkpot and threw its contents straight in the face of the man attacking her bridegroom. Astorre unhesitatingly ran him through as he stood blinded and spluttering, and the streams of ink turned red as they ran down his doublet.

Simultaneously Sigismondo, after an axe blow that halved the pike threatening him and sent the business end clanging to the marble floor, thrust his sword into the surprised man now short of it and, stepping aside, made way for him to stagger through the open window, meet the balustrade with force, and tip over it into the crowd below.

Benno, by this time disentangled from the two men still failing to choke each other, retrieved his knife and got to his feet to follow the Lady Minerva and protect her from the results of her courage. He squirmed away from a lunge by a pikeman on his right trying to transfix another who, falling backwards into a group of men using swords, then cannoned forwards past the pikeman and was seen to have a sword in his back. He too disappeared out the window and over the balcony. A roar came from below.

Benno forged on, looking to see where the lady had got to. What he saw was Duke Grifone, his right arm swordless and pinned against the panelling by Prince Livio's blade. It seemed that, as soon as the Prince could free his sword, the Duke would receive it in his heart, for his own had dropped from a useless hand. Prince Livio had seized the neck of the Duke's shirt and was dragging it open as he wrenched his sword free. Just as the Lord Astorre struck at the attacker's head, the Lady Minerva fastened her hands on the back of the Prince's cloak and, dragging it down with all her weight, sank to the floor. The Prince fell with a great howl that drew all eyes.

Grifone, snatching up his sword in his left hand, joined Astorre in making sure of the Prince's death.

Grifone helped the Lady Minerva from the floor and briefly kissed her hand before putting her behind him, close to the bloodstained wall, and surveying the room. None of the Prince's men remained standing. The small old woman in black hit a stirring Monteneran. In the quiet, a door to the banqueting hall opened, widened, and framed a group of pallid clerics, Torquato among them. There was no sound now but groans.

Sigismondo came striding over the prostrate forms. Grifone greeted him with some abrupt question, which he seemed to defer. He took the Duke's wounded arm. Tearing the sleeve, he bent his head to sniff at the wound. Astorre, with quick understanding and a face of alarm, took up Livio's sword and proffered its blade across his arm. Again Sigismondo sniffed and looked and shook his head. He pointed to the tiring-room, and the deep voice could be heard saying "water."

Grifone's Captain stood before him, in bloodstained black and white. The Duke pointed to this body and that. "From the balcony by the heels," he said.

There followed a surprisingly democratic interlude in the tiring-room, with the Duke having his wound cleansed by Sybilla while he chatted to Polissena, whose presence there clearly enlivened him. The Lady Minerva talked to her ladies on the window seat, pale and dazed but straight-backed. A protuberance in the hem of the blue silk table-cloth resolved itself into a black nose and grubby white fur, and Benno picked up Biondello and kissed him.

The Bishop was on his knees in the audience chamber now, reading their rites to the terminally wounded. One of these was of the Cardinal's Guard, and their Captain crouched over him as if helping him in his last moments. The Duke, in the midst of announcing that the ceremony of betrothal was merely to be postponed to a more suitable date, beckoned him.

The Cardinal's Captain, so severely wounded as to seem on the point of collapse and supported by two of his men swathed in extempore bandages, was brought to the Duke. He regretted the confusion, he said, when his men first entered; they had not known what was in hand. But in the latter part of the fray they had dealt with a force of Prince Livio's men trying to rush the stairs.

"Had His Eminence been spared to me, things would have gone differently today." The Duke shook his head.

The crowd below, after the first dead man's descent over the balcony, had hastily withdrawn as far as it could, leaving several trampled citizens and pilgrims to drag themselves, too, away out of the influence of what terrible events the Devil was busy with in the Bishop's very Palace. It was not until two men lay dead on the stones, and others began to try scrambling down, that the crowd caught the gist of what was happening, for all but one of these were in Prince Livio's colours.

Benno, his dog clutched to his chest, watched from the doorway of the tiring-room. He heard Sigismondo's voice from the banqueting hall beyond the audience chamber. The Duke heard it too and strode in there. Benno padded discreetly after.

Sigismondo was rising from the side of the lethal doctor. The brown robe had been removed; the face was contorted but, as they looked at it, the grimace relaxed, the eyes opened to gaze emptily at the ceiling. Breath ceased.

"Your Grace," said Sigismondo, "he tells me Prince Livio's army of mercenaries is at the border. They should already have crossed into Nemora."

32

You Can't Win Them All

Duke Grifone, Benno decided, was no more inclined to wait for things to happen than Sigismondo was. He instantly summoned the Captain of his guards—at that moment kneeling beside the Bishop, holding the hand of one of his own men and promising him that his widow would be looked after—and ordered him to take the body of Prince Livio, tie it across a horse, and at the head of his men follow the Lord Astorre to meet the condotta. There, Benno gathered, it was a case of asking mercenaries who had been prepared to fight for Prince Livio how they felt about carrying on with a corpse for commander, or whether, more to the point, they fancied dead men paid well.

"Tell them they *will* be paid." The Duke paused and gave his version of a smile, which would have graced a happy wolf. "Let them retire across the border and wait for word from me." He turned to the Bishop's Marshal, who had arrived and was hovering in the background, torn between a desire to be noticed and a dread of what might happen if he was. "Where did you place the Prince's sumpter mules with the Lady Minerva's dowry?"

The Marshal blossomed. Detail was his forte. He was able to tell the Duke that they had been accommodated in the Bishop's stables, and the coffers of treasure were, as he himself had previously arranged, under guard in the Bishop's strong room.

The Duke gave him, too, a smile, which he found less reassuring than the accompanying "Good! Prince Livio may have meant the money to grease a few palms with. Now the Lord Astorre shall take some with him to the border." He prodded the Marshal's chest. "Do you know a mercenary who wouldn't rather be paid *not* to fight?"

Benno saw Sigismondo going quietly out onto the balcony. Benno followed and found him crouching beside a man who lay against the wall, near the door from the tiring-room.

Sigismondo's hand cupped the man's head, almost lovingly, wiping away the blood that idled from the corner of the man's mouth. "The Cardinal," he was saying. "Tell me about the Cardinal."

"A priest." The man's mouth found words harder to produce than the blood that still trickled. "Confession."

"My son." Sigismondo pulled off the leather hood and bent closer so that the man's failing eyes could focus. "Tell me: the Cardinal?"

A spasm twisted the face. "He burnt 'Tonello . . . we paid him for that . . . bless me, Father—"

It was too late for blessing. Benno watched, shocked, as Sigismondo rose, crossed himself, and pointed out this body to the Duke's men for their attention. Benno pressed behind Sigismondo as he returned to the audience room. "You let him think you were a priest! You stopped him from getting absolution!"

He halted abruptly as his master swung round on him. The face was dark and serious. "We'll leave judgement in this matter to the Judge of us all. You are not here to tell me what I have done." The face relaxed a little. "Benno, there was no absolution to be got. A man who slays a priest can get absolution only from the Holy Father himself. Mm-mm-hm . . . what do you suppose a man who burns a *Cardinal* can hope for?"

"He killed the Cardinal?" Benno's amazement raised his voice, and the Duke wheeled to stare: "You know who killed Cardinal Petrucci?"

Sigismondo bowed. The Duke gripped him by the arm with a ferocity that made the Marshal step back but did not alter Sigismondo's expression in the least. "If you know who killed him, *tell me*. He shall know our justice."

"Your Grace. I've no confirmation as yet. I believe that one of the assassins hired by Prince Livio to kill you had the leisure yesterday night to pursue a private revenge as well."

The Duke impatiently waved aside his physician, who had

finally been found and was fussily anxious to examine the
Duke's wound. "A private revenge? For what?"

"Your Grace may have heard of one Antonello, a magician
whom His Eminence caused to be burnt last year in Bibbiena."

"I remember. He told His Eminence he would be dead before
this summer. Well, he was right, this Antonello; but you're
telling me His Eminence was burnt in revenge for this burning?
An eye for an eye, fire for fire—and to prove the prophecy?"

"So it seems, Your Grace. Those who burnt him owed
Antonello a life; the magician saved the son of one of them."

"These men: their names?"

"I know the name of only one: Achille Malvezzi."

"A brigand?"

"Your Grace has heard of him."

"He has been pestering our borders, robbing and killing our
people for some years. Petrucci hanged a man of his only last
year."

"When they tried to rescue Antonello, Your Grace."

"This Malvezzi—he was hired by Livio? Then he is here?"
The Duke surveyed the marble floor. The Bishop, still attended
by one of his priests bearing the holy oil, had just finished
anointing a dying man in the Duke's colours. The less wounded
had been helped away, some of the dead had been dragged to
the balcony, some carried to the antechapel, and a servant was
cleaning the smeared marble. Sigismondo shook his head.

"Malvezzi is already demonstrating Your Grace's justice to
the populace. He was the one dressed as a doctor, who was first
to try to kill you."

"Then I have killed him already." The Duke's whole bearing
showed his regret at the irreversible simplicity and speed of
Malvezzi's death. He looked sharply up as he added: "But you
said there was another? Who still lives?"

"No, Your Grace. He, too, has paid his price and hangs
there." The dark glance was turned towards the creaking ropes
made fast to the balustrade. "He was posted outside that
window to enter and kill the Lord Astorre when he came to the
table to sign the contract; that was when the attack was to
begin. So Malvezzi told me."

"But if Malvezzi meant to kill me, why give me time to draw
sword?"

"Mm-hm-mm . . . plans go awry, Your Grace. He was dressed as a doctor, and I believe that Prince Livio meant to approach you on his arm; but the Prince was surprised." Amusement had crept into the deep voice. "He did not expect to see his daughter."

The Duke stared. "Are you jesting with me, man?"

"Your Grace, I had no time to tell you—when I warned you at the city gate that Prince Livio plotted to take your life—that the bride was not the Lady Minerva."

"Was *not* . . ." The Duke leant forward.

"When the Prince was crazed by grief after the death of the Princess Oralia, he killed his son as Your Grace has heard. I was at his court then, delivering a letter from the Duke of Rocca to the Princess—"

"Ah. I understand. The letter you handed me." The Duke looked grim. "Continue."

"It seemed to me that the Lady Minerva was in great danger." Sigismondo glanced around the room. "If Your Grace will permit me to speak in private?"

The Duke's gesture, with his good hand, sent everyone but Sigismondo backing out of earshot. Benno watched wistfully from the window embrasure the shaven head bent towards the cap with the balas ruby that winked like the eye of an angry animal. He wondered how his master was explaining the abduction of the Lady Minerva, how he was representing the preservation of her chastity and honour, so essential to the Duke's future daughter-in-law. It crossed Benno's mind that perhaps his master had gambled too recklessly with her reputation. The Duke's face told him nothing, but he might surely never proceed with this marriage. Benno himself had seen the lady save the life of the Lord Astorre—but had the Duke? He must have witnessed her very bold attempt to save his own life, dragging the Prince down. Was that enough to reconcile this fierce man to his son's marrying the daughter of the man who'd planned to kill him?

In the tiring-room, out of sight of Benno and the rest, Minerva sat. Being a heroine was perfectly fine at the time, she had discovered, and she had never lived so intensely as in that

great room full of death on every side. The sight of Astorre
again—older by eight years than when last they met and,
unbelievably, handsomer, backed against a wall fighting a
giant—had snatched her into the middle of what was happening. She had certainly not stopped to think. It was thinking
about it now that it was all over that made her feel so peculiar.
Thinking about Prince Livio, lying on the floor with blood on
his face from Astorre's sword blow, conjured up the nightmare
sight she had successfully blocked all this time: her brother's
head looking up at nothing, looking up, it seemed, at her. She
put her hands to her face, but there was no comfort in the
darkness behind them.

"My lady?" Polissena was bending over her. "Were you
hurt?"

She shook her head. Where was Astorre? He had kissed her
hand and led her to the tiring-room and gone straight back to
his father. His face had said nothing. What would happen now?
Prince Livio, in the world's eyes her father, had tried to kill the
Duke. If I'm not *his* daughter, she told herself valiantly, I am
still the daughter of Princess Oralia, and my uncle is the Duke
of Rocca.

She became aware of a noise that had been going on for
some time, a yelling and booing from the crowd out in the
square. They had come to see her married. Could they now be
wanting to see her dead?

"My Lady. His Grace comes."

She managed to rise. She was of a sudden terrified. The
Duke was horribly pale and bleak. She saw the white rings of
curls under the velvet cap, the red eye of the ruby, the dark eyes
gazing at her. Now she would hear her sentence. Even
Sigismondo, standing behind the Duke, could no longer protect
her.

"Lady Minerva." He would put her in a nunnery. She would
never know love, never feel Astorre's arms holding her. "We
have considered all that has happened today." His voice was so
harsh. It would be prison, never to ride out on a spring morning
again. He took her hand, and she surrendered it, wondering if
it was to be death after all. "You may have thought to have
become Duchess of Nemora in the course of time, but your fate

has overtaken you. Your beauty is only matched by your courage. I have decided to marry you myself."

Duke Grifone raised her hand to his lips and kissed it. Behind him, Sigismondo shrugged.

You can't win them all.

33

✖

Looking for the Letter

✖

IT HAD BEEN A SORE DISAPPOINTment to the Bishop's Marshal to hear that the Cardinal's murderers had been punished already, but he was determined not to lose credit for what he had done himself in the investigation so far. He even overcame his awe of the Duke— who after all had commended him—to hurry forward as the ducal party was leaving for the Palazzo Corio and go on one knee before him.

"Your Grace, in the matter of His Eminence's death, there are others—"

"*Others?*"

He had all the Duke's attention now. "Three villains, Your Grace, that I arrested. They are in the Bishop's prison awaiting further interrogation."

"Bring them before us when I return from the Palazzo Corio. The Princess Corio will be glad to see them for her brother's sake. Bring your torturers too, they'll be needed. Come." He looked round for Sigismondo but did not see him. The smile vanished. He was not used to men who disappeared from his presence without asking his leave; he had still a few questions concerning events, but there would be time for that. Ignoring his physician's protests he mounted the horse, caparisoned in scarlet and gold, at the steps of the Bishop's Palace, and took his way across the square, cleared for him through a vociferous crowd whose cheers he acknowledged. They had been well satisfied with the display that afternoon and appreciated the excitement provided for them. The attack on the Duke, the effort to usurp the country, had produced a surge of popularity for a man whose activities did not always recommend him to his subjects.

Before bustling down to the dungeons, the Marshal surveyed the balcony and its dangling traitors with a glow of patriotic joy. The crowd was using the bodies for target practice, with such spoilt fruit or vegetables as came to hand, and some fresh ones too, such was their enthusiasm. By general opinion, the relics had won, and the Devil had got a good licking.

Benno watched the Lady Minerva, looking dazed, escorted by her respectful ladies—Sybilla grumbling in their wake—towards a room readied for her in haste by the Bishop's servants. There was a tremendous bustle going on in the audience chamber now, servants tidying the dais and the table and rehanging the tapestry, and tables were being set up in the great hall next door. They had just finished washing the floor. The lawyers had collected their documents, the windows had been closed, just in time: a turnip cast at a twirling traitor thumped against a pane, followed by something splashy and red that turned Benno's stomach until he remembered the offal that was being grilled at stalls in the square.

"Get out, rascal! Out of here, you and your dog!" The steward stopped himself in time from putting hands on the shoulders of Benno's greasy jerkin and directed a servant to throw him out. Benno, clasping Biondello, took the flight of stairs down to the door faster than his feet cared for. As he landed with a stagger on the flags of the entrance hall and Biondello winded him by springing free in search of something less insecure, a broad hand took him by the collar and effortlessly put him back on his feet.

"Come. The Palazzo Corio."

Benno, still rubbing himself, followed Biondello, who was trotting confidently at Sigismondo's heels.

The holiday mood in the crowd was so strong that even Sigismondo found an initial difficulty in getting through the square now that the Duke's train had passed. Then someone shouted that he was the man on the balcony, the one who'd killed a traitor in full view without anyone at the time knowing it, and a throng bore him on his way with great goodwill, slapping him on the shoulders and offering him everything from only partly used fried trotters to hysterical kisses. Benno in his wake had scooped Biondello up for safety and managed to forge a path behind a woman who pressed close to Sigismondo. She had a child on her shoulder whom she was urging to stroke the shaven scalp for luck.

The Palazzo Corio was a scene of confusion. The banner of
Nemora, a black gryphon on a white ground, sable on argent,
cracked in the spring breeze from one of the poles projecting
over the street; another pole had evidently held the Monteneran
banner of scarlet and yellow, for the ends of a piece of scarlet
cloth were being dragged through a long window beside the
pole when Sigismondo and Benno arrived. In the courtyard
knots of people—servants, grooms, guards of both Cardinal
and Duke—gossiped as though their lives depended on the
exchange of information. Inside the Palace they at once
encountered Battista, leading away a maidservant with dirty
arms who was blubbering into an apron thrown over her head.
His bitter face under its white thatch turned to them.

"I hear they've caught them. Pity they're dead."

The news of his master's murderers took precedence for him
over any minor affair of a Prince's death and a Duke's escape
from assassination. Sigismondo's reply was genially consoling.
"Mmmm. They may not *all* be dead. The Duke has some yet to
question." Benno thought with sinking heart of poor Massimo.
"His Grace believes the Princess will be glad to help."

"To help!" Battista snorted. The girl, who had been peeking
at Sigismondo, let out a fresh bellow and crammed the linen
over her face again. "The Princess is in the mood to question.
The whole house has been questioned from the moment the
Princess rose. Every corner has been searched."

"Searched for what?"

"A letter. My lady won't say from whom. Not that most of
this lot could read it if they found it. It's got no seal. She thinks
it might have been blown into a fire, and Maria here has riddled
ashes until she's covered with them and got nothing but blows
for her trouble. You come from the Bishop's then. Seen my
lady's nephew, Father Torquato, there? She's asking for him,
should be here to help her receive His Grace. Wonder he's not
here. Thought he must've been killed in the fighting to miss
such an opportunity—don't get a chance to suck up to a Duke
every day."

"Mmhm. He may be enjoying other opportunities. Who
knows?" Something in Sigismondo's voice made Benno sure
that his master knew very well. When Battista and the girl were
gone, Sigismondo was galvanised into sudden activity. With a

dismaying turn of speed he mounted a deserted side stair two
treads at a time and Benno had to scamper to keep up. Again
he wondered at Sigismondo's amazing ability to find his way in
places he didn't know. It was true they'd spent part of
yesterday evening at the Palazzo but, as far as Benno remembered, never penetrating corridors like the one they were now
taking at such a rate. He caught up with Sigismondo just as he
was ducking through a small doorway. The room beyond was
certainly the one he'd been heading for, as he was already
prowling round it, raising tapestries, running a hand over walls.

"You looking for the letter too then?"

Sigismondo gave him a preoccupied hum and then a grunt as
he felt round the base of the standing desk. The base was a box
between the uprights. Sigismondo opened the box and looked
through the papers in it. Then he put them all on the bed and
tapped the base of the box. Benno watched him feel along the
sides of the box with care, eyes half-shut like a man listening.
There was a sharp click and a sound between a grunt and a
laugh from Sigismondo. Benno, tidying himself up, came to
peer round his shoulder. The base of the box had sprung up,
revealing more papers.

"How did you know it would do that?" he asked.

"Sly people have sly desks." Sigismondo sorted through the
papers rapidly and selected two papers that he slid into a pocket
inside his black leather jerkin.

"That's the Princess's letter? How did he get that? Why?"

"That remains to be seen." Sigismondo was replacing the
papers, pressing the base of the box down until it clicked.
"Hand me those."

Benno picked up the papers from the bed and gave them to
him. Biondello, who had strayed out into the service corridor,
came in quickly, his tail clapped between his legs, and hid
behind the desk. Both men instantly reacted: Benno allowed
his mouth to hang open and his eyes to unfocus, Sigismondo,
hands behind his back, examined the tapestry.

"What are you doing here? Who let you in?"

It was Torquato—in a state of dilapidation that made his
indignant surprise funnier than he would have liked. One of his
eyes was already swollen and changing colour, promising to be
an ecclesiastical purple. Dirt mingled with blood on his face;

his gown was not only muddied but torn. He glanced at the desk, which, so far as Benno could tell, looked exactly as it had when they entered.

"Father, what has happened?" Sigismondo came forward, all concern. "Were you in the fight? Are you hurt?"

"I was set upon—" Torquato suddenly realised his question had been answered with another. *"What are you doing here?"*

Sigismondo inclined his head. "The Princess has been asking for you. His Grace is here."

Torquato was galvanised. He limped hurriedly to the curtain over the door to the landing, pulled it back, and shouted for a distant Tonio. When he turned there was no one in his room.

When Benno caught up with Sigismondo, he was laughing, all but silently. He stopped at a narrow window and they looked down together into the courtyard, where the Duke was gallantly handing a black-veiled Princess Corio into her black-draped litter.

Sigismondo's face changed. "We'll have to hurry, Benno. They'll be waiting with thumbscrews for Massimo."

34

Sauce for the Feast

THE MARSHAL HAD PROMISED HIS Duke three prisoners. On his return to his office across the square to bring them to the Palace for questioning—and no interference this time from that man of the Princess Corio's, he was confident—he found to his irritation that he had only two.

Stefano Delmonte had made a great deal of money in other ways than in being stupid and, although he was aware that his son had failed to inherit his brains, there was no reason why the boy should languish in the Marshal's dungeons on suspicion of being connected with the murder of Cardinal Petrucci. When word went round that the murderers were caught, were even now dangling from the Palace balcony, he hurried at once to the Marshal's office and, when he found the Marshal was at the Palace, he persuaded the Captain of his guard that the Marshal himself would applaud the release of Tomaso.

The Marshal was proud of his reputation for incorruptibility. The Captain of his guard, on the other hand, thought it perfectly proper to receive a little present for the happy task of reuniting father and son.

Tomaso, brought up from the dungeons where he had spent the worst night of his life, even though the straw had been clean, was furious with everything and everyone. He glowered at his father, broke from his embraces, and refusing all idea of being led home in prodigal style, fled and was lost to sight among the festive crowds in the square. Stefano Delmonte went home, consoled that his son was at least out of prison and that, should he need to find him, the boy would no doubt be haunting the house of that wretched courtesan.

When the Marshal had finished berating his Captain, he was

still short of a promised prisoner until he remembered the Jew.
It was true he had been told Duke Grifone habitually protected
his Jews, but he found it impossible to believe that the Duke
would not be ready to burn a Jew after all that had happened—
rather as one might burn a candle at a shrine in thanksgiving for
deliverance. He ordered the Captain to collect the Jew and
bring him to the Palace along with Iacomo and Massimo and
instructed his torturer to bring along the more portable of his
instruments. If they did not prove adequate, he could impro-
vise. The Duke, too, was said to be a man not short of ideas.

The Duke, when he arrived again at the Bishop's Palace, was
not so much short of ideas as running a trifle low in energy. He
was beginning to understand why his physician had tried to
stop him mounting his horse and had begged him to rest his
wound. Going to the Palazzo Corio to escort the Princess was
a courtesy with a higher price than he had foreseen. He hadn't
lost much blood, thanks to prompt treatment by that old crone
whom he must remember to reward, but the excitement of
overcoming a wholly unexpected enemy and surviving a
conspiracy against his life was starting to wear off. He began
to wonder about the ravages of time; wounds never used to
affect him like this. Deep in his mind he began to entertain the
idea that he was in fact no longer young.

He was not in a mood to be patient with the prisoners the
Marshal was to produce.

The Bishop had offered the hospitality of his Palace to the
Duke when he sent the news of the Cardinal's death. It had
been the Princess Corio who was to have entertained him and
his train and to provide the feast after the wedding. The disaster
of her brother's death precluded this. However, the Bishop was
not altogether happy to be host to his Marshal with prisoners
and torturers. He had already had a full, exhausting day,
hounded out at first light to exorcise a villa and a grave, both
of which had certainly needed it; returning to greet his Duke
only to be witness to appalling violence in his own Palace. He
had not yet had time to appreciate that the saints, in permitting
him to be knocked repeatedly to the floor during this, had
kindly saved him from worse. Then he had been moved, for he
was a compassionate man, at having to confess and comfort the

dying. And now, when he needed time to restore himself with prayer and siesta, the indefatigable Duke had summoned him to be present while the prisoners were questioned. He did not look forward to it. He knew himself to be lacking in the Duke's rigour towards wrongdoers. Yet after all the Devil, whose works had been so dreadfully apparent, had not been permitted to triumph. He thanked God, His Mother, and Saint Bernardina, whose relics (and the other heterogeneous items also procured by the Cardinal) had undoubtedly preserved the Duke.

Yet as he took his place in his great carved chair beside the Duke and watched the Marshal strut in, he felt a twinge of regret for Cardinal Petrucci. Although the Cardinal had not been an easy man to work with, this was the work that he enjoyed. He would have taken over everything, coped with Duke, Princess, and prisoners with the same ruthless charm; and the Bishop need have done no more than sit by, agree to everything, and twiddle his thumbs. Of course, had the Cardinal lived, none of this might have happened.

Benno and Sigismondo arrived just as the Marshal, with a flourish, presented the Duke with his Jew. "Your Grace, this creature was undoubtedly in league with Satan in this matter, for did it not take place on the eve of his accursed Sabbath?"

The Bishop made the beginning of a gesture here. As a scholar he knew, as probably no one else present did, that the Sabbath began at dusk. The information could, however, only do harm. Perhaps he ought to state that the Jew could certainly not light a fire, even under a Cardinal, during those hours.

The Duke interrupted his indecision.

"Is that all the evidence you have, Marshal? Your belief in his guilt? Was the man near the Palace when the act took place?"

"He was not *seen* there, Your Grace." To the Marshal this was clearly a proof of cunning rather than innocence. "The Cardinal had told him to expect a large sum of money. He may well have come to collect it."

"And did he?"

Not on the Sabbath, thought the Bishop.

"Why no, Your Grace. It was, I understand, left behind in the wretched rogue's haste to escape."

The Duke put a hand to his wound, which was beginning to throb. "You understand? From whom do you *understand* this?"

"From me, Your Grace. I was there." Sigismondo stepped forward, bowing with that supple back Petrucci had liked. "The Princess Corio asked me to conduct an investigation." He bowed again, towards the black-robed, black-veiled figure in the chair below the Duke's. She bent her head, acknowledging, and said, "I know him for a man who had been useful to His Grace of Rocca when his Duchess died. It is true there was a coffer of gold coins on my brother's desk that was not there before. My brother had told me nothing concerning it, and he had no secrets from me." She spoke with mournful confidence.

"And you, Jew, what have you to say?"

The Jew shrugged and spread his hands. He wore the chains at his wrists with the same dignity as the thick gold chain that lay on the fine cinnamon cloth of his tunic. "What can I say, Your Grace? I was not there. Why should I destroy someone who deigned to use my services and bring down on myself and my people a terrible retribution?"

The Duke was silent, watching him. Then he made up his mind. "Let him go. There is sense in what he says, and"—he did not add what the Bishop thought: *none whatever in what you say*—"no evidence against him. I will have no persecution of the innocent in Nemora."

That a Jew could be innocent was incomprehensible to the Marshal, but the Duke must be obeyed. Manacles were unlocked, the Jew bowed deeply and went.

"The other suspects, Marshal?" The Duke's tone intimated that they had better be more worthwhile than the last, and the Marshal, although piqued at having to release the Jew and puzzled by the Duke's views on evidence, felt confident of the success of his next offering. Iacomo was dragged forward, stumbling on his fetters and looking as if he had spent the night with rats strolling over him. He also looked confused and afraid, a most likely candidate for the balcony. The Captain of the Marshal's Guard gave the wrist chains a wrench to bring him to his knees.

"This villain, Your Grace, laid up oil and wood, by his own confession, to burn His Eminence. One of the rebels who defied Your Grace in San Sevino last year—"

"He was not there." Sigismondo's statement, quiet as it was, came to the Duke's ears and made him turn his head sharply.

"He was not there? This man's not one of the rebels?"

Sigismondo shook his head, and while the Marshal tried, with voice and gesture, to interrupt, he went on. "He is a stonemason, Your Grace, and was from home when his family fled for refuge to the tower—"

"Where His Eminence put an end to their treachery, Your Grace!" The Marshal, by shrillness—gnat against bumble-bee—managed to be heard. "He burnt the lot to a cinder!"

Iacomo contributed to the opposing sounds by banging his head on the marble and groaning. One look at the Duke's face had taken all hope of mercy from his soul, but he groaned nevertheless.

"Your Grace." Sigismondo stood, dark against one of the long windows leading to the balcony, his broad shoulders and smooth head conveying an impression of power that drew the Duke's eyes from the Marshal's attempt to speak. "This man did not in fact burn His Eminence. All that can be proved is that he had collected wood and oil for the purpose, not that he used them."

"He was in the street! The street outside His Eminence's private door! He was *seen* there!" The Marshal was panting, like a dog eager to be rewarded for bringing the game to his master's feet. "We have a witness. . . ." His voice faded as he recalled that should the Duke require this witness, he would be forced to admit to having mislaid him.

"What have *you* to say for yourself, man?" The Duke had so far commanded his temper, but there was the exasperating officiousness of the Marshal, not to mention the man's bleating voice; there was the pain of his wound; there was the stupid noise the stonemason's head intermittently made on the floor; there was even the silent attention of the man from Rocca, which he interpreted as critical. Everything made it possible that he would soon fly into one of his notorious rages.

"Speak up when His Grace asks!" The Captain gave the chains another yank, and the Marshal emphasised the importance of courtesy by booting Iacomo in the ribs. Iacomo was past speech and could only produce a spasm of coughing, followed by animal moans once more and a noticeably increased tempo of head banging. Sigismondo moved, dark against the window.

"If Your Grace permits, I will show him the fate that shall be his if he does not speak." He gestured towards the balcony outside.

The Captain hauled Iacomo to his feet, and Sigismondo took the chains and his shoulder to lead him to the window. A page opened it, and Iacomo was propelled onto the balcony, struggling with ineffectual vigour because he thought he was to be thrown over it at once. The spectators in the square had thinned out a little, but some who saw the men on the balcony set up a cheer, anticipating a tardy addition to the display.

Sigismondo's voice in his ear penetrated Iacomo's clouded mind. "Look well. Do you see any you have seen before?" Iacomo sensed no hostility in the man who held him, even when a hand on his neck made him lean and look down, so he did his best to carry out what was wanted. The faces slowly turning some way below were a good bit the worse for the macédoine applied by the crowd, and their original expressions had not been serene; moreover the angle was difficult so that he was bent far over, and he thought with terror of soon joining them there. As he peered, however, his attention fixed, and he pointed. "That one! He was there. I swear it was him in the street last night. Ugly bastard, I thought, when he turned in the moonlight."

Sigismondo leant too. They contemplated the twisted features of Achille Malvezzi, now wearing rotten egg instead of the doctor's cap. Sigismondo straightened up and drew Iacomo with him. "Where were you that he didn't see you?" If Malvezzi had seen Iacomo, he would have spared him all this suffering in one fast skilful movement. Witnesses to his presence outside the private stair would be the last thing he wanted.

"I shinned up some scaffolding when I heard people coming and kept still. After the girls had gone, and that swanky bastard in the sable cloak had taken himself off, I was going to get down; then the others came." He nodded at Malvezzi's heel. "They didn't see me. People don't look upwards." Iacomo spoke with the conviction of a stonemason who has seen some sights in his time.

"There were others then. Are they here?"

Iacomo leant to peer again, the effect on his stomach visible in his face. "Can't tell. Really I can't. That one turned round into the moonlight, he was sort of checking on the one in the cloak, the one that was all cloaked up as if he wanted to hide his face." The chains rang as Iacomo mimed the sweep of cloak. "I thought he'd heard me. He swung round a bit and looked my way and didn't move for a minute—like he was listening hard. I didn't dare move till he moved." Someone in the crowd took aim, and Sigismondo, humming, drew Iacomo away and back into the room where the Duke waited impatiently. The Bishop had been discussing the arrangements for a Mass of thanksgiving for the preservation of the Duke and the duchy next day, and the Princess made a sudden tense movement under her veils, as if to remind them that she would not be giving thanks for her loss. The Duke was not attending and fervently wished the Cardinal had been alive. With Petrucci, everything had run smoothly, all problems had been taken care of; and here was this stonemason villain being brought in again, and the torture might begin at any moment.

"Well? Does he have anything to say?" The Duke's question was savage. His wound prevented him from thinking clearly, and he could not now remember why he had let the man from Rocca take the wretched stonemason onto the balcony. What was clear, however, was the effect.

"Mercy, Your Grace! Mercy!" Iacomo was grovelling again. "I did not burn the Cardinal, I swear it by God and His holy angels, I swear it by the relics of Saint Bernardina, take me to the relics and—"

"Enough!" The crack of the Duke's voice made Benno jump, and he noticed he wasn't the only one. "Death is my sentence upon you. You may not have burnt His Eminence, *but you meant to*. Intent is the criterion, isn't it, Bishop? Let him be whipped to death and strung up like the rest. He wastes our time."

The Marshal stepped forward, delighted at this proof that his arrest was justified and they were at last getting somewhere. It took two of his guards to haul Iacomo to his feet and keep him there as he shouted and struggled. Sigismondo flung an arm round Iacomo's shoulders, in this one movement stopping his struggles and jovially cuddling him.

"A suggestion, Your Grace? At the feast tonight in honour of Lady Minerva's betrothal, would not this whipping serve as a sauce?"

35

"Here, I Give the Orders"

THE PRINCESS WAS ON HER FEET, her veils swirling. "Let him *burn!* Let him burn as my brother burnt!"

Perhaps the Duke saw this as a cliché. He demurred, and Sigismondo, clapping Iacomo's cheek fondly, as an ogre might treat his dinner, urged: "Princess, revenge is a dish to be savoured above all others. Burn a man, he suffocates from the smoke—pouf, it's all over. Whip him to death like a pig, and it will make your meat tenderer too."

Benno gulped, the Princess paused, and the Duke decided.

"Tonight, at the feast. He shall dine, for the first and last time in his life, with a Duke." Grifone's sense of humour had been deplored by his tutors, who felt that he derived an unnatural enjoyment from those tragic catastrophes in the classics meant not to entertain but to purge the mind. "Eh, Bishop? Shall he provide our music tonight?"

The Duke's spirits were rising as the Bishop's sank. He had to make an acquiescent sound, but he thought of the dinner his cooks had slaved over ruined—for him at least—by the screams of this poor man. The only civilised accompaniment to dinner was the music of a small orchestra such as he had got together over the years; expert players on a cither, a krummhorn, a viola da gamba—all to be wasted tonight. He had hoped that the Princess, in such deep mourning, would not be at the feast, but now it seemed as if she would be present to see, and hear, her brother's murderer—surely only would-be murderer?—tortured at it. He feared that he himself ought to have put in a plea for mercy, but against the combined wills of the Duke and the Princess it would have been even more ineffective than his suggestions usually were. He put up a quick internal prayer for the Duke's speedy departure from Colleverde and followed it with another for the quick exit of the shaven-headed foreigner who came up with such repulsive ideas.

"Is that the last, Marshal?" The Duke was nursing his arm now and frowning, but the Marshal was not a man sensitive to atmosphere. He threw out his chest and smiled like one proud to have saved the best for last. His Captain, at a sign, had gone to the door to fetch in the last prisoner.

"Your Grace, the Lord Bishop will have told you whence all this devil-work has come—Satan has had his home outside our city all this while and comes to try to overthrow Your Grace and foil our blessed Saint!" The Marshal paused for effect and then flung out an arm as the prisoner was dragged in and forced to his knees in front of the Duke. "The man from Fontecasta, Your Grace! In league with the Devil he came to Colleverde last night to burn His Eminence lest he discover the plot against Your Grace's life. See!" The Marshal bent and, with a clash of chains, held up the prisoner's arm. "Burns! The mark of his evil master's flames upon him!"

Benno watched in horror. He had to admit that, begrimed from his night in the dungeons, his small eyes reddened and glaring, his chin outthrust, Massimo made a very passable demon.

"Blessed Saint Bernardina protect us!" The Bishop, signing himself, leant forward to stare at Massimo. "This is the man whose grave I caused to be uncovered at Fontecasta only this morning—but how horribly young he has grown!"

"The Undead!" The Marshal was bobbing in his excitement now. "*He has fed on blood.* The Devil is here in Colleverde."

The Bishop, who had a habit of looking mildly worried, now looked distraught. His men had put a stake through the body at Fontecasta; he had exorcised its spirit. It was not possible that this terrible appearance should exist.

The Duke, on the other hand, was merely thoughtful. A month ago, and against his son's wishes, he had dismissed his astrologer for constantly making melancholy forecasts about malign influences and, in particular, a singular, sinister conjunction of planets from which the Duke could be saved only by a man from the East. Montenero lay to the East, and at such times as Grifone wondered if the astrologer might be correct, he had consoled himself with the thought that Prince Livio might be his salvation.

Prince Livio having conspicuously tried to be the opposite, the Duke was beginning to wonder about this fate. Prince Livio's astrologer had insisted on the betrothal's being brought forward to Saturday if the Prince were to avoid trouble.

The Duke grinned. The betrothal had not taken place today despite all the Prince's plans, and the Prince himself was at this moment slung across a horse in as bad trouble as anyone could get: dead and without absolution. Yet, if the Duke's own astrologer had been right as to the danger, so might he be about other matters. He beckoned to Sigismondo. "Where do you come from?"

"Your Grace?"

"Where were you born?"

The obvious irrelevance of the question in the matter of the demon from Fontecasta did not appear to disturb the man questioned. The Duke found this restful. Sigismondo looked merely attentive. "I was told, Your Grace, that I was born in Muscovy but"—he smiled of a sudden—"although I was there at the time, I can't be sure."

Benno's face of amiable idiocy was so habitual that it did not alter, although Sigismondo had told him he was born in Byzantium and told the Duke of Rocca that Spain was the lucky place. Duke Grifone, unaccustomed to frivolity in answers given to him, was very ready to overlook it now, for Muscovy was certainly to the East. This man, according to prediction, should know what to do. He gestured towards Massimo. "What is to become of him?"

Sigismondo surveyed Massimo, crouched and glowering, with a disparaging hum. "With all respect to my lord Bishop and his Marshal, this seems no demon. As I've told the Marshal, I worked for a short time at Fontecasta, and I know the man."

"But this morning—in the grave?" The amethyst on the Bishop's finger winked as it trembled. "The very same man, with white hair and blood on his lips!"

"His father, my lord, slain by Achille Malvezzi early this morning." Massimo sighed and drooped his head.

Grifone leant forward. "Malvezzi? The brigand who tried to kill me? What did he want at this Fontecasta?"

Sigismondo's hum was prolonged. "Your Grace remembers the magician Antonello whom His Eminence had burnt? For whom Malvezzi was taking revenge? No doubt Malvezzi had heard of the death of the Lord Giraldi and wanted some part of the corpse"—a rapid signing of the Cross was made by everyone present at this horrible suggestion—"for a spell, which Antonello may have taught him, to use against Your Grace. I have learnt that this man's father, when they killed him, was trying to protect the Lord Giraldi's grave against just such desecration."

Benno, like the Bishop, was devoutly praying. His prayer, however, was that the Duke would not enquire at all closely into the death, or indeed the life, of the Lord Giraldi or where his body in fact was. He wondered about Angelo at this moment and added a corollary to his prayer: Don't let Angelo make the Lord Mirandola draw cards for any of Duke Grifone's men that are out around town. If anyone did recognise the blind lord, even Sigismondo might have more explaining than he could cope with, and the beautiful Angelo could have told his last fortune.

"Giraldi?" The Duke's frown was back.

At his side the Princess stirred impatiently and burst out: "All this, Your Grace, is beside the point. This creature has the mark of fire on him, the Marshal believes he came to burn my brother. Let him be tortured until we hear the truth."

Before Sigismondo could speak, the Duke swung round at her. "Madam, here, *I* give the orders and *my* justice is done."

He turned swiftly back to Sigismondo and to Massimo, crouched on his heels and staring with the look of some gargoyle hoping for it to rain mercy. "You tell me that this man is innocent, that he came by that burn by other means?"

"There must be many of Your Grace's subjects at this moment burnt by candles, torches, braziers, and a thousand household hazards." Sigismondo's tone dismissed the evidence. "We have the villains already who dared to murder His Eminence," he nodded towards the balcony, "gone to a higher judgement."

"Very well." The Duke rose, holding his arm again. "Let him

go free," he said to the disappointed Marshal; and to a page: "Bring my physician. . . . Madam, we'll meet at supper. My lord Bishop, it would be fitting that His Eminence's Requiem Mass be held tomorrow also. Let the best scholar in your household make the oration, one who can speak with style. There must be full tribute paid to my most faithful counsellor." He paused and stared at Sigismondo. "And you. I wish to see you also at the supper tonight. You shall have your reward."

The Bishop had not been at all offended at the Duke's suggesting he find an orator and not speak the eulogy himself. He was a good classical scholar but not fond of making speeches at any time. He was aware that his sermons lacked style. His Eminence's nephew, Father Torquato, would be the one. It was a generous gesture to a quite minor cleric and a compliment to the Princess. She would need quite a bit of soothing, not only for her terrible loss but also for the public snub given by the Duke today: "Here, *I* give the orders." The Bishop really didn't know when he'd enjoyed himself more.

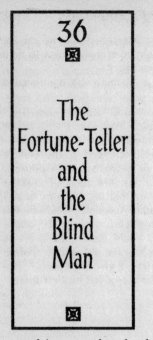

36

The Fortune-Teller and the Blind Man

MINERVA WAS LYING ON A BED IN the Bishop's Palace in a room that had been prepared in a hurry by the Bishop's major-domo. The Bishop, unlike many other ecclesiastics, did not keep a mistress either openly or secretly. The major-domo had sent out for pincushions, decorated hand mirrors, scented oils, and other things he felt suitable for a guest who, it appeared, was destined to become their Duchess.

This was what Minerva could not believe. Had she really come so far—been rescued by Sigismondo from what, now that she had seen the fight today, she was positive would have been certain death at the hands of her erstwhile father? Had she survived that raid on Fontecasta by night, done heroic deeds that very day, saved Astorre, only to be claimed by *his* terrible father? She was still startled by the rage she had felt at Prince Livio when she saw him threatening not only Duke Grifone's life but her whole future.

She lay on the bed, staring at the painted ceiling on which a mature Danaë opened her legs to a shower of gold with a very complacent expression. Minerva kicked her feet. Her ladies-in-waiting, three dim girls she used to terrorise—was it only a week ago?—sat in the window sipping wine and darting nervous glances at the figure on the bed. Beside Minerva, on a table inlaid with miello, was a silver-gilt dish of dried apricots and a cup of wine. She had not touched them.

What on earth could she do? It hadn't taken her a moment to decide that she could not tell the Duke she'd rather not marry him, she preferred his son. All the appalling stories she had heard about Duke Grifone chose this hour to come back to her. His wife, said Rumour, had been poisoned. He also, Rumour added, whipped his mistresses, had had one of them strangled with her own braids. He smiled like a wolf. He was old, at least forty. And Astorre, the handsome Astorre whose life she had certainly saved with a strategic inkpot, was she never to lie in his arms? Was she to be his *stepmother?*

She made a violent grimace at Danaë, who continued to smirk at the invasive gold.

Of course, some people might think she was lucky. Duchess of Nemora meant showers of gold all right. Grifone might die at any time, she had heard that; but then anyone might die at any time even if they were in much better health than the Duke—today was proof of that! She tensed at the memory of the blood and screams such a short time ago; but even if Grifone did die, she could never marry Astorre if she had married his father. No pope would grant a dispensation for *that*, no matter how much money she paid.

She beat a tattoo with the heels of her satin slippers on the brocade bedcover. The ladies-in-waiting started but decided against coming to ask her if she wanted anything.

She wanted Sigismondo. He had got her out of one mess, and he could get her out of this one. She had begun to have a confidence very like Benno's in Sigismondo's ability to rescue a situation. She refused to think of the unlikelihood of even Sigismondo telling Duke Grifone not to marry someone he had decided to marry; he would certainly find a way.

Having decided this, she felt much better. She hoped Astorre would complain at his father's plan. She could place little trust in his protests' power to move his father, but it would be humiliating if he tamely acquiesced. . . . She put her head on one side and looked Danaë over. Her own figure was much better than that. All those rolls of flesh . . . ugh! She sat up, drank most of the wine at one draught, and ate a dried apricot. Her ladies, who had been speculating on the unlucky fact that they were Montenerans in a city where Montenerans would obviously be far from popular, jumped up and hurried to see if they could ingratiate themselves in some way. They would have some protection, at least, if the Lady Minerva really became Duchess of Nemora.

Some miles away, on the banks of the river border of the two countries, Astorre had successfully exhibited the body of Prince Livio to the good-sized band of mercenaries waiting for the hour to race towards Colleverde. Their leader, initially inclined to challenge the authority of the young man barring his way, had become open to conviction when the man who was to have paid him handsomely for the burning and looting looked at him upside down from over the saddle.

The deal was clinched when the young lord produced a useful amount of retainer in gold, slung in a coffer on muleback. They discussed the new contract to be drawn up, for the one under which they were here had automatically been cancelled by the death of the signatory on one side, Prince Livio.

The mercenary leader saluted Astorre and, with only a few regretful glances towards the unburnt villages and the even more inviting towers of Colleverde, which were to have been theirs to subdue, took his band back across the border to make their encampment and await word from the Duke.

Astorre turned back towards Colleverde. He believed his father would be pleased with him, and he was looking forward to seeing the Lady Minerva again. Having left before the Duke had questioned Sigismondo, he had no idea that he had already lost his bride.

A sudden doubt made Astorre frown, giving him, to the Captain of the Duke's Guard riding at his side, a disturbing resemblance to his father. It had occurred to him that the political situation wasn't in the least straightforward: Would his father still be eager for him to marry the daughter of the man who had done his best to kill them both and take the duchy? A pain nearly physical came to him with the thought of not marrying her—such beauty! He had been transfixed when with that flying gesture she threw back her veil—such courage! She had appeared when that brute in the fight was pressing him hard, like his guardian angel shining in silver. Perhaps she had saved his life. . . . He was reluctant to admit, even to himself, that the brute had been getting the better of him, but he had become too much aware of having a young man's strength against a heavy fighting arm—but no matter. She had looked wonderful! What would such a girl be like in the embraces of love!

The Captain, glancing again at Astorre, thought that when he smiled he did not at all resemble his father.

† † †

In the Bishop's kitchens, cooks were putting the final touches to the banquet. Wild boar had been parboiled, seasoned with pepper, nutmeg, cloves, and ginger and then baked in a pastry coffin. There was hashed hare in broth and wine, and roasted hare covered with finely grated manchet bread and cinnamon. Rissoles of dried fruit and nuts had been dipped in batter, threaded together, and wound round spits, a favourite of the Bishop's. He was fond of pottage, too, of fruit and almond milk and, now that Lent was over, of meat.

In honour of the occasion, of the Duke's victory and the arrival of the relics, there was a spectacular piece to be carried in at the end: a subtlety of translucent marchpane, pistachio nuts pounded with expensive amounts of sugar, and moulded into a representation of Colleverde Cathedral, every pinnacle faithfully reproduced, and, kneeling on the steps before the open doors, two figures. These were, originally, the Duke and the Cardinal, but it took only a skilful compression to change the Cardinal's hat into the Bishop's mitre. There had been a consultation, which degenerated into acrimony, imprecation, and the producing of knives, as to whether to include the bridal couple, but the major-domo, intervening only just in time, had ruled that since the Duke was visiting Colleverde as much for the relics as for the wedding, they could be omitted; and now that it was rumoured that the Duke himself intended marrying, the chief confectioner congratulated himself on not having put in extra figures, the removal of which might have damaged the structure.

At the Palazzo Corio, the search for the missing letter was continuing, after the Princess had vented some of her suppressed rage at Grifone's rebuke on her nephew, for not having been there to receive the Duke earlier. He, furious for a number of complicated reasons, took his own reprimand with ill grace and a Latin quotation, which his aunt did not catch, and retired to his chamber, sending to the kitchen for more raw meat to put on his rapidly swelling eye.

Not only the appearance of his face but also, by bad luck, his clothes, which the Princess had observed being carried away for cleansing, attracted a further visit for another series of comments from his aunt, who gave her full opinion of clerics

who got into street brawls without regard for their cloth or, in
this case, for the name of the family so recently bereaved. His
inability to be discreet, she had added, was one of the reasons
his uncle had not given him the advancement he was always
whining for. As she left she remarked that his room had an
unpleasant smell.

Because she went off to range all over the house, having
hearth ash sifted again, turning out drawers in desks and
boxing ears as she went, Torquato set himself to compose a
stiff note of complaint to the *maestro della strada* about the
filthiness of the street where he had fallen; he judged it wise
not to look again at the place where he had hidden his aunt's
letter, lest she should come in. It was perfectly safe where it
was.

As the hooves of Astorre's band clattered over the stones of
Colleverde, the welcoming arches were being dismantled, the
machinery Fortune had so distrusted reduced to its component
parts under the eye of the Florentine in charge.

Astorre, coming into the Cathedral square and approaching
the Bishop's Palace, had his attention caught by a flashing in
the evening sunlight. He sent a groom to enquire and waited
at the door of the Palace, smelling the food cooking in stores
and shops, realising that he was hungry. He did not notice that
he was being watched by folk in the Square. The groom told
him that the crowd was around a fortune-teller juggling with
knives who used a blind man to draw the cards and was said to
have foretold all that had happened that day. Astorre had a
sudden hope. He had not been at ease since his father dismissed
the court astrologer who had forecast trouble for the future—
exactly such trouble, Astorre thought, as they had just been
through. If he was going to marry the Lady Minerva, what
better present could he offer than happy prophecies for their
life together? His father would be glad, too, for he must now
see the truth of what had been foretold.

"Bring them to the Palace. The fortune-teller and the blind
man."

His father was fond of the weird. He would be bound to like
the blind man.

37

Witchcraft Abroad in the Palace!

When the Duke had retired with his physician, word was sent round the Palace that there must be quiet to allow him to rest. The Bishop's major-domo was therefore anxious to trace and stifle the source of a noise that broke out downstairs.

He had no way of knowing that the old crone he found hitting and cuffing one of his servants was the one who had done the Duke such signal service earlier in the day. The servant, who had had his shins kicked, his ears pulled, and his livery torn, was apprehensive as well as indignant. He had found her fingering the brocade hangings, laying her dirty hands on the very things that were to adorn the canopy of the Duke's chair at the feast. He was only trying to do his duty in throwing her out, but he was very much afraid that she was one of the Devil's manifestations here in Colleverde.

She was bundled in black like all old women, but under a crooked cap her white hair was in elflocks, her eyes were fierce—and listen to her! Those must be spells. You couldn't understand a word, and that had to mean they were evil.

"Old woman, where are you from? How did you come to be here?"

The major-domo knew it was a priority to set the servants' minds at rest. The banqueting hall was only half ready, and all work in this room below it had stopped. They were staring and crossing themselves and all set, he could see, to bolt and bring every preparation to a stop with rumours of witchcraft in the Palace. The crone glared at him as if she were deaf. With those tanned, ruddy cheeks she would probably turn out to be some poor countrywoman come into town to see the procession and the relics. She must have come gawping into the Palace in the dreadful confusion of the past few hours and now couldn't find her way out. He raised his voice to penetrate her ears and what was likely to be a simple mind. "Where do you come from, woman?"

Unexpectedly, she cackled. "*Fontecasta!* That's where I come from!"

In an instant the servants became like a pack of hens with a fox among them. Squealing and shrieking, they scattered out of the room—the last one jammed in the doorway with a bucket and shouting Hail Marys till she exploded into the corridor. Even the major-domo, left alone with the creature, muttered a prayer. He was still telling himself that she was a cracked old peasant who just happened to come from Fontecasta hamlet near that accursed villa, but it was best to be sure of heavenly protection. She seemed to ignore the effect she produced; almost as if she might be used to it. She had bundled off suddenly to the window that looked out into the courtyard. Being on the ground floor it had bars and night shutters, not glass; she peered out as though something had caught her eye. He followed her, debating on whether it was safe to lay a hand on her shoulder. He was going to have to do the job of throwing her out himself, degrading but necessary if he were to get the staff calmed down in time and the banquet ready. The garlands were not nearly finished, the canopy not hung.

"Massimo! *Massimo!* Over here!" The screech was like a gull's cry, hurting his ears. His hands, stretched to grab her, retreated to hold his head. Why was there never a guard when you needed one, when they were always cluttering up rooms you needed to work in?

"MASSIMO! Here!"

Hands pressed to his ears, the major-domo stared in shock. A horrible face, under fuzzy hair all on end, a face streaked with dirt, jaw thrust out, was pressed to the bars as though the small reddened eyes sought something within the room.

The major-domo himself rapidly launched into a decade of Hail Marys. The face vanished, and the major-domo stopped praying and addressed himself anew to the task of evicting the old woman—witch, whatever—into the courtyard where she could commune with her familiar for all he cared. It was imperative to get the servants back, the garlands finished and up, the curtains hung. He gritted his teeth and extended a hand to her shoulder again, but it was not there. She had gathered up her skirts and was making for the door.

He followed cautiously, hoping to see her off the premises so that he could get the servants back, when the door ahead of her burst open, and the frightful face appeared. It belonged to a thickset fellow in dirty, torn clothes who ran limping to meet the crone.

"Sybilla! Where's the master?"

The master! This wasn't the Devil himself, of course not; there was another . . .

"Massimo!"

The next person through the door was the half-wit. Here the major-domo was on surer ground. Benno's general appearance made everyone feel instinctively that he should be displaced, at once, from wherever he was. The major-domo pointed at the door with his wand.

"Out! Out, all of you!" he cried. At this juncture he was passed, to his immense relief, by the Captain of the Duke's Guard. Lord Astorre must have returned from the border, and here was a saviour of the situation. Luckily, the Captain grasped the urgency at once. He turned to wave on the guards in the Duke's livery and gestured at the old woman, the sturdy man, and the half-wit, still with their heads together.

Pikes can be persuasive. The major-domo smiled as the guards prodded the invasive three, but they, least of all, expected the next event. The crone ducked under a pike and, with both fists together, slung a professional punch into the stomach of the pike's owner. As he doubled up, she seized his pike and swung it sideways, swivelling, and knocked another guard into the Captain himself, who went down on all fours as if searching the marble for cracks. The demon called Massimo delivered a kick to the Captain's rump that sent him sprawling on the major-domo's feet. The half-wit had sat down against the wall, and his chest heaved strangely.

"Can I help?"

It was the man from Rocca, or Muscovy, or the back of beyond, who had been investigating the Cardinal's death and whose advice the Duke himself had asked. He had the disturbing appearance of being a soldier by build and a priest by his shaven head, but he was oddly comforting. The major-domo was starting to explain when a half-seen sudden movement made him turn his head and look at the half-wit: to his horror he saw the creature's chest burst open and a dog's head pop out. A familiar! Mother of God, these *are* devils.

He clutched the arm of the man from Rocca. "She's from *Fontecasta!*"

"So am I and can vouch for them all. The Bishop exorcised the place. The old woman fought on the Duke's side this morning; he plans to reward her well—"

The Captain had risen and was glaring about him to find who had kicked him. Sybilla thrust Massimo aside and fisted her two hands together, ready for another punch. But the Captain had seen the first one, grabbed her locked fists, pulled her off balance, and dumped her on the floor. A guard with his pike at Massimo's throat kept him quiet. The Captain was not to be humiliated before his men by a vicious old woman, and he cuffed her about the head.

"Witch!"

She was not daunted, shrieking, *"Canalla! Dologone! Skatapedo!"*

The man from Rocca was suddenly between them, helping the old woman to her feet; the Captain's last slap fell on muscle that hurt his hand. He remembered this man as wonderfully conspicuous in the fighting with Prince Livio's men. Now he was helping to dust down the hag's skirts and talking to her in a foreign language, a precise, clipped, but flowing language, and she stared, shrieked again—"Oréa!"—and flung her arms round his neck.

The major-domo plucked urgently at the Captain's sleeve. "She's in favour with the Duke. He'll be furious if she is harmed."

The Captain, through his teeth, ordered his men to ground arms. He and the major-domo stood watching while the old woman kissed the man from Rocca on the nose, the cheeks, the mouth, while she held his face by the ears. If the stranger had authority and the ear of the Duke and was known to these three, he could deal with them. The Captain, having only just got back from escorting Lord Astorre to the border and back, was tired and thirsty, and he would be on duty this evening again.

The major-domo had been greatly reassured to perceive everyone concerned was, after all, human, and to be reminded that Fontecasta had been properly exorcised by the Bishop himself. Now, he must round up the servants, remind them of the same thing, and make them, at all costs, *hurry*.

So it was that Sigismondo, Sybilla, Benno, and Massimo found themselves alone, with Biondello circling them in satisfaction that danger was past. Sybilla, her arm tucked under Sigismondo's and her hand enclosed in his, raised her face to him and chattered, not in her usual gibberish, so far as they could tell, but in that same tongue full of foreign sounds that he had spoken to her. The words poured out of her as though they had been dammed up for half a lifetime, and Sigismondo did no more than insert an interrogative or two into the cascade. It is true that one of her answers sent his eyebrows up. He drew her to the window and a long bench there, and they sat while she, gesturing with her free hand, patting his that held hers, pinching his cheek, and beaming continually, still talked.

Massimo looked abruptly at Benno. "The master? He's not with him?"

This being suddenly obvious, he ran to Sigismondo. "Where's the master? Is he dead?" He seized Sigismondo's free hand, brought his face to within an inch and, either begging or threatening, demanded: "*Where is he?* Is he in danger?"

Sigismondo's hum was prolonged. "Mm, mm, mm, mm, I've no doubt he is. We *all* are. He's in the city, Massimo, in very good hands."

"But the Duke's men are in town! Suppose he's recognized?"

"Who'd believe what they saw? A man who fed the wolves eight years ago? *That's* a miracle for Saint Bernardina. There are blind men in plenty around the city; we'd be unlucky indeed if he got picked out."

Unlucky indeed, on the other side of the Palace, the fortune-teller and the blind man——fetched by order of the Lord Astorre——were put into the guardroom, where they were enthusiastically welcomed, to pass the time until the Duke sent for them.

38

The Best Gift a Man Can Have

EVERYTHING WAS READY FOR THE feast. The Duke, who had refused to be bled as his physician wished, was feeling more himself after his siesta. His Captain reported the success of his mission with the Lord Astorre, his wound hardly throbbed at all, and he was invigorated by contemplation of the dangers he had overcome and the pleasures yet to be enjoyed. He sent two of his pages to carry a little coffer of ivory carved with cupids and blue velvet lined to the Lady Minerva. In it she found a collar of pearl with a pendent ruby heart, which she would have liked very much if it had come from Astorre. She guessed it was originally intended as a gift from a father-in-law, so she felt entitled to have her ladies clasp it round her throat. Her speech of thanks to be conveyed to the Duke was formal and noncommittal but as prettily phrased as her upbringing ensured.

Prince Livio had not wasted space on bridal gear, but the silver brocade lent by Polissena had only a spot or two of blood on the hem, which she set the palace maids to clean off. She hoped it wasn't Prince Livio's blood and that if it were, cleansing was a symbolic act. She wondered how she would have felt about him if she had been close to him; if she had ever talked to him as she had talked to the Lord Mirandola; if he had not been the remote, seldom-seen, on occasion furiously affectionate personage he was. The three ladies were whispering together again. The silly creatures had not lived through what she had lived through this last week. She was quite sorry for one of them, Louisa Montalba, whom Prince Livio had forced to impersonate her and who very likely would have a terror, for some time, of letting her face be seen.

Minerva was perfectly happy with her own face. Looking at it in the silver hand mirror she observed the colour in her cheeks, the sparkle in her eyes, and thought that fighting suited her. The pearl necklet looked remarkably well, but the ruby heart reminded her of the balas ruby in Duke Grifone's cap and the bleak face beneath those white curls. Suppose Sigismondo couldn't think of a way to stop the Duke from marrying her. . . . She frowned, resolutely put the idea from her, and ordered Louisa to take some of the hair out of the braids she was plaiting for her and arrange it in ringlets before her ears. Astorre was bound to be at the feast.

Astorre had only a short time to strip off the clothes soiled by blood, sweat, and dust that he had worn since morning, during the fight, and on his journey to the border. They were very fine clothes of silver velvet with sleeves of gold brocade over silk, with which he had hoped to impress his bride, but she could hardly have seen them. He had, of course, brought many more suits of fine clothes for the anticipated feasts and ceremonial appearances. His servants had unpacked the trunks and laid out a choice for him to decide upon.

They had also spent the time quarrelling among themselves as to who should tell him that he had lost his bride to his father. The scripter was already at work on the new marriage contract. They hoped someone would tell him before he arrived, but they knew it was unrealistic.

As far as Colleverde was concerned, the marriage was still on. The cast had changed, that was all. With any luck the fountains in the Cathedral square would run wine on the day of the wedding—a miracle dukes could work better than saints, in most people's experience. Some women expressed pity for the bride at not getting the handsome young lord, but, as others pointed out, she would be Duchess a lot sooner than she could have hoped.

Who was going to tell the Lord Astorre? He chose the scarlet velvet with silver scroll embroidery and silver damask sleeves, and, as they helped to dress him, they were all thinking he had chosen it to go with a certain dress of silver brocade.

The one person in the Palace not engaged in preparation for the feast could be excused on grounds of health: Cardinal

Petrucci lay in state in the Bishop's private chapel. The Duke had commanded a Requiem Mass the next day in the Cathedral, which he and all the dignitaries of Colleverde would attend. Today, already dressed in black velvet slashed with gold damask, he knelt in the chapel's chill gloom beside the catafalque. The smell of damp stone, resinous incense, and candlewax was underlaid by a fugitive but stomach-turning smell that rosemary and scented oils seemed to emphasise rather than hide. The Duke contemplated the pale face with its dark patches of scorching and the mercifully gloved hands crossed on the cape of scarlet watered silk.

What secrets had Petrucci carried to the grave? At least one secret was known: the identity of his murderers. Perhaps from somewhere he looked down on them hanging by their heels. It crossed the Duke's mind that, had his own wound been mortal, he might have died like Petrucci without absolution—unless the Bishop had been very quick. He did not doubt that Petrucci's murderers had taken this into account in their plans so that their vengeance might pursue him beyond this world.

"Father. What's this I hear?"

The fierce voice was muted because of where they were, an effect the Duke appreciated. He had been waiting for this, and he crossed himself and rose. Astorre, magnificent in scarlet and silver in the candlelit gloom, was furious, and the Duke thought fondly that he resembled his mother, with whom there had been so many satisfying quarrels. "What do you hear, my son?"

"That *you* intend marrying the Lady Minerva."

The Duke drew his son to the foot of the catafalque and pointed. "Petrucci, while he was alive, would have advised me what to do. I've been praying for guidance. And I think I have the answer."

Astorre could scarcely subdue his voice. "You *shall* not take her from me, sir! I love her!"

The Duke opened his dark eyes at the inadequacy of the reason, but he smiled, patted the brocade sleeve, and said: "You are seduced, as I was when I knew the whole of it, by her courage. She will breed you good sons to hold Nemora against our enemies."

Astorre's face was amusing to watch. "Then you—"

"I propose to see you betrothed tonight and bedded with the

lady." He turned from the catafalque and Astorre followed close at his side. "My physician tells me that I cannot expect to live forever, my confessor that I should prepare for death at all times. The man from Rocca, from Muscovy, tells me that he believes the omens for Montenero—which mourns a hopeful young prince—are for youth." Grifone's predatory grin returned. He paused to look down at Astorre, who had seized his hand and knelt to kiss it.

"Montenero, my son, will more gladly accept you as its Prince than it would me. When you marry the Lady Minerva," he continued briskly, "you'll need to fight for your inheritance in one way and another. You shall ride to Montenero tomorrow with your wife, at the head of the condotta that Prince Livio meant to use against us—I have drafted their contract and send it to them for their approval tonight—before the leading citizens of that headless State have time to decide what they should do. My spies have long told me that the Prince did not command the allegiance of all the great families there; the Lord Eugenio's family for one must be disaffected by his impromptu execution, and the Vanozzi have been in my pay for years. You should not, claiming in the Lady Minerva's right, have too much trouble in establishing yourself." He raised his son and gave him a fierce one-armed embrace. "Come. We must honour Bishop Taddeo's feast. What you need," he added, half to himself, as they passed from the chill air of the chapel, "is a good adviser, an experienced counsellor, another Petrucci, to help you govern in Montenero."

The group of courtiers, approaching, bowing, were fascinated that the Duke and his son seemed on excellent terms. What in the world could have consoled the Lord Astorre for the humiliating loss of his bride? One of the more frivolous among them speculated on a possible consolation the considerable wealth of the Princess Corio, although the unavoidable addition of her person might prove daunting for even their Duke's son.

"Congratulations, Your Grace," someone dared, followed by general murmurs of congratulation. They took refuge in ambiguity as to whether they congratulated him on his escape from death or on his rumoured marriage.

They had not been able to assist their Duke in the struggle,

as Prince Livio's insistence on a private ceremony on account
of mourning had led to their exclusion in the Bishop's garden.
They had heard fighting and found themselves shut out, unable
to get into the house until one of the Cardinal's Guard unbarred
the door when all was over.

Their good wishes, however, reminded Astorre of the
present surprise he had arranged for his father. By now his men
would have brought the fortune-teller, and finding out the
immediate future's luck had become of prime importance.

The major-domo was making a deep obeisance before them,
silver-topped wand in hand. It was not every day he had the
honour of telling a duke that his dinner was ready, nor was it
to be his immediate lot. The Lord Astorre had sent a page
scampering off urgently, and he was speaking to the Duke, so
the major-domo had to wait. He hoped desperately that the
dinner would prove as accommodating. Great folk never failed
to be annoyed when their own delays spoiled a perfect dish.

"Excellent! Where is this pair?" The Duke had some time
ago come to the conclusion that he had been mistaken in his
treatment of the astrologer, no matter how lugubrious the
fellow was, and he had never so much needed to know what the
stars' influences were as now. He was seizing the chance of
adding Montenero to his duchy, and he wanted to know, too, if
this marriage of his son's, this alliance with hostile blood, was
favourably aspected. "Bring them here. He shall read the cards
at once!"

"He has a blind assistant, sir, who draws the cards for him.
They are said to have foretold all that happened today."

"A pity the Prince didn't hear them."

Everyone laughed dutifully and made way for the returning
page, who ushered in a young man in faded yellow and blue
clothes who in turn led by the hand a tall man in an ancient
ragged cotta and a straw hat. The hat was snatched from his
head by a scandalised courtier as he came into the Duke's
presence. In the speculative silence the young man bowed,
pulling on the hand he held so that the blind man bent too; and
as they straightened the Duke stared, then strode forward,
taking the blind man by the shoulders and turning him towards
the light.

"God's bones! I don't believe it!" The handsome, sightless

face sustained his gaze. There was even the suspicion of a melancholy smile. *"Mirandola!"* The Duke shook the man, almost in affection. "So you didn't attend the wolves' banquet after all! But you shall attend mine. If you've come to tell my fortune, I can tell yours first: You have plenty left to lose besides your eyes. Yes, you shall dine with me for the last time tonight, Mirandola, and see—oh no, you shall *hear*—the punishment of one who plotted Petrucci's death as you did mine."

The Duke, in high spirits, turned to his son and embraced him again. "My thanks, Astorre my son, for bringing me the best gift a man can have—*his enemy!*"

39

⬕

Not to Be Disturbed

⬕

TRUMPETS ANNOUNCED THE DUKE'S arrival at the feast, and the company bent and dipped in acknowledgement. While they waited there had been plenty to occupy their tongues: the main topic, of course, was speculation over the coming marriage and intense curiosity over the bride. Never had the dignitaries of Colleverde been so spoilt for choice of gossip—the fighting that morning, the near loss of their Duke to a wicked foreign conspiracy—they were used to native ones. They now looked forward to seeing the bride and wondering how she felt at being so abruptly orphaned and having to marry either her father's killer or his son. There was a whisper that she, with mother, father, and brother dead, two or perhaps all three having met violent ends, must herself bring bad luck and have been born under an evil star. It was felt that the Duke's ex-astrologer might have known what he was talking about.

The Duke's entrance gave everyone something else to puzzle over. True, he led by the hand an amazingly pretty bride, her ringlets silver gold and her skin fashionably white, her head held high. She was placed at the table between the Duke and the Lord Astorre, leaving everyone still on tenterhooks as to who was to be her groom. Next to the Duke on the other side, however, a man was led to sit, a man evidently by his scarred eye sockets blind, but more astonishing still, dressed in rags fit only for a peasant. The Duke, strangely, seemed delighted with this disabled rustic, whom he had seated in the place that was to have been Bishop Taddeo's, though nothing in the Bishop's face suggested that he regretted losing this honour. One or two among the older members of the Duke's suite had begun to murmur among themselves about the extraordinary resemblance of this blind peasant to someone rather untidily dead and certainly disposed of years ago.

The most awful thing for Benno, standing on the stairs and seeing them pass to the banquet, was that his master had made a mistake. The worst had happened. Putting the blind man boldly in the open had not worked.

A little commotion at a side door drew attention now. The Marshal arrived, with assistants and a wild-looking prisoner, and was making a fuss over having a pillar stripped of decorative garlands of bay so that a chain could be hitched round it to secure the prisoner. The guests were realising that the entertainment usual to a feast, omitted tonight out of respect for the Cardinal and for the bride's mourning, was to be provided—after a fashion. The allegories so frequently presented in entertainments were to appear in a different form. This must be one of the plotters. An announcement that he had planned the Cardinal's death and that he was to die for it before their eyes took away some guests' appetites, although others thought the spectacle would add spice.

Either way this would not be an event anyone would forget.

As the servants crowded on the staircase with Benno to see the great folk go in to supper began to disperse, reluctantly, to their duties, he was left with his appalling problem. He must alert Sigismondo at once that the blind lord had got into the Duke's loving clutches again, but he had no firm idea where Sigismondo was. "I must go the Palazzo Corio, but I'll be back soon" was all Benno had been told before Sigismondo vanished with his usual disconcerting speed. Well, back soon, that's fine, Benno thought, but what about the blind lord? There's Angelo marched off by the Duke's men somewhere, and I've been left to keep an eye on Massimo and Sybilla . . . at least the major-domo, perceiving Sigismondo's authority, had ordered that these, his apparent belongings, should be fed. He had sent them into the inner courtyard, no doubt giving consideration to the havoc Sybilla could cause in kitchens busy serving up the feast. Benno had left the pair on a stone bench tearing a roast capon to pieces, attended devoutly by Biondello.

He must find Sigismondo, and he must not leave these two in case they wandered off—particularly as Massimo was anxious to find Mirandola, for although Massimo trusted

Sigismondo, the only "good hands" he wanted his master to be in were his own. Earlier, Benno had been all but throttled by Massimo before he swore, on his parents' souls, that he didn't know where Mirandola was. It was true, he told himself at that time. Angelo could be anywhere in the square. Lucky Massimo had asked him then and not now.

Hurrying out to check that the pair was still in the courtyard, Benno sent up a prayer of thanks for their absence when the blind lord had been led in. He followed this with a prayer to the kind Saint who had saved him from hanging, that she start thinking seriously about those who were in danger of worse. He added a rider: that she send Sigismondo—fast.

Sigismondo had arrived at the Palazzo Corio soon after the Princess left in her litter, for the second time that day, muffled in black and dripping with gold, to attend the feast where the Duke had promised her the screams of her brother's would-be murderer as sauce for her meat. The doorkeeper admitted Sigismondo with a bow of recognition. He had been to and fro on the Princess's business in the past few days, and if he now arrived when she had just gone, he still wasn't the kind of man you bothered with possibly irrelevant questions. He was probably on an errand for the Princess.

The courtyard lay empty, the long evening shadows across it like fingers pointing to the golden stone of the Palace itself. The stone shield with the Corio crest looked down on Sigismondo as he stepped over the threshold. The hall, too, was empty, but a diffuse hum and clatter in the distance suggested the household was at dinner. No one was there to see Sigismondo pass up the stairs.

He cast about, listening, glancing in at several rooms, and at last found on the top floor, under the roof, a dormitory still-warm from the day's sun and a soldier of the Cardinal's Guard standing at a small side door, leaning on his pike. An empty bowl on a nearby chest showed that he had supped. At sight of Sigismondo he straightened up and gave a quick salute. This was a man he had heard about: One or two returned from the Bishop's Palace to speak with awe of the shaven-headed one who chopped men with his axe like logs.

"The Captain's in there? Is he still alive?"

"Sir. The Princess had him brought here and sent her

physician to bleed him that left not a quarter hour ago. He's not to be disturbed, sir. Express orders." The guard put his pike apologetically across the doorway as Sigismondo made to enter. "Not to be disturbed, sir. No one to go in; Princess's orders. Whatever happens."

The Princess had perhaps not had in mind what did happen, but it left the guard in a peaceful heap. Sigismondo caught the pike as it fell and put it out of his reach. Stepping over him and pushing the door open, he smelt at once the cloying odours of a sickroom: sweat, urine, herbs, and, above all, the sharp smell of fresh blood.

The Captain of the Cardinal's Guard lay on his back on the pallet bed in the small room, his eyes half closed with only the whites showing, his face yellow under the purplish map of scars. He was naked at least to the waist, with a coverlet roughly thrown over the rest. His left arm, where the physician had opened a vein, hung over the edge of the bed. The bandage had been put on so loosely that it had slipped off and hung on the edge of the cupping basin on the bare boards below. An uneven trickle ran slowly down the arm to the basin, which had overflowed, and a red pool was slowly creeping out round it. The Captain was being bled to death.

40

The Duke Doesn't Know He Wants Him Yet

BENNO DID NOT CARE FOR DECISIONS. Perhaps the main advantage of being a low-rank menial all your life is that there are no decisions, only orders. Since he had attached himself to Sigismondo there had still been orders, and he had still obeyed — not without question, for he was insatiably curious, but without hesitation. Now he was driven to disobey. If there are two dangers, Sigismondo had said, juggle them and see which is lighter.

Benno scooped up Biondello by the hind legs and stuffed him into his bosom. Sybilla was now concerned with the state of Massimo's burnt arm. With any luck, Benno thought as he started off, that will keep her busy and him involved for a bit; I've got to find the master.

Sigismondo had spoken of the Palazzo Corio. As Benno trotted rapidly among the strollers in the square, he wondered if his master would be in a relaxed, question-answering mood when he found him or if it'd be hold the tongue and guess. He thought that the news he carried would not be relaxing.

The Corio doorkeeper, recognising him as follower of the man with the shaven head, condescended to tell him his master was in the Palace. Once indoors, Benno set down Biondello: "Go find. *Find.*"

Biondello started to cast about, nose down, from side to side. Suddenly, he pricked up his one ear, set off busily down the hall, through an arch, and began to lollop up the twisty backstairs. Benno followed.

When, coming into the long dormitory, he saw Biondello sniffing with interest at a large man in the livery of the Cardinal's Guard, apparently taking a nap on the floor with his pike propped neatly against the wall, he knew his master was

near. Sigismondo had a magic touch with insomniacs, somewhere under the ear, he believed.

"Benno. Didn't I tell you to watch Massimo?"

Benno's jaw was having difficulty relocating enough to let
him speak. He thought that Sigismondo, now leaning over the
man in this little room stinking of blood, had murdered him.
Then, as he saw that he was actually finishing a bandage round
the man's arm, he had to lunge forward to prevent Biondello
from investigating the bowl on the floor.

"I had to come with the news."

"Find wine. Or brandy."

Benno fished in his clothing and produced a small flask no
one had been attending to very closely at the Bishop's Palace.
Sigismondo took the flask and held it to the lips of the man,
whom he had now propped up on his own shoulder. As the man
stirred and gasped at the brandy finding its way into his mouth,
Sigismondo turned to Benno. "The news? What's happened?"

"The blind Lord. He's been took. I saw the Duke sort of
cuddling him like he was feeling him over for what damage he
could do him, and he's sat him next to him at dinner."

"Angelo?"

"There's to be fortunes told after dinner, I heard someone
say. It could be him, they took him off somewhere . . ."

Sigismondo supported the sick Captain still and was tipping
the flask with care. "Angelo's alive at least. We must hurry, or
Iacomo won't be. I had his punishment delayed as long as I
could."

"Oh, he's been put off till after dinner. Something about
having respect for ladies' stomachs. The servers were pleased;
he'd been strung to a pillar right in everybody's way. The
Duke's being ever so kind, he's said to be in a specially good
mood what with not being dead and everyone else about to be."
He watched as the wounded man coughed a trail of brandy over
the hand that held the flask. "Thought he was the bloke you
were fighting earlier on."

"Indeed. He's the Captain of the Cardinal's Guard."

At Sigismondo's introduction, the man's eyes opened wider,
and he rolled his head to stare at Sigismondo.

"You!" The Captain was hoarsely incredulous at seeing who
was nursing him, but it also stirred his energy. Sigismondo

helped him swing his feet to the floor. His hose were torn and bloodstained.

"Benno. We need some servants and a litter. The Princess will have men for that."

Benno stopped at the door, looking back. "What do I say? Where're we going?"

"Tell them the Duke wants to see the Captain. Immediately."

That note in the deep voice sent Benno out down the dormitory fast. They were following the litter across the square, with people making way for the Princess's livery, before he finally ventured to ask, "What's the Duke want with this Captain then?"

"The Duke doesn't *know* he wants him yet."

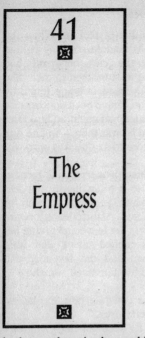

41

The Empress

MINERVA'S MIND WAS IN TOTAL tumult. It hadn't taken long for Astorre to tell her that he and not his father was to be her bridegroom after all. He had conveyed this with delicate courtesy, implying that his father had naturally responded to her beauty and her courage, without thought of consequences, as any man would; but that for dynastic reasons . . . By this Minerva understood that it was thought more sensible for her to bear children to a healthy young man than to a ruler who had made a habit of tottering on the grave's edge.

Astorre's words were discreet, but his eyes were not. His gaze did not roam over her offensively; it was an ardent glow that implied he had no need to look anywhere in the world but at her. She knew she blushed and was glad to dip her head to the gilt winecup. As she drank, she thought she must have misheard. Surely Astorre had not gone on to say that they were to be married this very evening?

"His Grace believes it wise I should go to Montenero before any can attempt to dispute your claim to the inheritance." Astorre paused, avoiding what was in both their minds: *since your father killed his son, his heir, your brother, before my father killed yours* . . .

What can he think of me, Minerva asked herself, not revenging Prince Livio's death, not refusing to marry his slayer's son? Surely I shall be condemned for it. I should pick up this knife, and thrust it into his velvet chest . . . and I might, I suppose, if I thought Prince Livio was really my father.

The man she believed to be her father was at table, beside Duke Grifone, who was feeding him the best pieces from his own plate with the loving attention bestowed by keepers of an animal just before it is to be slaughtered. Her capacity to think

seemed paralysed by too much conflict of feeling. When she
had first caught sight of the Lord Mirandola standing behind
the Duke as he greeted her before the feast, her hands had
prickled with fear, her heart seemed to stop, then to race. She
had known all along the danger of Mirandola being found by
Petrucci, his deadly enemy. There must have been another raid
on Fontecasta by Grifone's men, which had captured him after
she left, but how had the Duke heard he was there? And he was
not likely to have asked him to dinner to say he was sorry for
the past, so why was he here?

The arrival of the Marshal with his prisoner and the buzz of
comment as Iacomo was chained to a pillar hardly ten feet
away gave her a fresh taste of what she might expect for
Mirandola. She shuddered and felt cold. Astorre leant forward
to address his father across her, asking her leave and giving her
an intoxicating close view of a tanned cheek and long
eyelashes. He smelt of fresh linen and the lavender and
sandalwood it had been kept in, and his hair smelt somehow of
the open air.

"Your Grace, may I beg that we consider how the ladies'
appetites may suffer from unmannerly cries?"

The Duke turned, his face with its deep-cut lines and dark
eyes suddenly a threatening version of his son's. Minerva felt
trapped between them. The Duke, however, was in an amiable
mood, his hand on Mirandola's as it lay on the cloth.

"True! Let the rogue wait for his death. Why should we
oblige him? We'll see his blood for our dessert. Your boon's
granted, my son." He turned back to Mirandola, taking the
gilded ewer from the page and pouring the wine himself into
the cup, folding Mirandola's fingers round it, while Mirandola
sat in his darkness smiling his secret, ironic smile. Minerva felt
her heart flood with love for him, for his bravery, his calm.
Would the Duke grant her a boon too if she flung herself on her
knees? But what should she ask? *Spare my father.* . . . If she
said that, all reason for marrying her would vanish; she would
openly accuse her mother; she would join Mirandola in death.

She scarcely knew how the feast went. Dishes were put
before her, and she tried to eat a little here and there as she had
been taught. She drank more wine than her mother would have
allowed her. *Where* was Sigismondo?

She turned attentively to Astorre's conversation, which she could not summon the wits to follow. He did not seem to expect more than an appearance of interest. Perhaps he was as conscious as she of the extraordinary things that had happened that day. Could he know, though, that she had dragged down Prince Livio because he was a terror to her and no longer a father? Astorre was speaking pretty compliments, which were much more strongly spoken by his eyes. His regard was so intent, when she met it, that she was conscious all at once of the marriage's being put forward. She was aware of the poor wretch, half-stripped, trying to ease his arms that embraced the pillar, putting his forehead to the marble. Occasionally the Duke would give her his attention, but he was engrossed by Mirandola, who, he was delighted to find, could not control a slight start whenever his cheek was patted.

Astorre had assured her that he would plead for Mirandola's life, that he regarded him still with affection, but that his father had already told him rulers could not afford to forgive — justice must not only be seen to be done but done in a way no one was likely to forget.

The feast was almost over. The dishes were removed, the cloths drawn. Grifone held up a preventing hand as the servants were about to take the trestle tables down and called, "Where is the fortune-teller?"

Voices rose in amusement as he was brought in. When he threw back his golden hair with a shake of the head, a different note came into the women's voices at least. He saw the Duke and marched up the hall as if he were not under guard at all. When he reached the high table, the company fell silent to hear what would pass.

"You shall tell the fortune of your companion here," Grifone said. "I know already what it is to be, but let us see what you make of it."

"I make nothing, Your Grace," the young man said. "It is all as Fortune sends."

Minerva stared as the young man took out a small silk bundle and unwrapped it. How had this strange creature come to be Lord Mirandola's *companion?* His accent was foreign, his garments shabby, his face exquisite; it was as if a guardian angel had disguised himself. He shuffled and laid out cards in front of Mirandola. "The cards are before you. Take one."

Mirandola reached forward and found where the cards were. His hand hovered a moment, seemed to be drawn down. He took a card and turned it over. Minerva saw even the Princess Corio crane forward. The card was a woman throned, with symbols about her Minerva could not see.

Angelo raised grey eyes to the Duke. He said flatly: "It is the Empress. It means great fortune."

The Duke flung back in his chair. "Great fortune! Look again, fortune-teller. Be advised."

Angelo shrugged. "I can only tell what the cards show. Should I deal and let him pick again?" His tone said it was useless; *Great Fortune* would reappear. The Duke, rubbing his chin with one thumb, regarded him for a moment, then abruptly said: "He will no doubt be a king in Hell. Satan will advance such a notable traitor."

The fortune-teller gathered his cards with speed and wrapped them. "The tarot must be honoured in silver or gold, Your Grace, when it's consulted."

"Much silver and gold you've seen!" the Duke said. "You shall have some. It shall be put molten into your mouth! Tie him up there—let us have symmetry. You sheltered my enemy, and *your* fortune is not far to seek."

The Marshal, delighted, hurried across to the right-hand pillar and supervised its denuding and the fastening of Angelo's hands. The tables were carried away, the Bishop's little band of cither, lute, rebec, and krummhorn struck up again, and the Marshal, visibly swelling with pride, bustled across to provide the special music the Duke had asked for. Beside Astorre, the Princess Corio, who had scarcely eaten or said a word in response to his polite formalities, leant forward, the black gauze of her headdress like a thundercloud round her white face. This she had been waiting for. She had missed the deaths of the real murderers, but this man had schemed and planned to burn her brother.

The Marshal's torturer came forward, unleashed the coils of his whip like a great snake hissing along the floor, and sent it sailing in a preliminary crack that made others beside Minerva jump. One woman could not repress a little scream at the circling lash, as spontaneous as the Princess's sudden clap of her hands.

Hardly had the third lash spattered the rushes with blood when the curtain at the hall's far end was drawn back and a strange procession entered, preceded, backwards, by a protesting major-domo. Then came servants in the Princess's livery of dark and light grey carrying a litter, on which lay a man swathed in the Cardinal's colours, eyes closed in a face wax pale but mottled with scars. Beside him, walking at the pace of the litter, tall and grave, in his usual black, came Sigismondo.

42

⊠

A Proposal of Marriage

⊠

DUKE GRIFONE HAD SURVIVED AS Duke thanks to the speed of his reactions. He raised a hand to check the flogging so that he could hear better, leaving Iacomo slumped in temporary relief against the pillar, and called, "He shall approach," thus removing the major-domo and preventing an officious rush by the Marshal. Sigismondo escorted the litter up to the dais. Minerva and the Princess had, oddly, made identical gestures on seeing the procession. Both had clasped their hands and raised them to their mouths. They might therefore be supposed to share the same feelings, in Minerva's case joy as well as surprise.

Sigismondo directed the servants so that they brought the litter round sideways to the dais, giving Duke Grifone a clear view of the man on it. He himself stood by the Captain's head and bowed deeply. The Duke leant forward, forgetting even Mirandola in the inexplicable sight of a moribund man brought to him for dessert.

"Who? And why?" The Duke was beginning to believe that the man from Rocca, to whom he already owed much, had as many surprises in stock as a conjuror.

"Your Grace, it is the Captain of His late Eminence's Guard. He has something to confess to you."

Beside Astorre there was a rustle of heavy silk as the Princess spoke suddenly. "The man has a fever. He should never have been brought—he is in no state—"

"Peace." The Duke delivered his second snub to a woman he found too fond of interfering. "Let him speak if he can."

There was silence in the hall, except for the spluttering of torches, as the man struggled to speak. Sigismondo knelt to

prop him with a strong arm. The words came out as if the
energy to produce them could hardly be found.

"His Eminence . . . my orders from him . . . to aid Prince
Livio."

"*Prince Livio!*" The Duke started out of his chair. "*Petrucci*
told you to fight for him *against me?*"

Behind him the Princess was on her feet, eyes huge in her
white face, indignation and rage personified. The Duke now
had hold of the wounded man, trying to drag out further words.
"Petrucci? Did he plot with Livio *against me?* Do you swear
this as you hope for salvation?"

Looking round, the Duke saw the Bishop, strode back across
the dais, seized the Bishop's pectoral cross of amethyst and
gold on its chain, and dragged it down to the man on the litter.

"Swear."

The Bishop, who had been forced to stumble after the Duke,
bent over the Captain as his cross was pressed to the man's lips,
and the sight of the ecclesiastical countenance and purple silk
damask cape seemed to impart a touch of life to the Captain.
His next words were quite distinct: "I swear to the truth of this
on my hope of Heaven."

A shriek cut into the end of his testimony. The Princess left
her place, rushed from the dais, and jabbing a finger at him
again and again past the kneeling Bishop cried: "Liar! Perjurer!
My brother was never a traitor! Never! Kill him for his lies!'

The Duke, without looking at her, swept an arm back,
catching her across the midriff and sending her staggering.
Astorre started forward as her heel caught the dais edge and
lent his arm to help her to her chair.

The Bishop, his cross freed by the Duke, took one matter
into his own hands. He spoke quietly to the Duke, summoned
his chaplain with a glance and directed the litter-bearers
towards the next room, the audience chamber; and while the
chaplain went to get the stole and holy oil, the Bishop followed
the litter at a dignified pace.

The Duke returned slowly to his chair and stared at
Sigismondo almost accusingly. The hall filled with the sound
of people marvelling in whispers. The great Cardinal, the
faithful counsellor, the murdered friend of the Duke—a

traitor? In league with Prince Livio who had only that day tried to kill their Duke? It altered everything, casting new and revealing light on all that had gone before.

"How did you find this out?" Grifone's voice was measured, cool. Sigismondo in return was deferential but confident. "I saw him deliberately attack one of Your Grace's men before I engaged him myself."

"But with my own eyes I saw his men engage Livio's."

"After you killed the Prince, Your Grace. Only a fool fights for a dead man."

"And only a fool obeys one. Why did the Captain still follow his orders? Petrucci died yesterday."

Sigismondo bent his head in acknowledgement of the Duke's point. "His Eminence died, Your Grace; but the orders were renewed." Sigismondo paused. "The Captain told me that the Princess Corio instructed him this morning that all was to go forward as her brother had planned, that Prince Livio and she would reward him fully for his services."

The Princess was on her feet again, almost spitting. "Lies! Lies! Your Grace, this man is a stranger, an agent from Rocca. *He* is the one who plots against you. Your Grace knows how my brother served you. This villain tries to turn your mind against those faithful to you. How can he be believed?"

"How can you be believed?" The Duke passed the question coolly to Sigismondo.

"By this, Your Grace." Sigismondo drew from inside his black leather jerkin a flattened roll of parchment that the watching Benno recognised. "Will Your Grace read it?"

He came forward and, twisting the letter away from a sudden desperate lunge of the Princess, put it in the Duke's outstretched hand. "You will find it a proposal of marriage to the Princess."

The Duke unfolded the paper and stared. "Signed by Prince Livio!"

"Your Grace perceives—" Sigismondo caught deft hold of the Princess's wrists as she attempted to snatch the letter from Grifone's hands "—the lady had good reason to renew her brother's orders. The success of the plot would have made her Duchess of Nemora as well as Princess of Montenero."

Now there was no checking the buzz of comment in the hall.

The Princess had never been a popular figure in Colleverde, and there was intense pleasure in seeing her ambitions dashed just when their true audacity was revealed. She twisted in Sigismondo's hold, and as she ducked to sink her teeth into his hand, he unexpectedly let go and stepped away from her. Benno wondered afterwards if he had guessed what she was after and let her go on purpose.

The Duke had motioned the guards forward. Before they could reach her the Princess took her chance. To Benno it seemed that she repeated the action she had attempted a minute before, but this time she bit her own hand. Only as she threw her head back did he realise she had bitten not her hand but her ring. She put a hand to her throat, then her heart, as if she traced the poison's path. Benno had time to think how awful, she's dying without absolution, just like her brother, she'll join him in Hell, before she swayed, sank rather than fell, and lay, in a whirlpool of black silk, at the Duke's feet.

43

Time to Rejoice

THE WHOLE ASSEMBLY SEEMED TO make a single sound as the Princess collapsed. A babel of cries and screams broke out, which only the raised hand of the Duke could quiet.

"Condemned out of her own mouth." The Duke smiled at the play on words. "Who could now doubt her guilt? Let her join Prince Livio in Hell and the Devil celebrate their wedding there. As for her brother! Petrucci, whom I called my right hand!"

He wheeled suddenly and plunged at the silent Mirandola, seized him by the upper arms, and hauled him up to his feet. "You. You warned me. When I condemned you, you warned me. *'Do not trust him,'* you said. *'He is ambitious and only waits for your death.'"*

Mirandola, who had flinched at the unexpected violent grasp, was impassive.

"By God, the Duke's eyes saw everything!" Grifone turned, half releasing him, pointed to Angelo, and said: "Free him. And you, and you," the finger swung and pointed at two of his courtiers, "look after the Lord Mirandola. Find him clothes to wear—"

"Father—"

"Ah yes! No doubt you want to attend to that. The boy was pleading for you, Mirandola, not an hour ago. But you must be dressed for his wedding. Hurry. After that we shall have much to say to each other late into the night."

"Your Grace," said the distinctive, harsh voice. There might have been a trace of resignation in the slight smile.

"God's bones!" said the Duke. "I'd forgotten that voice." He kissed Mirandola and pushed him towards the attendant courtiers and the waiting Astorre.

"Your Grace," Mirandola repeated.

The Duke paused. "What is it?"

"Honour the tarot." And Mirandola reached out a hand to be led away.

The Duke laughed. He worked a ring from his little finger, a heavy shank of gold set with a carved agate, and flung it. Angelo, who had been rubbing his freed wrists as if mobility were his prime concern, flashed out a hand and caught it.

"And now." Grifone swept the crowd with his dark, intimidating eye. "Time to rejoice. Where's my Lord Bishop?"

The Bishop proved to be finishing his prayers over the body of the Captain, who had barely survived his confession. In the audience room, absorbed in the needs of the dying man, he had heard nothing of events and, summoned to the Duke's presence, he came and halted, staring, to see the woman he had so dreaded lying lifeless at the Duke's feet. His own servants were coming timidly forward at the Duke's summons to carry the body away.

"She took her own life, my Lord Bishop. You must decide later where she can be buried."

Silently praying for forgiveness at his profound sense of relief, the Bishop was pondering on this new task when the Duke, with that terrible smile of his, took him by the sleeve and distracted him entirely.

"A wedding, Bishop, a wedding. We must concern ourselves no longer with the death of traitors but with the heirs of Nemora. Have fetched what's necessary. All here shall witness the betrothal of my son Astorre and the Princess of Montenero. We shall celebrate their wedding later, at Nemora in splendour; but meanwhile, lose no time."

The Bishop, his head spinning, called his chaplain. Grifone's restless eye noticed a little group frozen where they had been halted.

"Marshal, what are you at? Release that man."

Iacomo was helped from his chains and stood, head low like a baited bull, his back crossed with only the three lines of red.

All this time Sigismondo had not moved, yet people had constantly eyed him. He was not a man whose presence one overlooked.

"And you," the Duke said, "I'll hear your part in this too, after the ceremony; for you know far more than you've said."

Sigismondo bowed and backed away.

The servants were making a poor job of bundling up the Princess as though they were afraid of her still. They struggled to rise and, with a sudden clatter, a thick chain of gold from round her neck caught in the veiling of black gauze with which they had tried to cover her face and fell in a heap on the dais. The servants almost dropped her, recovered, and hesitated. One reached for it, but the Duke was swifter. He stooped, swept up the chain; and in the same movement flung it towards Iacomo.

"Take it, rascal. Take it for trying to do what I should have done long ago. You're a stonemason. I've a cathedral building at Nemora. Go to my chamberlain; he'll see to your employment there. For all I know, without Petrucci to advise me, I'd have had no rebellion on my hands a year ago, and your folk might not have burnt." He regarded Iacomo, on his knees now and stammering bewildered thanks. "Take comfort, man. Petrucci burns in Hell for sure—what's their few minutes against his eternity?"

With this consolation the Duke left them. Minerva, caught in the sudden and overwhelming realisation that her marriage to Astorre and then its consummation were within the next few hours, followed with burning cheeks. Her ladies hastily fell in behind. An old woman in black, with white hair and ruddy cheeks, among the crowd of servers pressed against the tapestries by the wall, put down the bowl of water she had appropriated to establish her right to be there, took the napkin she had likewise snatched, arranged it into a kerchief for her head, and joined the small procession. Sigismondo, who had observed her all along, called out what were to the crowd unintelligible words, and she, walking crabwise, threw some quick gibberish back at him before she disappeared.

"Where's Massimo?" Benno took a drumstick out of his mouth in sudden appalled recollection. "I forgot to look for him. And that was Sybilla, and he wasn't with her!"

"She tells me he tried to break into the banquet when he heard the Lord Mirandola had been discovered to the Duke." Sigismondo ate a slice of venison in his fingers and wiped them on a damask napkin supplied by the now-solicitous major-domo. "He's in prison again."

"The Marshal won't like it when he has to let him go, will he?" Benno saw from his master's calm that Massimo's fate was but temporary. He renewed his assault on a dish of roast boar in wine, something he might not have had a chance at if he had just stood behind Sigismondo at dinner as had originally been planned. A pair of forepaws now beat on his thigh, and he dropped a piece to Biondello.

Sigismondo, Benno, and Angelo were sitting at a small table set up for them in an oriel overlooking the piazza. At a discreet distance stood a server, ready to fill their cups or bring more to eat. The major-domo had registered how much in favour they were with the Duke.

"The Marshal would have liked to get his hands on me. I'm just his kind of vagabond." Angelo showed the crooked teeth that made his angel face a devil's as he chewed on a chicken wing. "Now he's had to hand my knives back all polite, right side round."

"Did he get them all?"

"All but a couple." Angelo was examining with a professional eye the ring the Duke had thrown to him. From somewhere he produced a thin cord, which Benno imagined he kept handy for any garrotting that became necessary, and threaded the ring onto it. As Benno watched, the ring seemed to vanish. He thought the Marshal's men had done very well to find as many of Angelo's knives as they had.

With the easy gesture of one who all his life has been waited upon, Angelo summoned the server to pour his wine. When the man had retreated, he asked Sigismondo casually, "How did you come by that letter?"

"I stole it. From one who had stolen it before."

"Her nephew. Father Torquato." It was seldom that Benno had information to supply, and he was proud of it. Angelo's glass-grey eyes turned to him. "Her nephew? Why? He was family."

Sigismondo replied. "He was family, and his uncle the Cardinal and his aunt the Princess didn't do enough for him. Or so he thought. He saw a chance to exert a little pressure on his aunt with that letter. A murmur from him that he could show it to the Duke, and the Princess would have parted with quite a bit of gold."

"If she didn't poison him first," Angelo said. "How'd he get such a letter? Not a thing you'd leave lying about."

"I can't be exact," Sigismondo spoke around a candied plum. "In the letter, the Prince wrote that she must burn it immediately, which she neglected to do. I fancy only a Cardinal in flames would have distracted her into leaving the letter unguarded. Though I didn't know it at the time, I saw it myself under her hand before I smelt the smoke from his room. Perhaps she dropped it, and Torquato seized his chance soon after that. There was enough confusion to cover any theft. And with the Cardinal dead, Torquato may have thought the conspiracy unlikely to succeed, so the letter would be worth having."

"You saw the thing yourself. Did you know who it was from?"

"You'd make a fair lawyer, Angelo. I had some idea, yes. A slip of the tongue. She was trying to sound me out on how Duke Ludovico might take the killing of his nephew by Prince Livio. I thought her more interested on behalf of the Prince than I'd expected. She spoke of a ruler's need to marry, and she mentioned his future wife as *Princess of Nemora* and stroked the paper under her hand. I don't think she knew that she did it."

"Where's this Torquato then? The Duke's not going to kiss him to death if he turns up now his auntie and his Eminent uncle have gone to dine with the Devil."

Sigismondo crooked a finger at the server for another pitcher of wine, filled Angelo's cup, then Benno's, and wagged his head sadly. "Vanished. I saw him stealing away when his uncle was accused. On his way to Rome, I shouldn't wonder, to try his fortune."

"Without Auntie's gold."

"True, Angelo. But also without the Duke's noose round his neck."

Benno remembered how he had last seen Torquato. "Someone had a go at him today, all right. Wonder who'd beat up a priest in the street like that and why. Everyone's been a bit excited today, but it's a bit—I mean, a priest."

Sigismondo offered a bit of peacock to Biondello, who bolted it. "I asked Polissena to keep Torquato busy while we searched his room. She'd told me he'd envied his uncle there for years, and he jumped at the chance."

"*She* didn't beat him up?"

"No. No. Though I paid well and doubtless she'd have done it if that was what he fancied. No, it was Tomaso Delmonte, her admirer. The Marshal's Captain had freed him in good time for him to be languishing at her door and see Bianca lead Torquato in. There's a limit to what a man can take."

44

✠

You'll Have Guessed the Rest

✠

ALTHOUGH THE DIGNITARIES OF Colleverde and their wives carried away with them that Saturday night the news of the betrothal and bedding of their Duke's son, it became general knowledge only on Sunday morning as people were on their way to Mass. Evidently the formal wedding celebration was to wait; rumour had it that Lord Astorre had been plighted with such speed to consolidate his claim to his wife's inheritance and that he was going—had already gone—to meet the condotta that only yesterday had been crouched on the city borders waiting for the signal from wicked Prince Livio to invade; they were now to enforce his taking of Montenero. This was widely approved.

Another item of news spread rapidly through the town: Although the Duke would attend a thanksgiving Mass that day and pay formal respects to the relics, there was to be no Requiem Mass for Cardinal Petrucci. Incredible to think of the Cardinal as the Duke's enemy, but his haughty sister, the Princess Corio, had poisoned herself, so it was true. There was no conspicuous sorrow for the Princess, but the Cardinal's frequent visits to the city, his residences at the Palazzo Corio, had lent Colleverde a certain importance, and it was disagreeable to know that he must have intended the city to become Prince Livio's property. Everyone had much to thank Saint Bernardina for.

Sigismondo had been early summoned to the Duke's presence, where he found Minerva and Astorre on their knees for the Bishop's blessing, Minerva in a dress she had achieved from somewhere, of plum-coloured velvet banded with gold embroidery, and wearing the Duke's gift. As the Bishop laid a hand on each head, Astorre's own hand came out to take

Minerva's, and the Duke smiled. The blind lord was there, too, standing by the Duke, and when the Prince and Princess of Montenero had kissed the Bishop's ring and risen from the blessing, the Duke led Mirandola forward.

"My present to you both. I give you, my son, a counsellor who will never be false to you as he was never false to me. He will help you to govern Montenero and keep you safe from treachery."

He embraced Astorre and kissed Minerva's cheek, whispering something in her ear that made her blush. The blind lord was looking very grand today in olive velvet, and there was no mistaking the balas ruby pinned to his collar. The Princess of Montenero had something to give Sigismondo: a purse of gold links that looked satisfactorily heavy and her hand to kiss. Benno could not suppress the memory of Sigismondo tossing her the reins of his horse before he went into the haunted villa. Perhaps she wouldn't forget that either.

At the farewell on the steps outside the Palace, the crowd, shouting and throwing caps in the air, was kept at a distance with some difficulty by the Bishop's Guard. The Lord Astorre was mounted on a great black stallion that tossed its head, whickered, and stamped the cobbles at the noise of the crowd. The Lady Minerva was on a white horse with gold tassels on its bridle, and she looked every inch a Princess, in spite of the tears in her eyes.

It was with a not unpleasant sense of anticlimax that Benno followed Sigismondo into the Bishop's garden. Bishop Taddeo was a civilised man and, after the pleasures of the table, he enjoyed his garden. He was interested in the latest fashions, and antique statues—bought at great expense—stood in classical niches or contrived natural arbours. Sigismondo paused before a Diana, her huntress tunic kilted up, bow in hand, and crescent moon poised on her curling hair, looking across the gravel paths and box hedges towards a stone stag beyond.

"The Bishop knows how to spend his money." He looked about, sniffing the air, and brushed the top of a small box tree clipped into a ball, standing in a terra-cotta jar; the hot spicy scent was released. "He will be able to come and walk here and forget all about what happened yesterday, I hope."

"I bet he's glad the Cardinal's not just dead but a traitor too.

Bet he's glad the Princess Corio isn't here to boss him either. Wouldn't have lasted long as Prince Livio's wife, would she? He wouldn't take to being ordered about. Have a fit and off goes her head. Seemed to me he threw a sort of fit when he saw the Lady Minerva yesterday."

"I was *counting* on that." Sigismondo was twirling a sprig of bay under his nostrils, inhaling. "His substitute daughter told me she was not to take off her veil at all. He'd planned to get up to Duke Grifone, leaning on his fake doctor and his assistant, and give him a warm embrace." Demonstrating, he clasped Benno's arms to his ribs. "You see? The chance for Achille Malvezzi to ram his stiletto somewhere between the fourth and fifth vertebrae," he tapped Benno at the base of the neck, "above any coat of mail the Duke might be prudent enough to be wearing under his shirt; and once Malvezzi's friend posted outside on the balcony had come in and dealt with Astorre, Nemora would have had a new ruler."

Benno thought about this, shuffling the gravel at his feet into little heaps. Then he said, "If Prince Livio thought his wife's lover was buried in that grave at Fontecasta, what was he going to *do* with him?"

Sigismondo hummed and shrugged. "A jealous man can think of things to do to the body of his wife's lover even though it's too late for the lover to appreciate it properly."

"Welcome to the severed-heads collection, you mean? Didn't give up revenge easily, did he? Like that lot, Malvezzi and his mates, that burnt the Cardinal for his burning their magician friend. Bet they'd not have lived long if Prince Livio discovered they'd burnt the person he was counting on to help out the conspiracy. And it might have worked, too, if the Cardinal had been alive. And if you hadn't been there."

Sigismondo stood, thumbs in belt, contemplating the pattern made by the box hedges, a foot high, that divided part of the garden into a winding route that seemed to lead nowhere but had a centre where a fountain played. "Nice, isn't it," Benno continued, "everything ending happily like that? I'm glad the blind lord went off with Lady Minerva. I mean, he's her proper father, isn't he? Though, of course, she can't ever let on."

"Exceedingly unwise," Sigismondo agreed.

"What's Massimo and Sybilla doing?"

"Massimo's been let out of jail. . . . I understand he's happy to go back to Fontecasta now he knows his master is safe. The Duke's made the villa over to Lord Mirandola—he's going to buy it for him from the Giraldi family. He'll entertain the Lord Astorre there when he goes hunting. Sybilla's gone there too. She's anxious about the goats."

Benno glanced sideways up at his master, summoning up courage for a question that verged on personal. "That language . . . the one you talked to Sybilla and she was telling you things in. Wasn't Muscovite, was it?"

"Greek, Benno, Greek. Sybilla was marched off from her home and sold as a slave by Turks long ago when her hair was still black and she was more vigorous, she told me, than she is now."

Benno drew breath at this dismaying prospect. "Then how'd she come to be at Fontecasta looking after the blind lord? Did he buy her?"

"He wasn't in time. The old Duke of Rocca beat him to it by thirty years. She was brought north from Calabria where she learnt her Italian. . . . He bought her for the Princess Oralia."

"Princess Oralia?" Benno's eyes widened.

"Sybilla became her nurse; and the Lady Minerva's too, for the first year or so of her life. They didn't take to her at the court at Montenero." Sigismondo walked on along one of the paths, smiling. "The Princess thought it wise to let her retire, make her retire, to Rocca, where she gave her a house and a little land."

Benno was silent for a minute, then he said: "The Duke liked the fortune Angelo told for the Lady Minerva and her lord this morning, din' he? That Empress again and the lovers and the other whatsit: good fortune, happiness and all they could want, though he didn't say about sons—"

"Surely part of the good fortune."

"And I thought it was dead cheeky of Angelo to ask the blind lord to draw the cards now he's got grand again. Made the Duke laugh though."

Sigismondo came to a closed end in the maze and stopped. Biondello, who had been following him, jumped the tiny hedge and looked up enquiringly. Sigismondo smiled and stepped over after him.

"You see, Benno? He shows us what to do. You come to a dead end? Ignore it. The right path is just to hand."

Benno shook his head. "You didn't come to any dead ends, did you? The Princess asked you to find out who murdered the Cardinal, and you did: that Achille Malvezzi and his mates."

"Mm-mm. They were glad to do it because they had personal reasons. They were acting on orders though."

"Orders?" Benno reviewed possibilities and hesitated. "They were working for Prince Livio, right? But didn't he want the Cardinal alive to help the conspiracy? You don't just go and set fire to all your arrangements like that. And anyway, why should he want to?"

"For the same reason that he went that night to dig up a grave."

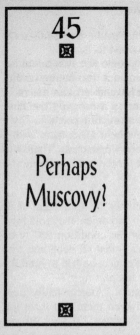

45

Perhaps Muscovy!

"TO DIG UP . . . *JEALOUSY?* OF the *Cardinal?* How could *he* be the Princess Oralia's lover?"

"Because he was in holy orders? It doesn't take a cynic to see that other people don't do as they should. He visited Montenero, just as he visited Rocca—a Cardinal isn't confined to one State."

"But the Princess?"

"Polissena told me His Eminence was a most attractive man."

"You mean it was Prince Livio come to burn up the Cardinal that was with Malvezzi in the street, the bloke Iacomo saw—Holy Mother! You *said* Iacomo saw one of them muffled up, hiding his face; I thought it must be the blue man hiding his scars. And then he swung round, and Iacomo thought he was on to him, and he stopped still . . . and it was Prince Livio, right? In one of his fits, like when he saw Lady Minerva put her veil back."

Sigismondo looked up at the sky, almost cloudless and hyacinth blue. "Excitement, I think. I've seen others with the falling sickness. They don't fall always. They may go into a trance and not know it. It can last one moment or many—a fatal moment for the Prince in the end. But it had to be someone like Prince Livio. Only someone Petrucci thought he could trust would have been allowed in and could have overcome him without giving him time to raise an alarm. And only Prince Livio was likely to have brought so much gold."

He began to step over the tiny hedges. Benno, dazed, came carefully after, saying, "So *Prince Livio* burnt the Cardinal because of the Princess and then tooled off to Fontecasta to damage another lover's body . . . only, why didn't he kill the Lady Minerva when he saw her?"

Sigismondo reached the bench and sat down. "I never had

the opportunity to ask him. . . . She was dressed as a boy. He may have thought he saw his son's ghost."

Biondello, at a second try, jumped onto the bench and sat beside Sigismondo. "It may be he had a fit. At any event, Malvezzi and the others lost their heads and left him. He must have managed later to join the procession bringing the false Minerva, while they came straight away full pelt into town with a tale of ghosts. Angelo tells me he'd upset them with a bad reading that day. He'd seldom seen worse cards. Thanks to him I could tell the Duke the reason for the gold on Petrucci's desk."

"You could?"

Sigismondo laughed. "You remember he told them their fortunes a second time? They'd had a bad omen, they told him; but they were counting on fulfilling the condition set by an astrologer—I imagine Prince Livio's—that all debts must be paid if they were to succeed. Either Petrucci helped to fund the conspiracy or he had to be paid for his part in it."

Benno sat down beside Sigismondo. "Angelo really does know how to read the cards. If I'd been them, I'd have left Colleverde straight off, no option, whether I'd paid off old debts or not."

Sigismondo was tousling Biondello's head and scratching him under his one ear. "Hey, you can't escape Fate."

"You mean if they'd left Colleverde and not helped the Prince, they'd have fallen off a cliff or bumped into a wild boar?"

"Meeting Duke Grifone's sword was perhaps only one of the alternatives."

Benno was silent. What Malvezzi's nameless colleague on the balcony had met had been, apparently, Sigismondo's dagger; and who could tell who had killed the pockmarked man?

Sigismondo shielded his eyes; on his hand shone the Duke's gift, a ring of amazing mass, set with a sapphire darker than the sky overhead. It looked large even on Sigismondo's hand.

"You'll have to tie that round your neck on a cord like Angelo did, or it'll be, excuse me, sir, can I borrow your ring for keeps, sorry about your throat."

"Better than that. I take it to Master Ispano the Jew, and he'll give me a token I can turn into money when I need it."

This sounded like magic, and Benno felt he had better not know more. "Why did Prince Livio *want* to marry the Princess Corio? You wouldn't think anybody would."

"As I see it, he wasn't leaving anything to chance after burning Petrucci. He needed to have his commands enforced after Petrucci's death, so he gave her a motive, an interest, an overwhelming interest in the success of the conspiracy. We can't doubt that her brother had taken her into his confidence about that. Livio had only to make sure Petrucci didn't tell her he was to be there that night."

Benno sat up straight. "Well, yes, that would have put paid to the marriage. What a *twister!* He'd got it all fixed up."

Sigismondo stretched out his long legs and lifted his face to the sun. "You must have heard the saying, Revenge is a dish best eaten cold. Livio had calculated it all."

Sigismondo stirred, and Benno saw, going along the side of the maze garden with his back to them, the distant figure of Bishop Taddeo, head down, pacing slowly. He might be telling his beads or reading or musing.

"We'll leave His Lordship in peace." Sigismondo stood up. "He's had much to disturb him. The Duke's announced that the Bishop is to be present at the trial of Cardinal Petrucci shortly."

"The trial? But he's dead. He's lying in the Bishop's chapel."

"Not any more. He's to be roped to a chair and arraigned before the noble families of Colleverde. Then the Duke plans to have him thrown into the river."

There was silence again as they stole away from the pacing figure who didn't seem to have noticed them. Benno began to giggle. "The Duke doesn't give up, does he? Any more than Prince Livio meant to."

"It takes immense determination to stay in power, wherever you rule. Perhaps more in this part of the world than most."

Benno tried, and failed, to visualise another part of the world. Surely even Muscovy couldn't be so different from Italy, except he'd heard there was more snow. By now their retreat had taken them to the other side of the hornbeam hedge, and Benno was happy to find another balcony, more pleasant than the one overlooking the square with its dangling traitors.

This one swept the length of the hedge with room for two to walk side by side and gaze over the prospect below. They looked across at the far hills, smudged blue only a little darker than the sky. Benno pointed. "That's Montenero, isn't it? Hope she's happy, with the Lord Astorre. And her father."

The hum was negative, vibrating. "Not her father."

"The blind lord's her father, isn't he? The Lord Mirandola? You said she thinks he is. *Wasn't* he one of the Princess Oralia's lovers?"

"I don't believe that he was. The Princess found him left to die. She must have guessed who he was. She sent for Sybilla and had him tended at Fontecasta, which belonged to the old Lord Giraldi she'd known in Rocca. But more than that, I think not."

"So it was Lord Eugenio after all?"

Sigismondo turned to look at him. "Didn't I mention any other lover?"

"You mean . . ."

"Cardinal Petrucci was the father of Minerva and Marco. Sybilla told me. She was one of two people who knew. The other one must have been tortured by Prince Livio after his wife's death."

"So he found out. No wonder the Cardinal went up in flames." Benno turned back to the view, seeing nothing. "Not a very good thing if that bit of news got about. Fancy the Duke's son married to the daughter of the devil Petrucci."

The deep voice went on. "If the Duke thinks, as he may, that Mirandola is her father, he'll be tolerant of that now as long as the world believes she has the right to Montenero."

A lark sang insistently. The shadows shifted across their shoulders, the breeze touched their faces. After a bit, Benno said plaintively: "I wish Angelo'd told our fortunes before he left. Wouldn't you have liked to know?"

"Never. Not knowing our fortunes, that's where the fun is, Benno. We're for Rocca, after the Cardinal's trial, and after that, who can tell? I'm getting too well-known in these parts. Perhaps Muscovy?"

Benno tried to think of the distant hills covered in snow. His mind spread out towards unknown and strange places. One thing was sure. Wherever they were going, life would not be dull.

A distant trumpet sounded, and Sigismondo levered himself off the parapet.

"Come. We must not keep the Cardinal waiting."